ALSO BY SOFI OKSANEN

When the Doves Disappeared

Purge

Norma

Norma

SOFI OKSANEN

Translated from the Finnish
by Owen F. Witesman

ALFRED A. KNOPF New York
2017

THIS IS A BORZOI BOOK
PUBLISHED BY ALFRED A. KNOPF

www.aaknopf.com

This translation has been published with the financial support of the Finnish Language Exchange.

F I
L I

Library of Congress Cataloging-in-Publication Data
Names: Oksanen, Sofi, [date]. | Witesman, Owen, translator.
Title: Norma : a novel / by Sofi Oksanen ;
[translated by Owen F. Witesman]
Other titles: Norma. English
Description: First edition. | New York : Alfred A. Knopf, 2017.
Identifiers: LCCN 2017011797 | ISBN 9780451493521 (hardcover) | ISBN 9780451493538 (ebook) | 9781524711290 (open market)
Subjects: LCSH: Mothers and daughters—Fiction. | Magic realism (Literature)—Fiction. | Beauty, Personal—Fiction. | Paranormal fiction. | BISAC: FICTION / Contemporary Women. | FICTION / Fantasy / Contemporary. | FICTION / Mystery & Detective / Women Sleuths.
Classification: LCC PH356.037 N6713 2017 | DDC 894/.54134—dc23
LC record available at https://lccn.loc.gov/2017011797

Jacket illustration by Winnie Truong
Jacket design by Kelly Blair

Manufactured in the United States of America
First United States Edition

Norma

One

If everything goes well, by August we can sit back and enjoy good food, sleep, and spa treatments. We can raise a glass to a future in which you receive everything you've never dared to dream. Then my work will be done, and I won't regret the price of your new life one bit.

After the funeral, nothing went back to the way it had been. As Norma fell behind the other guests and slipped onto the road leading to the cemetery gates, she still tried to make herself believe it was possible, though. Her mother wouldn't have been offended that she'd already ordered a taxi, and Norma didn't care about any of the rest of it: relatives she hardly knew, scheming heirs, the fate of the ancestral home of the Naakka family, which was sure to come up over the Karelian pasties and savory sandwich cake as her grandmother interjected observations spun from her brittle memory. Norma would leave the farce behind to try to return to normal life and meet her mother's death head-on. No more avoiding places that reminded Norma of her. No more being late to work. No more taking taxis instead of the metro, and no more bursting into tears each morning as she tore at her hair with a metal-toothed comb. She wouldn't forget to eat or drink enough, and she wouldn't let the life she and her mother had spent so much work building together fall apart. She would prepare for her workday the next morning just as before: she would pick the lint from the back of her blouse and pack her purse with baby oil to tame her curls, diazepam and meclizine to calm her mind and body. Into the bottom of the bag she would toss a travel-size bottle of Elnett hair spray because that was the smell of a normal workday, the choice of women who had their lives in order. That was the kind of woman she intended to be.

After armoring herself for the day to come, she would enter the Sörnäinen Metro Station, melt into the flowing mass of humanity, and allow the escalator to carry her to the platform as on any other day. The air current would flap the hem of her skirt, people would browse their phones and free newspapers, and none of them would remember the tragedy that had happened on that same platform. Only she would think of it as she prepared to confront the tension that had dominated her workplace through months of labor negotiations. She would realize that nothing in her life had stopped other than her mother's life.

There was no sign of her taxi. Norma leaned against the cemetery fence and allowed relief to swim into the bubble formed by the benzos and scopolamine. She had survived the funeral. She hadn't spotted deception in anyone's commiseration, or hypocrisy in words of sympathy. She hadn't fainted, vomited, or had a panic attack even though some people had come close enough to hug her. She'd behaved like a model daughter and was finally ready to remove her sunglasses, which had begun to slip down her nose from sweat caused by the heat. Then, just as she was shoving them into her bag, a man she didn't know came up to her to express his condolences. Norma pushed the glasses back on. She didn't want company.

"The others already went that way." Norma motioned toward the restaurant where the reception was being held and pulled the brim of her hat down lower. Instead of leaving, the man extended his hand. Norma ignored the greeting and turned away. She had no interest in interacting with strangers.

But the man didn't give up. He grabbed Norma's hand. "Lambert," the man said. "Max Lambert. One of your mother's old friends."

"I don't remember her ever mentioning you."

The man laughed. "Did you and your mother talk about all your friends? It's been ages. When we were younger, Anita and I had some real adventures together."

Norma pulled her hand away. She could feel the man's grip on her fingers like a stamp pressed into her skin against her will, and he had used the past tense referring to her mother. It sounded like an insult. Norma hadn't moved on to that stage yet, and this man didn't look like one of her mother's friends. Norma and Anita Ross's life had been cloistered, their social contact limited to the circles required for their work. What few acquaintances each had had, the other knew, and this man was not one of them.

The man's hair was slicked back, and his hairline with its widow's peak looked like that of a younger man. The same couldn't be said of his skin. The harsh rays of the sun had carved deep lines in his face, and his tan couldn't conceal bags and broken blood vessels beneath his eyes from years of devoted alcohol consumption. The previous night's beer stank on his glistening temples. The man's suit was also yesterday's vintage, the knees of his trousers hanging loosely. Everything about him sagged, fitting poorly with the serenity of the surrounding conifers. However, he spoke politely enough, his suit was a black appropriate to the occasion, and the fabric looked expensive. His cologne was fresh Kouros, not something that had been sitting on the shelf for years, and his shampoo was salon quality. That was where Norma's examination ended. Her nose was plugged by drugs and sorrow, and the antinausea patches behind her ears pumped hyoscine steadily into her veins, so she couldn't read the man any more carefully. When she noticed a lock that had escaped from her ponytail twisting like a corkscrew, she panicked and glanced at the clock on her phone. The taxi should have come by now.

The man took a pair of mirrored sunglasses from a pocket and put them on. "May I offer you a ride?"

"No, thank you. I have a taxi coming."

The man's laugh was that of an old gambler, and he sidled up closer to Norma. Something in his voice reminded her of the chatter of a gaggle of tourists. You could always find some wag in the group who talked louder than the others and cracked jokes that everyone laughed at even when the punch line fell flat.

"Well, please get in touch soon. We can take care of all this unpleasant business so you can continue your life."

The man produced a card from a tarnished case that must have been silver and shoved it into Norma's hand. The gold chain that encircled his wrist glinted in the sun. He might have won the case in a game of cards or stolen it. Cinematic possibilities flashed through Norma's mind: What if her mother had had an affair with this man, and what if Norma had sisters and brothers she didn't know about? Even worse, what if this man was her real father instead of Reijo Ross? Why was she even thinking like this? What if the man had simply come to the wrong funeral?

By the time Margit called, the taxi was nearly in Kallio. Norma answered after the sixth ring. Lambert's card still rested in her lap, and she snapped its corners as her aunt attempted to persuade her to come back to the reception. The cardstock was sturdy and expensive, a cream hue with embossed gold lettering. There was no title and no address. On a whim, Norma asked her aunt whether Max Lambert had come to the memorial service.

The name didn't mean anything to Margit. Norma's guess about the wrong funeral must have been correct, and she was just about to roll down the window and throw the card into the wind.

"Wait, do you mean Helena's ex-husband?" Margit asked.

Norma started in surprise. She must have numbed herself too much for the funeral. That was why she hadn't made the connection: her mother's best friend had the same last name as the man who had just introduced himself.

"Why on earth would Max Lambert come to Anita Ross's funeral?" Margit asked. "That's impossible."

"I think I just saw him. Isn't he there now?"

"No."

"Could he have come in Helena's place?"

"Don't you remember how Helena and Lambert split up? Your mother would never have wanted that man here."

In the background of the phone call, Norma could hear the muted voice of the priest and the clinking of plates. When she heard Lambert's name, Margit had sounded bitter, but now her tone turned impatient. Even so, she spoke of Helena with respect, as if Norma's mother could hear them—no one treated Helena with as much compassion as Norma's mother had. And for a moment, her mother was alive again, in this conversation that still adhered to her wishes.

"Those years resulted in a few good children but otherwise only sorrow. Think about what happened to Helena." Margit took a drink of something, and the glass tinkled. "Forget the whole thing. You must have been mistaken."

Crazy Helena's husband. Norma's mother couldn't abide anyone calling Helena names, and she had rarely spoken of her visits with her friend. However, over the past few years, her mother visited Kuopio more and more often, and Norma had deduced that Helena was either better or worse. But she hadn't asked. Hospitals reminded Norma of the fates that deviants always faced, and she'd already heard plenty of those stories from her mother. She had enough torment. And she didn't know Helena personally—she could barely remember her. It wasn't until this very moment that she realized she hadn't asked Margit whether anyone had notified Helena of Norma's mother's death, if Helena was even lucid enough to understand anyway.

"Those friends were only trouble." Margit was becoming agitated again, but her words formed slowly and her mouth was full of cotton, as if she'd taken a sedative.

"Friends, what friends?"

Norma wondered whether Margit would recognize Lambert anymore. He'd left for Sweden decades ago with Reijo Ross, and neither had been seen in the old town since. They hadn't even come home to bury their own parents.

"Do you mean Reijo? Is anyone there from Reijo's family? Maybe Lambert came with one of the Rosses."

"Rosses? Please! The past is the past. No good will come of digging it up."

Norma's aunt was probably right, and her mother would have agreed. She had wanted to keep these people where they belonged, in the past. But if no one had been in contact with Reijo, Lambert's old friend, or with Helena, where had Lambert heard about the accident? Norma didn't remember what the obituary said, whether it mentioned the funeral. Margit had handled that too. The report in the newspaper had definitely not included her mother's name: *A woman died after falling under a metro train in Sörnäinen. According to the police, there was no foul play.*

Norma pressed another pill out of its blister pack and dropped the business card into her bag. Directory Information said that the man's phone number was either private or a prepaid account with no address attached. Her mother would have known what to do. Although the false ebullience of the summer radio playlist didn't fit the day, Norma asked the taxi driver to turn it up. It covered the sniffing. The helplessness. She was over thirty and still used to her mother solving most of the difficult problems that confronted her.

Her mother would never have left her alone to cope with a shady old man who affected her hair like an electric shock.

Back at the reception, Marion glanced at Alvar, who shook his head imperceptibly. There was no sign of the girl. Nor of Lambert. Marion cursed to herself. She wished she could have talked to Norma first.

"More coffee?" The woman who asked was in her fifties and seemed a little lost. A restrained smile was frozen on her face and had remained even when she accidentally tried to enter the men's restroom and ran into the door.

"Beautiful ceremony. Just like Anita would have wanted." Alvar's familiar tone dispelled the need for an introduction. He acted as if they were Anita's old friends and trusted that the woman would blame her own weak memory rather than presuming to ask who they were.

"We didn't really know what to do," the woman said. "The funeral home said that in cases like this, cremation is most common. But we decided to do the burial this way because of my mother's condition. She would have been too upset if we'd violated tradition."

So this was Anita's sister, Margit. She had stood next to Anita's mother at the grave. Elli Naakka had seemed frail and distant, just as confused as Anita had said. The old woman had been startled when the other woman burst into tears and faltered as earth fell on the casket, patting her hand as if offering comfort to a passing acquaintance. She hadn't recognized Margit or understood that they were burying her own daughter. That had reassured Marion, but she still wished the elderly woman could have understood what was happening. She wanted to see her tears.

Alvar placed his hand on Margit's shoulder and took the coffeepot from her. "I can help you pour. Your decision about the burial was very considerate."

"Of course we didn't tell Mother what happened," Margit said. "If you speak to her, don't be surprised if she talks about a stroke. You must be one of Anita's friends from the post office."

Marion extended her coffee cup to her brother to buy time to think, but Alvar simply said yes. Apparently Anita hadn't mentioned getting fired or her new job at Shear Magic. That wasn't unusual; people were always ashamed to lose their jobs, even these days, and Anita definitely wouldn't have wanted to explain her new work to this crowd. The speeches during the reception all recounted memories of summers at the old house in the country and other such drivel. They had little to do with Anita's real life. Marion felt the irritation smoldering in her breast flare again. People who didn't know Anita shouldn't be seeing her off. Anita would have hated an event like this. She would have wanted wine and dancing and ABBA. And Helena, not Lambert. As the priest spoke at the grave, Lambert had whispered to Marion that they'd worried for nothing, everything was going fine. No one brought up Helena, and no one seemed to remember Lambert, let alone his children, Marion and Alvar. Time had done its work.

"We had no way to know that Anita was dealing with anything like this," Margit continued.

"Depression can be treacherous," Alvar agreed.

"You didn't notice anything either?"

"Maybe Anita was a bit more withdrawn lately," Alvar said, turning to Marion for confirmation. She would have to say something. But she couldn't. She fumbled in her pockets for a tissue but couldn't find any unused. Alvar handed her a napkin. Marion pressed it to her eyes.

"Anita was never very social," Margit said. "I should have called more often. I should have made her tell me how she was doing."

"How is Norma holding up?" Alvar asked. "This must be hardest on her."

"Norma is so much like her mother. She keeps things to herself."

"If there's any way we can help . . ."

"Thank you. I'll remember that," Margit said. "I'd like to talk to some of Anita's other co-workers, but I just don't recognize any of them." She then reported how she'd called the switchboard at the post office to ask them to let everyone know about Anita's funeral, but the woman who answered the phone hadn't known Anita.

"The post office has so much turnover these days," Alvar said.

The conversation was beginning to move in a bothersome direction. Marion would let her brother handle the rest. She edged away, and Alvar gave a small nod as he continued to pour coffee. Margit seemed to have forgotten all about looking for Anita's co-workers by the time they reached the second guest with an empty cup. The coffeepot had been a cunning move on Alvar's part, allowing him to circulate naturally through the entire group.

The men of the family still stood around as they had in the cemetery, stiff and uncomfortable in their suits, hands clasped behind their backs. Lambert had done the same. It was a masculine way to express piety. But it didn't fit Lambert, least of all at Anita's funeral. It seemed false. As Marion moved among the guests, words flitted by her that expressed shock and confusion, lamentation that no one had sensed anything—as if any of them could have, given how few people had even seen Anita since she moved to Helsinki. Marion didn't understand why this crowd had shown up. Perhaps to assuage their guilt at having lost touch or in order to be able to gossip to the other people in the village about the tragedy that had befallen the Naakka family. People's reaction to violent death was always the same. They were hypocritical but full of curiosity, and the rumors would continue for decades, especially if the death couldn't be explained with rationality but rather its lack. Marion would still try to reach the girl, but then this charade would be over and she would leave.

Norma climbed out of the car, ripping the scopolamine patches from behind her ears and inside her elbows, and lit a cigarette. She would throw these clothes with their cemetery smell into the backyard trash bin, cut away the sorrow of the day, and open the bottle of red wine she'd stashed in the kitchen cupboard to make waiting for tomorrow morning more bearable. She just had to open the gate and enter. Over the past few weeks, that step had become the most difficult.

Twelve years before, everything had been different. The same gate had welcomed her and her mother, opening as if by itself—their move to the city had felt like the best decision ever. Norma had just received her graduation cap when they left behind the Naakka home and the oppressive village community surrounding it. They'd found perfect apartments in the same building, considering it such a stroke of luck that they celebrated by riding from one end of the metro line to the other and back again.

Twelve years later that symbol of urban life had ridden right over Norma's mother, one day after she returned from a vacation to Thailand. Norma couldn't help wondering whether she could have stopped it. Would she have picked up on some sign of her mother's mental state if she'd called that night? If she'd climbed those few extra stairs to her apartment?

Instead she'd spent her evening out with an occasional lover. During those hours her mother had sent one final message to Norma: *Dinner tomorrow? I have presents!* Norma hadn't read it until the morning. Even if her mother had called, she wouldn't have answered. She'd needed to forget the mood at work after spending the last week watching the expressions of the managers and the executives as they slipped down the stairwell. The janitor, who was always in the know, had begun avoiding the smoking spot, which was a sign that the negotiations were not going well. The thought of having to rehash all that with her mother as soon as she returned home made Norma anxious. Instead she had focused on her glass, a forgettable man, and emptying her mind. She would see her mother the next day.

When Norma received the call at work, she thought it had something to do with the labor negotiations and hurried to the conference room, ready to show off her best qualities. But what she found was a pair of police officers. The female officer's hair smelled of birch shampoo, healthy living, and high doses of vitamin C. Norma's locks curled tighter, and the thought flashed through her mind that she was going to survive the cutbacks—no one would fire a person who had just lost her mother in a tragic accident. Later this embarrassed her. In that moment she should have been thinking anything else.

News spread instantly through the building, and her purse filled with crisis hotline cards. Her closest co-worker whispered about an article she'd read in the paper, according to which the metro hired only drivers who could survive seeing someone throw herself on the tracks, because it always happened sooner or later. This reminded Norma that the train operator had been the last person to see her mother alive. Her mother's last second, last step, last breath. Probably everything had happened so quickly that the driver hadn't registered any of it. But that person should have been Norma, not a train operator, not the perfect strangers on the platform.

When the old woman's gaze came to rest on Marion, Marion realized she had made a mistake. Confusion parted like a curtain as the old woman stood up with surprising agility and attempted to spit at her. The priest standing nearby jumped, and heads turned toward Elli Naakka. After a moment of silence, everyone began covering up the embarrassing incident with the clinking of coffee cups, spooning more food onto their plates.

"Maybe she thought you were Helena," Alvar said.

Her brother had appeared unobserved at her side and began leading Marion, who stood frozen in place, toward the door of the restaurant.

Marion's mouth was dry, and her hands trembled. This was exactly why she didn't want to see anyone who remembered Helena. "I don't look that much like her," she whispered.

"Of course not, and no one else here would connect you to her." Alvar brushed her hair out of her eyes. "Put it out of your mind. Anita's mother has dementia."

But Elli Naakka's gaze was sharp and full of accusation. She did understand she was at her daughter's funeral; she blamed Helena and wanted to say that this never would have happened if not for Helena's deranged presence in Anita's life. No, Marion knew she was letting her imagination run away with her. Elli Naakka didn't understand what had happened. Marion had approached the old woman only so she could tell Lambert that she'd tried at least. She'd been sure she couldn't get anything out of Elli Naakka, that the old woman wouldn't even recognize her.

"Try to calm down. Remember why we came here. Is there anyone you remember seeing with Anita?" Alvar asked.

Marion shook her head. They were spying on Anita's funeral, and that was sick. Marion glanced at her brother's pupils. Normal. Only the slightest tension in the wrinkles around his eyes revealed that her brother must have recognized someone he'd fought with as a child, maybe someone who'd chanted Crazy Helena. And yet he was still able to be here sober and converse with these people politely. After Marion left, Alvar would join the ring of smokers outside, passing around the flask in his pocket and creating a natural connection with the men of the family. He would probably be able to find out everything they needed. Lambert would be pleased and give his son another bonus. Marion never got those, unless you counted having her own salon.

Alvar noticed his sister's fingers tearing a napkin and took the shreds from her. The floor looked as if a molting chicken had been walking around.

"Do you need anything?"

"No, I'm fine."

"Give your own eulogy for Anita later at home. I'll tell Lambert you did your best here."

The window was open: street dust covered the sill and had blown onto the clothes lying on the couch. Margit's shirts covered the pile of Norma's mother's dresses. The dishes on the counter were Margit's, not Norma's mother's. The disk in the CD player was Suvi Teräsniska, one of Margit's. The smell of Shalimar had been replaced by an imitation scent. The apartment no longer felt like her mother's home, and Norma began to sense that she'd made a mistake allowing her aunt to ensconce herself here and handle all the funeral arrangements. She had accepted the offered help, because after one attempt she hadn't even been able to go into the apartment. The sight she met on the threshold was unbearable: the apartment looked as if her mother were simply out running an errand and would be back at any moment. That was why she'd let her aunt find her mother's favorite dress, let her remove the ABBA concert ticket attached to the edge of the mirror, let her take the Shalimar off the dressing table. Margit collected all the things her sister would have wanted in her casket, even though she didn't know anything about her.

Only Norma knew why the Shalimar should go with her mother. In the hospital after Norma's birth, her mother had awoken to the smells of bergamot and lemon and had suddenly been utterly, completely sure that everything would be fine. They would survive, despite it all. They would survive together, just the two of them, and they wouldn't need Reijo or anyone else. Later her mother had recognized the scent in the village drugstore and purchased the perfume, ignoring the cost. This was the smell of the greatest turning point in her life. Norma lit a cigarette. She alone had let her aunt foul the scene of the crime—when she noticed herself thinking of her mother's home as a crime scene, she was startled and swept her hair aside as if wanting to brush the thought away. As she tried desperately to find a rational reason for her mother's actions, she strained to see mystery where there was none. Max Lambert's appearance probably had a perfectly natural explanation.

Norma lifted the lid of her mother's laptop, then closed it again. The computer wouldn't contain anything from her mother's youth, which was where the hunt had to go. All the photos from when she was younger were in an album in the closet, but now that shelf was empty. Finally the photo album turned up on the nightstand, blank spots on its previously full pages. Margit had made it here first, too. According to her aunt, Norma's mother hadn't left her a letter, and Norma had trusted Margit, but now she didn't know why she had. Her mother hadn't even told Margit about being fired, let alone about her new job. Margit didn't know Norma's mother, not as Norma did. She wouldn't have known where to look, and it was beginning to seem that Norma's laziness might have led her aunt to destroy some piece of evidence connected to Lambert. Norma nearly called Margit to press her about the photographs. She even took out her phone but then threw it back in her purse. Her anger was unreasonable. Margit had a right to a few pictures. She had gone to so much trouble, taking care of the funeral and handling the rent for June and July so there wouldn't be any rush clearing out the apartment and she would have a place to sleep if Norma needed her support a little longer.

Norma shoved the computer into her bag, along with the bank

codes she found on the table. Then she lit another cigarette and began leafing through the album. Her aunt had wanted shots that included herself and Norma's grandmother, rejecting photos of Helena and Norma's mother as young women, or of Helena with her children holding cotton candy at an amusement park. In the pictures, Norma recognized Helena's daughter, Marion, who as a teenager looked like a young Helena. The madness hadn't taken root in Helena until later. The Helena of the photo album had a direct gaze and a dulcet smile.

Norma turned to the final page and was about to stand up when she noticed a photo of two couples enjoying a jovial summer day: there were her mother and Reijo Ross leaning against each other looking at the camera. Next to them a younger version of the man Norma met today had his arm around Helena. Under the portrait was a Polaroid snapshot. In it a later edition of the same man smiled alongside Marion, holding a baby in his arms. On the back of the photo was an inscription written in a shaky hand. It was signed by Alvar. He had taken the photo himself and asked Norma's mother to visit soon.

Marion's phone chimed as a message arrived, but it was a client, not the girl as she had hoped. Marion's texts, the greeting she'd left on voice mail, and her emails had all met the same fate: the girl remained silent.

"I have a meeting in two hours," Alla said.

Marion looked away from her phone and grabbed the tape remover. Alla didn't inquire about the funeral, instead feigning indifference as she had since she stepped through the door of the salon, as if she knew that Marion hadn't learned anything. It was her way of rubbing salt in the wound, of demonstrating her position and authority.

"I haven't tried this hair yet in such warm weather. Do you think that will make any difference?"

"It'll stand up to anything: chlorinated water, diving, Vietnam," Marion replied. "Not a single client who's gone to the tropics has complained. Some swimmers have even stopped wearing caps."

The Hanoi trip was awhile off, and Alla's hair was in good shape. Still, she had wanted new extensions right now, on the day of Anita's funeral. It was an obvious attempt to torment Marion, made worse by the way Alla kept chattering about the quality of various weaves and current styling trends.

Of course, Alla had already talked about the funeral with her beloved husband, but if Lambert had extracted anything from the girl, Alla wouldn't have been so calm. Or maybe Lambert sent Alla to gauge Marion's behavior, to ensure she was staying on the rails and could still handle her work. Maybe that was it. Maybe it wasn't intentional harassment, it just felt like it.

"Show me the reservation book," Alla said.

Marion handed her the book. Alla hummed in approval. Everyone was enthralled with the Ukrainian hair, and even Alla's girlfriends had switched to Shear Magic to get it. Marion didn't dare touch their reservations, which made rearranging Anita's appointments even more difficult. She didn't want to move reservations related to weddings; Shear Magic was responsible for the success of those celebrations, and they weren't going to let that slip. But for other clients, she had been forced to find new times, some even months away. Still, they were hard pressed. Tonight the final client would come at nine in the evening, the first tomorrow morning at six. She wasn't going to survive the wedding season without help.

Alla continued inspecting the reservation book as if she were reading the Bible. For Lambert, the revenue at the salon was small change, so his attention to its profits was purely superficial. They didn't care about the happiness of the customers as Marion did, and Marion was never going to find another apprentice like Anita, let alone an experienced professional. No one could soothe a woman fretting over her hair as well as Anita could. She had been a born hairdresser with a sixth sense for topics people didn't want to discuss. Contrary to Marion's fears, during her first days at work, Anita hadn't brought up Helena or anything else about the past. She hadn't even commented on the way fate had brought them back together after nearly thirty years. When Anita stepped through the door of Shear Magic the first time, she didn't exclaim how much Marion resembled her mother or lay a single word of guilt on Marion for not visiting Helena. Longing stung like a barb in Marion's chest. No one had understood her like Anita.

Alla flicked the names in the reservation book with her nails, then placed the book in her lap.

"How much more Ukrainian do we have in stock?"

"Enough for a week. Two if we mix it with Russian."

Alla sighed and glanced at her phone, which was flashing again on silent, angling it so Marion would be sure to see who was trying to reach her. The Japanese woman again. Alla dropped the phone onto the salon cape that covered her lap. Maybe she wanted to emphasize the fact that she didn't speak with important clients when Marion was listening. Or she wanted to demonstrate her own power: Alla would answer when it suited her, even when it was the Japanese woman.

"What are you planning to offer after that? Max and I were just discussing it. You can have a week. Within one week, you have to fix your mess."

Marion felt like grabbing the scissors and plunging them into Alla's neck. The desire was so strong that for a moment Marion had to grab the tool cart and squeeze it tight. Alla had influence over the clan's business and also over what Marion's future would look like.

"Max was much more effective at the funeral than you were. I won't even bother asking what you've accomplished to fix the situation, but the clock is ticking. Tick-tock." Alla tapped her Rolex, a gesture she'd learned from Lambert.

Marion's eyes itched. Maybe it was pollen. Or the dreams that had been destroyed because of Anita's death. A day before their return to Finland, they had sat at a Bangkok rooftop bar and chosen cocktails named Sweet Dreams. They'd toasted the future, and everything had seemed so clear. Marion had thought she might go visit Helena after all, with Anita, someday.

Marion looked through the display window to the street. That day would never come now. The parking lot was empty. That was where she had last seen Anita. Anita had been sitting in the car, back straight, eyes forward, chin up. When Marion finally built up the courage to go outside, she was already gone.

At ten to eight, her mother had rushed to the metro station even though she should have been on her way to the salon, which was just down the street. According to eyewitnesses, she had nearly been running, but in the morning a lot of people were in a hurry, so no one took any particular notice. Norma breathed in the scent of the coffee roastery, the same smell that would have been here on her mother's final morning, and crossed Vaasa Square, as her mother had. Quickly she passed the crowd waiting outside the market for beer sales to begin, trying to see anything that might have influenced her mother's decision, something that could make it comprehensible. Norma had chosen some practical ballet flats, capris, and a collared cotton blouse, her normal work attire, the same sort of thing her mother had been wearing that morning too, and rushed down the escalator to the platform, as her mother had done, repeatedly begging pardon as she hurried past rubes who didn't know to keep right and blocked the entire width, just as she and her mother had done after moving to Helsinki, too. Once at the platform, she sat on the bench that her mother had not sat on. No, the metro had careened into the station too soon. Her mother had simply tossed her shoes and handbag under the bench, and then she had been gone.

Norma set her bag in the same place her mother had put her own and dropped her shoes onto the gray stone paving. Her mother's shoes and bag had been delivered to her without any message. She'd removed the lining of the bag in case something had slipped behind—but no, there was nothing, just old receipts, a grubby Band-Aid, the detritus found in any woman's handbag. The smells of the salon. Hair particles. This was her mother's work purse, not her vacation purse. A hair dye stain. A couple of hairs stuck in the zipper, one from an Indian extension, and one blond, presumably from a customer. Her mother had left her phone at home. When Norma's aunt brought it to her, she'd been sure she would find a message from her mother concealed in its depths. Disappointment had made her throw the thing at the wall. The last calls were from the week before the Thailand trip, and the messages were about changes to appointments and graduation hairdos. All the messages and calls were connected to Shear Magic. Her mother had been the salon's Facebook page administrator, and she'd written the latest post just a few hours before her departure: After she gets back from vacation, Anita will be available again to conjure up an unforgettable style for your special day! On sale now: genuine tape-in human hair extensions!

Currents of air brushed Norma's ankles as train after train zipped past. Metro guards came and went. Clubs, bulletproof vests, combat boots. Open, close, in, out. Signals warning of shutting doors. The mandarin-colored sides of the cars. Sausage advertisements, smiling celebrity chefs, birch benches on the platform. The heavy velvet skirts of the Finnish Roma, hands carrying beer bottles, methadone teeth. People returning from vacation. People leaving on vacation. Roller bags, homeless people carrying bundles, faded plastic sacks. Efficient briefcases rushing to work, quick steps, skirts smelling detergent fresh. Jackets, nonslip summer panty hose new from the package, without toe reinforcements. New high-heel tips. Virgin hair weaves, Indian and Russian, a few Malaysian. Bonding glue, melatonin pills, hormone therapy, tenderloin, expensive hair nutrients. Her mother's final scenery.

The clock moved past noon. Her mother hadn't gotten to see the slower steps of the midday passengers on the platform or their less careful grooming. She hadn't smelled the cheaper perfumes, the forgotten deodorant, the uncut hair, the sweaty smells of yesterday's food and beer, cola drinks and mustard, Imovane and antidepressants. She didn't notice the Somali girls and the glints of light on the pins in their carefully folded headscarves, the quick weaves the immigrants used, the stay-at-home dads with their strollers, the bearded ones with brand-new sneakers, rolled-up pants, and dandified baseball caps. She didn't smell the wake of incense trailing the ones headed for Goa for the coming winter, the hot chilies, the sugary sweetness of the pot.

Norma still sat on the bench.

The spoons she stored in the freezer had calmed the swelling of her eyelids from crying, but the effect had worn off as the morning went on. The spoons were one of her mother's beauty tips. She and Helena had also used them to curl their lashes when they were younger. Norma pressed her fingers to her eyes. All these people, all this bustling. As they returned to the platform and climbed back aboveground to look for a streetcar or a bus, everyone on the metro that morning had known before her that something had happened. At the moment when she was still spraying Elnett into her hair and hoping the labor negotiations would end, they had all known. Hundreds of people had cursed the change in their routine, their missed meetings, and had known before her.

A few years before, she and her mother had experienced the same thing together. They'd been traveling on the train toward Helsinki, and suddenly Norma's hair began to curl. They had chosen seats in the allergy compartment, so there were no extra irritants. She was startled. Her mother suggested cognac, and then just at that moment the train stopped. The announcement didn't mention a reason. Even so, everyone had known instinctively that soon officials would arrive to begin collecting body parts from the tracks. Everyone traveling on the train had known before the family of the person who walked in front of it. Norma's mother had seen her reaction then and had still chosen such a brutal way—of all the metro stations, this platform was on Norma's way to work.

The vibration of her phone snapped Norma back to reality. A guard who seemed to be watching her had appeared near the bench. Norma moved closer to the other people loitering on the platform. The call was from Shear Magic again, from Marion. Norma didn't answer. She wouldn't know how to be natural with Marion, and she didn't want to talk to her, let alone see her, even though Marion would know what mood Norma's mother had been in during her final days at work and might have an explanation for her own father's strange behavior. Norma had run into Marion a couple of times when she and Norma's mother had been leaving work at the same time. A cloud of salon scents had surrounded Marion, disgusting Norma, who avoided looking her in the eyes. That was why she had retreated from Marion at the funeral, hiding behind the other mourners. What Helena did had scarred her entire family for all eternity. People treated them with either unnatural empathy or irritating curiosity. Never like normal people. Her mother had hated that, but now Norma had acted exactly the same way.

Alvar turned the key in the lock. While Marion removed her sandals in the entryway, Alvar tromped right in, heedless of the rattan basket from which Marion grabbed a pair of Anita's guest slippers. In the draft, the dust on the windowsill in the living room took flight. Marion wiped her cheek, and as she swallowed a sneeze, Alvar was already pulling open drawers in the dressing table, rummaging through their contents as if doing accounting, with the same exactness, the same alertness, ready to latch on to any clue. Alvar trusted his own eyes more than he did Lambert's guard dogs, who had visited the apartment immediately after the accident and copied the contents of Anita's laptop. They hadn't found anything noteworthy on the machine, and Alvar had been waiting for this moment with the empty apartment. One of the boys watching the building had called Alvar as soon as the coast was clear.

"Look for any address books, postcards, scribbled notes, credit card bills, plane tickets, hotel receipts, or rental car paperwork," Alvar said. "Other phones, memory cards."

Marion saw from Alvar's expression what he was thinking: that he should have handled this whole job himself. Then mistakes like this wouldn't have happened. They would know who had delivered the Ukrainian hair to Anita, Marion wouldn't have to worry about what to replace it with, and Alvar would receive one more of his numerous bonuses. This episode, which had shocked the clan, would be wiped away, and they would be safe again.

"Margit lived here for more than a week, and plenty of other people have probably been here, too," Marion said, even though she knew the surveillance had begun immediately after Anita's death. The clan's mongrels already knew everyone who lived in the stairwell, their families, their pets, their daily rituals. Any strangers would be recognized instantly, and Lambert had probably also sent to the funeral one of the boys who stood guard outside Anita's building. Otherwise her brother wouldn't be so sure that Margit was the only one of the funeral guests who had visited the apartment. No one slipped through Lambert's network of thugs, ever.

"Tell me one more time what you saw at the funeral."

"How many times do I have to repeat this?" Marion said. "Ask your men why they didn't find anything here." She glanced at the clock. Norma was at work, and Margit was away, so Alvar had the whole day. He didn't need Marion here, and she didn't want to be here. She shouldn't be here. She felt like crying and wiped her cheeks again, mumbling something about allergies. The clan just wanted to torment her. That was why she had to come along. Alvar was still tossing the dressing table, lifting bottles and jars, opening boxes. In one drawer, he found a picture of Anita and Helena in long flowery skirts from sometime long ago. Marion turned her head away.

"Think more carefully," Alvar demanded as he shoved the picture into his pocket. "Maybe you forgot something."

"Margit could have taken anything."

"I understand she didn't take much. All she put in her car was a small roller suitcase, a garment bag, some plastic sacks, a few houseplants, and an old tube radio," Alvar rattled off. "Norma helped her carry it all, and then they hugged. Margit hung on Norma, who only looked bored. You knew Anita best. If anyone can find a clue, it's you."

Marion glanced at the shelves: art books, hair books, medical books, genetics books. Three English biographies of Elizabeth Siddal, two of the Sutherland sisters, one of Martha Harper, and three guides on doing extensions. No wonder Anita had been so good at her job—she had read practically everything about the hair industry.

Alvar grabbed a book off the shelf titled *The Belle Époque,* flipped through it from cover to cover, and put it back.

"The last bundle went for five thousand dollars per kilo."

"I know!"

"Lambert can send someone to search Margit's apartment. We should've come here ourselves after the accident."

Alvar's complaining was pointless. Anita's actions had put everyone on edge, and before making any moves, they'd had to make sure no one else was watching the apartment. They didn't want another ambush; the leaders of the clan had to be able to keep an appropriate distance. But by the time the building had been declared clear, Margit had already ensconced herself in Anita's home. The lights had shined through the night, and apparently her wailing had been audible all the way down the stairwell. According to Lambert's dogs, the woman hadn't gone out at all other than to visit a funeral parlor and then only briefly. Norma had stayed home with no sign of guests.

Alvar stopped in front of a camera on a shelf. It was new and expensive. The memory card was missing. Alvar placed the camera back on the shelf and returned to Anita's dressing table. The edges of the mirror were crammed full of postcards and photographs from Tenerife, Rhodes, Stockholm, Tallinn, Athens, Rome, and Antalya. The Canary Islands. Costa del Sol.

"If Anita had been traveling to Kiev for years and had distant relatives in Ukraine, why aren't there any cards from there?" Alvar said. "What if the hair is really coming from somewhere else? No one at the funeral had heard of any Ukrainian relatives, not even a Ukrainian girlfriend or wife."

"Where else could it have come from?"

"Anita must have been getting it through a go-between. We need to find that intermediary."

Marion glanced at her watch. She had to get back to the salon. Her next customer was coming in half an hour. She grabbed Anita's spare keys from Alvar in case the girl came to get some of Anita's things. Keys to the attic and cellar hung from hooks by the door. Alvar could handle those.

Two

By August we'll be able to laugh at all the old stories and the will we made out for you. You won't need to be afraid of accidents, and I won't need to lose sleep wondering if you'll be run down by a car just when I'm unreachable by phone or I'm too far away to get to you at the hospital, or worse, at the morgue. You can forget the cremation.

The sweat of the previous victim lingered on the beige chair, and fingerprints were visible on the armrests in the grease each employee had left while awaiting his or her fate. Norma moved her hands to her lap. Words flew past about challenging times and unavoidable course corrections. Apparently the decision about Norma Ross had been made ages ago. Those words were repeated several times as if in an attempt to emphasize that the recent tragedy had nothing to do with the termination of her employment. Crisis hotline cards were offered once again. The thought of a therapist trying to handle her problems was laughable, but Norma swallowed the giggle that tickled her throat. She had to act normal.

What had made this job exceptional was the large number of sight-impaired people among the clientele, so she rarely had to worry about sidelong glances. The guide dogs were well trained and didn't pay her special attention the way animals usually did. The ventilation in the building was good, recently renovated. She'd thought she would be able to hold on to her secretarial position because previous firings had helped her learn to avoid the worst pitfalls: workplace romances and excessive sociability, involvement in internal power struggles and criticizing management. She knew how to create relationships wrapped in friendship-like gestures, and she had attended the theater and other workplace outings in order to seem normal. *I could stay here,* she had told her mother. A series of positions lost at short intervals encumbered her résumé—not an advantage during a downturn. Landing a job at the Central Association for the Visually Impaired had been a stroke of luck.

Her boss carefully ticked off the reasons for her termination. Then his voice rose when he noticed Norma's dry eyes. Her pink slip was her own fault, a testimony to her obstinacy and slackening morale, to her rebellious influence at a time when an entirely different attitude was required. Norma Ross was frequently late for work despite repeated reprimands, and her defiant behavior had clearly increased of late. That Norma could not deny. She could only secretly blame her hair, which had become increasingly difficult during the labor negotiations as it absorbed the anxiety of everyone around her. At times it had become nearly impossible to cut, like barbed wire or hemp rope, which made her late in the morning and dragged out her lunch hours. Its weight had grown as if preparing to defend her in a war. Her wrists hurt, and she decided to complain of repetitive stress injury from using a mouse. And then her mother's death had come.

Her boss clearly expected anger and unhinged behavior that would confirm the grounds for her release and ease his conscience. Norma felt the cuticles of her hair opening as if she were in a hot shower, but she refused to fulfill the man's desires. His forehead and temples were so damp that a spoon would have stuck to them. His sebaceous glands had worked hard all day without the table fan appearing to have helped much. Norma stood to leave, took a pen from her boss's desk, and on a company notepad wrote the words "Ducray Sabal."

"This will help with your scalp. I doubt the management considers careless hygiene among their hirelings particularly good for the association's image."

She didn't stop until she reached the doors of the office complex and realized she was shaking. Her mother would have mourned Norma's lost job more than she did, seeing a replay of all her daughter's failed attempts to find her place in the working world, all the times Norma had been forced to leave. They used to joke afterward about all the situations she ended up in because of her hair. Once a colleague had seen her hair the wrong length. Another time someone had made it curl. Sometimes a workplace just hadn't given her anywhere to cut it during the day. There would be no more jokes now.

Norma heard her name being yelled just as she was turning out of the store toward home. Reflexively she stopped but immediately regretted it. Max Lambert's teeth shone under the faded awning of the Golden Palm—his suntan made them look whitened like an American's. Norma didn't have any reason to stay even out of politeness. She didn't know this man, so she tried to walk away, but Lambert fell into step nimbly alongside her.

"This is quite a coincidence," Lambert said. "I've been waiting for you to call." Even though the paper towel package hanging from Norma's fingers indicated she must be on her way home, opening the door a few meters ahead felt impossible in this man's company. Norma passed her stairwell and continued walking. The terrace of the Straw Hat Pub approached, and Lambert took a few running strides to catch up with her again.

"Could I offer you a beer or some other summer refreshment?"

"No, thank you. I'm not really in the mood for company."

"Sometimes it's important to talk about things. Is there anyone you can unburden your heart to?"

Norma's increasing pace didn't seem to bother Lambert. They quickly sped past the row of bars, making oncoming traffic get out of their way. Dogs lifted their noses, and women guarded their handbags. This scene from a summer evening comedy would have been humorous if Lambert's intrusive behavior hadn't begun to seem like stalking.

Norma didn't understand what he wanted. Lambert couldn't have any business with her, and she hadn't found any clues in her mother's apartment that might explain his sudden interest. Still, her hair urged her on. It wanted out of here. A sculpture depicting a working-class mother approached, marking the intersection with Sturenkatu, and Norma listened for an approaching streetcar she could jump onto. Or maybe this had to do with her father. But if Reijo Ross had heard about her mother's death, why would he have chosen a messenger Norma didn't know, Helena's ex-husband? And why would he want to contact Norma at all?

The heat took her breath away. Norma couldn't walk any faster. She leaned against the corner of the streetcar stop and set down her bags. She felt uncomfortable, and her hair retreated in from her forehead in tight twists. She shoved her double ponytail under her dress.

"I thought you lived on Vaasankatu, above Anita. Or was it below? Anita had a beautiful home," Lambert said.

The heat had stuck Lambert's shirt to his chest. As they stood, out of breath and dripping sweat after having rushed to the stop together, they looked like a father and daughter who had been assigned to bring the drinks for a family party but were late. A young couple who came to wait for the streetcar didn't see anything strange in the situation, and another pair who hurried by with Nordic walking poles didn't even glance at them. After her breathing leveled off a bit, Norma realized what Lambert had said: he had been in her mother's apartment.

"I thought the two of you were only childhood friends."

"That too, that too."

Lambert produced a cigarillo case and offered Norma one.

Norma shook her head and glanced at the timetable. Eight minutes until the next car. A taxi would come faster, so she brought up the number on her phone. But she didn't call. The phone returned to her handbag.

"What does he want? My father. This has something to do with him, doesn't it?"

Lambert's brow furrowed.

"Please be so good as to leave me alone. That's what you can tell him," Norma said.

Her mother would have said exactly the same thing. Nothing personal. As colorless and polite as possible. The voice had come from her of its own accord, and Norma had clearly succeeded in throwing Lambert off balance, at least a little. Satisfied, she stood a bit taller. Had he expected tears and blubbering followed by a toast with the wine peeking out of her bag?

"Reijo was really sad you lost contact. He missed you a lot."

Norma bit her lip and swallowed the question she didn't even want to think about. It just slipped into her mind. What was her father like? This man knew, but she did not. Now she wasn't going to be able to get any answers from her mother to the questions she had always put off asking. Norma had nothing left of Reijo Ross other than his last name.

"As I already said, we could talk about this somewhere more comfortable," Lambert said.

His tone was probing, and Norma was shocked at its effect. Even though the tingling in her scalp reminded her that the man standing next to her was a threat, she wanted to hear what Lambert had to say about Reijo Ross, which made her feel like accepting his offer. Surely one glass wouldn't hurt. But as soon as the idea crossed her mind, she felt the roots of her hair constrict as if scolding her, and that brought her back to her senses.

"I don't want to hear about my father."

"Unfortunately my business has nothing to do with your father. I haven't seen Reijo in ages. We made our last trip together ten years ago."

Norma's cheeks flushed at her stupid, fleeting notion that her father might have been interested in her. If he hadn't shown interest in three decades, what would her mother's death have changed?

Suddenly Lambert slapped his forehead in a wide, arcing gesture appropriate to a silent film. "But wait . . . ! Didn't your mother tell you? It didn't even occur to me that I should introduce myself in more detail. Anita was one of my employees. I own Marion's salon."

Norma sat on the bench, which was hot from a day in the sun, and Lambert flopped down next to her. No, her mother had not told her. Maybe she hadn't known who owned the salon. There could be no other explanation. Her mother would never have done this, not to Helena. The burning plastic under Norma's thighs made the sweating worse, and her ponytail, now curly at the top, swelled under her dress like a tumor. Saliva pooled in her mouth, and she felt nauseated.

"I've been traveling so much," Lambert said, "it's no wonder we haven't run into each other. However, I do drop in on the salon from time to time. According to Marion, Anita seemed somewhat distant during her last few days, perhaps even sad."

"Sad how?"

"Marion interpreted it as a kind of goodbye."

"How could she tell?"

"Just in her expression. And her words. Anita asked Marion to look after you if anything happened to her."

Lambert's body temperature rose at his temples and along his hairline. The lie was obvious.

"Some of Anita's things are still at the salon. Would you like to come by and get them?"

The clattering of the streetcar approached, and Norma stood

up. Was she imagining it, or had Lambert's tone changed? At first Norma couldn't find the right word, and then she realized what it was: *fatherly*. He sounded more fatherly. Lambert grabbed her shopping bags before Norma could stop him.

"This is the wrong moment," Lambert said. "But someone has to say it, since apparently you don't know . . ."

The streetcar stopped. The folding doors opened.

"There's no point in beating around the bush. Reijo died in a boating accident in Thailand. A while ago. He was like a brother to me, and I have many stories I could tell about him. Our family is prepared to help you any way we can. We always take care of our own."

Norma rode until the streetcar completed its loop and returned to her street in Kallio. Lambert hadn't been lying about her father. But the news didn't arouse any feelings in Norma, and the sentimentality that had bothered her at the streetcar stop did not return. Her skin tingled, but it didn't have anything to do with Reijo—it was from the hug Lambert had foisted on her before he lifted Norma's purchases onto the streetcar. Only now did Norma remember that Lambert still hadn't told her what the unfortunate business was he had hinted about at the cemetery gates. And she realized she'd been looking for clues about her mother's relationship with Lambert in the wrong decade: he had been part of her mother's life recently.

The laptop. There could actually be something there.

Lambert's gaze was glued to the screen. Once again he was playing back the security camera footage sent from the Bangkok clinic. The footage that had led to Anita being found out. The footage in which a woman recognizable as Anita questioned a girl handcuffed to a bed. The video was from the closed wing and clearly showed that Anita had a camera in her hand, that she had recorded the conversation.

"Turn it off," Alla said. "There isn't anything new in it."

"Where the hell is that camera?" Lambert asked, tapping the screen. "Whoever was doing business with Anita knows that she got caught and that she's dead. Why aren't they reacting?"

Alla looked out into the yard at her children playing with Ljuba and dabbed layer after layer of gloss on her lips. The layers began to build into waves that would soon run into the wrinkles around her lips. Two of Lambert's mongrels stood at the edges of the property, alert to every movement and sound, whether it was the boy distributing junk mail who sped by, the banging of a lawnmower motor, or the popping of beer bottle caps after sauna on the other side of the fence. Alla had demanded around-the-clock monitoring for her children as soon as suspicions about Anita's activities had surfaced, and she never went anywhere alone anymore. She had changed cars to one with bulletproof glass, and the home security system had been upgraded. These measures had calmed Alla, but not completely.

"If the Russians have gotten mixed up in—"

Lambert interrupted Alla by raising his hand like a truce flag. "Anita's modus operandi was not the traditional Russian way of handling conflicts. The Russians would have made themselves known after her death."

"But if they are involved, we need to blow the whistle," Alla said. "We aren't going to war. That would be unacceptable."

The applicator pressed hard against Alla's lower lip. Done with dabbing, she dragged it across her mouth as if scratching a rash. Her intermediaries still hadn't heard anything out of the ordinary. Business in Ukraine continued without interruption. There had been no threats against dealers, no plundered or burned stockpiles, and no broken windows. Except for Anita's exposure, nothing indicated a turf war—unlike when Alla had been establishing her Russian hair logistics chain. Lambert still remembered too how Alla had driven off a few Americans who were trying to muscle in on the Ukrainian market.

Alla dropped the lip gloss and picked up her nail file. The thought of war toppled the imperiousness from her like a meringue onto a plate, and for a moment the person leaning against the window was the girl who had been dating a Uralic hair mogul when matters got out of hand. The power struggle in the hair industry had become so intense that her partner got a bullet in the brain, the man who had been hunting Alla lost his own head, and that man's right hand had fled to Congo. Now Alla ruled her corner of the market from Finland with the aid of an army of helpers, but her iron grip had clearly slipped. Brittle from worry, she glanced at the kids running around on the grass, her hand clutching the file as if it were a weapon.

"The Ukrainian could just have been bait. A way to get Anita inside," Alvar pointed out. "No one could resist that hair."

Lambert ground his teeth. They had drawn a blank at Margit's, Norma's, and Anita's apartments, and the clan still didn't know the origin of the hair. Lambert cursed his blindness. The clan had made a mistake and forgotten caution. They should have suspected something immediately when Alla's contacts in Ukraine didn't know where the hair was coming from, who controlled it, or from whom Anita was getting it. But they had been smitten by the possibilities the Ukrainian hair offered and let the mole burrow in close.

"Whoever is selling it can continue doing business with us. It's too good to leave to the others," Lambert said.

"Sounds like war," Alvar said.

"We're only taking what belongs to us. We'll follow the trail until we find whoever the hair is coming from. Then we'll also find Anita's real boss and lay down the law," Lambert said.

"That's a war."

"Fine!"

Lambert slammed his fist onto the table. Their opponent was devious, more devious than any of Lambert's other enemies. He had known to find a mole from Lambert's past, a woman his children would trust.

Folake's salon was closed, but the drone of sewing machines was audible from the threshold. The girls in the back room were still working, and Marion would be able to take the finished hair soon. They had everything: sew-in, hot fusion, tape-in, all top quality as always. No one would notice that there was Russian mixed in. Folake was sure of that.

"We still won't give this to hypersensitive customers," Marion said.

Folake nodded. The Russian raw hair had been treated with the normal chemicals, but for the Ukrainian, just a wash and a hypoallergenic dye were enough. It had become a hit in Nigeria because it worked for people who were allergic to human hair. Before, hypersensitive clients had been forced to use synthetics, but now they could have the real thing.

"When will you get more?"

"Soon. It's just a delay."

Marion smiled her most convincing smile and took the glass of juice Folake offered. The logistical disturbance caused by Anita's death had to be fixed before Folake began to suspect that Anita had been behind everything. Marion glanced at her phone again. She had to continue calling the girl. She must know her mother's friends. She had to pick up Anita's trail even though no one in the clan seemed to believe she was capable of doing so. At the family meeting she'd been left out of the discussion as if her countdown had already begun. Air—she was only air to the clan even now.

The sew-ins would still be a few minutes. Marion sat to wait and looked outside. The mango juice in her hand was evidence that she wasn't under suspicion. She knew that. Otherwise she wouldn't be sitting in Folake's salon—she would have met Anita's fate. She would have been picked up at the airport just like Anita. She had been lucky that they always took different flights just to be safe. Even though her plane had landed a full two hours earlier, she'd stayed to wait. While she was getting her Starbucks, she noticed Lambert's men. First she was paralyzed, then she tried to call Anita, with no success. When the doors of the baggage claim area opened, Anita had walked right into Lambert's arms, and Lambert's fingers snapped around her wrist like a handcuff. Later Marion feigned confusion—she had no idea Anita had followed her to Bangkok. She thought Anita was on vacation somewhere else with friends. The clan believed her because they thought she was so stupid.

The droning stopped, and Marion was given the box of extensions, each bundle carefully packaged.

The other businesses on the street were already closed, but farther off the sounds of the pub patios were picking up. There was no sign of any gangs of immigrant boys or Lambert's mongrels. Contrary to Alla's advice, Marion had declined the offer of extra security. Still, she felt Lambert's eyes on her back. Ever since the moment she realized Anita was gathering evidence of the clan's business activities in order to blackmail them, overthrow them, and claim their territory, those had been the eyes of a predator sharpening its teeth.

The upper corner of the display began to scroll through a list of unread emails from the past several weeks, all from customers. The emojis in the subject lines pricked her heart. Norma had put off touching her mother's laptop because she knew that a wave of salon garbage would tumble out as soon as she opened the lid. But the good news was, what she saw on the screen was obviously her mother's doing, not anyone else's. Unlike Norma, her aunt didn't know the password: *Elizabeth Siddal.*

Norma logged into her mother's bank account. The final transaction was a grocery store purchase the day before her flight to Thailand. She had paid her May rent before the trip, leaving 250 euros in the account. Nothing about the transactions seemed strange, until she realized that despite all the traveling her mother had done that spring, she hadn't made any large credit card payments or any large cash withdrawals before each trip. Norma tried to count. Her mother's travel expenses exceeded her income. Had she taken out a loan and not mentioned it? Nothing in the account information indicated that.

The browser history had been cleared. She found messages to Marion in the sent folder, but they only touched on reservations and shifts at work. Norma moved on to the salon Facebook page, which her mother had administered under the name Anita Elizabeth. The account had been created for her in the spring, and she'd used it only for work. Other than Marion, all her Facebook friends were clients. Norma lit a cigarette and thought. Just a few hours before her flight to Thailand, her mother had confirmed some customer reservations. Why would she have done that if she was planning to end it all?

The notification sounds for the unread messages distracted Norma from her pondering. She turned off the computer's network connection, as she'd also done on the phone. Her mother would never be online again, and there would never be a need to water her houseplants again, contrary to the reminder that had appeared on the screen.

Norma placed the pot of angel's tears on the counter and said she wasn't interested in houseplants. Under her care they would just die.

"This was Anita's."

The florist hadn't heard about her longtime customer's demise. She knew someone had jumped in front of a metro train while she was in the south vacationing, but not that it was Norma's mother. The woman sat down and sighed.

Norma allowed time for condolences before presenting the seedling she had brought from her mother's balcony. "Mother meant to plant this almond bush in the backyard."

"You still could."

"No, you plant it somewhere."

The woman inspected the plant—it was rare at this latitude. In recent years, Norma's mother had begun tending the garden at their apartment building to make it more welcoming. The almond bush had been a gift from a grateful client just before her trip to Thailand. Norma had already turned to go when the shopkeeper began rummaging for something under the counter.

"Anita left her spare key here."

The woman gave Norma a padded envelope. It was glued shut, with no writing on the front.

"Did my mother do that often?"

"Whenever she left on a trip."

Norma didn't understand. She already had a spare key to her mother's apartment, and Norma thought she kept another at work.

She tore open the envelope. There was no key inside. Instead she found a flash drive and a memory card.

The screen showed an open suitcase with clothes tossed in. Norma's mother was operating the camera and couldn't seem to hold still, constantly walking around and occasionally checking the stove. Norma recognized the package of lamb fillets. The garam masala and almonds. This was the last meal they had shared, so the video on the memory card must have been made just before, the day before her mother left on her trip. The display began to tremble, and the light was so dazzling her eyes watered. Norma turned her head and took a sip of wine to force down the lump that had formed in her throat. She had been looking for her mother's message in the wrong places, thinking she would have written to Norma even though she'd never been a writing person. She handled things by calling or coming to visit. She talked. Norma should have realized that.

~

When I started this last year, I had no way of knowing where it would lead. The first time I picked up this camera, I thought I was only going to document things your grandmother remembered, for you. That wasn't what happened, though.

I ended up on an expedition that took a surprising turn. Hopefully I'll have enough courage to figure out everything myself. If not, I'll give you these videos in Bangkok. I can't deny I'm nervous. I'm so close. It feels like the night before a big holiday.

Her mother was excited. She wasn't saying goodbye. This wasn't her final message to Norma, and Norma wasn't meant to be seeing these videos yet. Norma paused the image. She dimmed the display, but the light still hurt her eyes. She tasted almonds in her mouth and smelled roasting lamb. The strangling feeling had returned, and drinking wine didn't make it go away. Brushing her hair didn't bring any relief either. She stared for a moment at the trash can icon. The videos might show her something she didn't want to know.

As Norma turned over in her hand the flash drive with its backup copies of video files from the memory card, she tried to force an unpleasant premonition from her mind. She moved on to the first file, recorded in May 2012. Only then did she notice how much her mother had aged in the past year: new lines had appeared, and her eyes had sunk into her face. The eyelash extensions Marion had applied were of little help—same with the new gel nails and the hairdo Marion had styled. Norma glanced at the index of videos again. Every file was named "For Norma." Watching them would take dozens of hours.

Three

When I met Lambert for the first time after all those years, the memories came flooding back. I could see in his expression that the same thing was happening to him. But we acted as if they didn't exist, as if we had no common past, as if no wrong had been done to Helena, as if Marion hadn't experienced any loss. It was easier that way, for both of us and for Marion, too. She was so nervous about our meeting. Eva had counseled me to maintain my composure no matter what happened. No one could suspect anything.

May 9, 2012

Grandma's condition isn't improving, and her prognosis doesn't promise any change. She still has moments of clarity when her mind works, which is why I have to talk to her about Eva. I can't put it off any longer. The first time I tried, she flew into a rage; the second time she only turned cranky and cried. Grandma claimed she didn't remember any Eva or intentionally confused her with Eeva from next door. Then she began scolding me, for my eyebrows or my hair. The nurse has already warned me about the agitation my visits are causing. I'm not giving up, though.

Today I tested whether a picture would help. I went to your grandmother's nightstand and picked up the family Bible. I took the picture out of it and put it in front of her face and told her this was the woman I meant. Grandma jumped and tried to grab the picture. I wouldn't give it to her. After that she started sobbing and forgot where we were. She was like a child again and asked me to braid her hair better so her mother wouldn't get upset.

The picture was a black and white postcard from the early 1900s and had been in that Bible as long as I can remember. When I was little, I would sneak looks at it. Once Grandma caught me, and I got a beating and had to spend the night in the shed. Back then I didn't know who the woman in the picture was. But the picture's place in the pages of the family Bible meant that she was someone, as did my mother's reaction. I never brought the woman up again in our house and never dared to ask anyone else about her. I shared my secret only with Helena and always went to look at the picture when no one was around. Her unnaturally long hair made her look more like a fairy-tale creature than a real person. It wasn't until I learned to read that I understood the words on the card and the name of the woman on it, and I realized that she was related to us. I'd never heard anyone talk about someone named Eva Naakka.

After you were born, I went through every possible drug I'd taken and everything I'd eaten during my pregnancy. I worried that I'd traveled somewhere a woman expecting a baby shouldn't go, accidentally eaten radioactive mushrooms, or visited a farm that used DDT. It was totally irrational for me to have a daughter whose hair grew more than a meter every day. Just as absurd was the idea that this might be a recessive genetic trait, or at least a predisposition to unusual hair growth, but the picture of Eva Naakka pointed that way. If the cascading hair in the picture was genuine, she was the same kind of exception as you, and in that case at least I hadn't made you the way you were by something I did.

I started to search for people like you in books and pictures, and I always came back to the photograph of Eva. Maybe it had some connection to my own mother's obsession with hair. When I was a child, she braided my hair so tightly it made my eyes squint. I always had to loosen the braids for school—Helena tightened them again before I came home. Grandma disapproved of free-flowing locks, considering them a sign of a loose woman. That had to come from somewhere. Eva's peculiarity could be enough of an explanation if Grandma knew about it. I suspected there was something else hiding in this, though.

May 10, 2012

According to the postmark, the card was sent from New York City, but the date was smudged. On the back a man named Antero reported finding a familiar-looking face in the window display of a Harlem wig shop: "Isn't this Eva Naakka in this picture? I wouldn't have noticed if I wasn't shining shoes out front," he wrote.

Antero was a stranger to us, but a few years later we caught wind of him in a chance encounter at a funeral. The deceased, Helmi, had lived to ninety years old. Around the coffee table, a conversation started about whether her son Antero was still alive and in America, since he hadn't shown up to pay his respects. Helena's aunts began reminiscing about the Civil Guard Crisis and how the freshly appointed commander of the guard, Karl Emil Berg, shot himself under all the pressure. The Communists had been waiting for the situation to reach a head and now saw their opportunity. Helmi had lost a lot of sleep because Antero had a habit of getting mixed up in just that sort of thing.

When a card came from Antero after Berg's suicide, the rock rolled off of Helmi's chest. The card was evidence that her son was still in America, not involved in the troubles in Finland. As they talked about the card, Helena's aunts leaned over their saucers and whispered about whether it was that card.

The date was easy to figure out. Karl Emil Berg shot himself in 1921. The same year Helmi received the card from Antero. At some point before then, Eva had to have been in Paris where the picture was taken. I didn't understand that until after I talked to Johansson, the art dealer.

My great-grandparents' portrait fell to the floor one day while it was being dusted, and I was sent to have the frame fixed at the art shop, which was a sort of combination framing and antique shop. While Johansson worked, he handed me a box of old photographs to pass the time. The letters "PC Paris" on Eva's picture had always bothered me, and now I noticed the same letters on many of the photos in the box. Johansson told me that it referred to a very respected postcard publisher. PC Paris postcards were world famous. The people who modeled for them weren't just anybody, Johansson said, and began presenting his collection, which mostly consisted of landscapes and women. I saw immediately that Eva was more beautiful than the belles in the pictures, hands down. The collection also included cards in color, like Eva's. Johansson said the only artists who knew how to add color to pictures that way at the time were in Paris and Belgium. They couldn't make cards like that in America even of their own film stars, so those were made in the Old World too. "All by hand, of course. Coloring was women's work, and many of them were poisoned because they would wet the brushes in their mouths," Johansson whispered.

June 3, 2012

Helena and I spun all sorts of adventures for Eva. We were convinced she'd been in beauty contests and wondered whether that was the reason for her shadowy reputation in the Naakka home. The only sure thing was that she went out into the world and became a star. She was the one from our village who became something. Our Eva in a Parisian studio. That affected the decision Helena and I made: we would leave, too. We didn't have Eva's beauty, but we would find another way to make our mark. Helena dreamed of a career as a singer, while I just wanted to see the world. We didn't have money for a trip to America or Paris, but we could hitchhike to Sweden.

When we fled to Gothenburg and started work at the Volvo factory, we added sparkle to our days of punching time cards by continuing to investigate the mystery of Eva. We pored over art and photography books in the library and also took a trip from Gothenburg to Stockholm to check the secondhand bookshops. One of them paid off. Eva was easily recognizable. One of the cards had been sent from Opatija in Croatia to Dinard in France, the other from Brighton to Boston. One was dated 1922, the other 1924. The pictures were very elegant, though they didn't carry any mention of the studio or photographer: In one, Eva's locks spread toward steps leading to a fountain. She posed as a gypsy with a mandolin in her lap, despite how white she was. In the other, she flirted coquettishly with a lapdog, her left hand holding a comb, as if about to set it to her hair. An oval mirror was positioned so that it also gave a view of the back of her mass of locks.

I asked the shopkeeper about the series numbers—I'd noticed those on most of the cards from the famous French publishers. But they were missing from the PC Paris picture and the ones we had just found. The shopkeeper laughed. Series numbers weren't required, but the signature of a famous publisher raised the price even though it wasn't always genuine. This explanation disappointed me. Eva might never have visited Paris. The setback didn't discourage Helena, though. She wanted to know whether the shopkeeper had any other cards depicting models with unusually long hair. The shopkeeper winked and set a box before us full of French postcards. His own favorite was a picture of an *adelita* wrapped only in bandoliers and her own hair. These words were new to us, both *French postcards* and *adelitas*, the female *soldaderas* who became symbols of the Mexican Revolution. The card was exceptional because the model was blond and the face had been scraped away. The shopkeeper guessed that the woman wanted to conceal her identity since the picture was so risqué. But there was no way to mistake the hair or the pose. It was obviously Eva: the shape and position of the hands were the same as in the girl with the mandolin. And the same as in the picture at home in the Bible.

Later on, I continued tracking pictures of Eva using the Internet. I found only a few new French ones, but there are plenty of copies of the existing pictures out there. People have collected them for decades and used them on confetti boxes, perfume bottles, book covers, advertisements. The name Eva Naakka is never mentioned despite the fact that her blond exoticism had the potential to make her a permanent celebrity at PC Paris, like Miss Fernande. Something or someone must have prevented that from happening.

Since I was so far away in Sweden, I finally worked up the courage to make a long-distance call to our parish at home and ask for information about Eva from the church records. Mother found out about my call and brooded over it for years. When I returned home with you after you were born, she finally unleashed her anger. Supposedly I was trying to shame her. Again that shame. But now I thought I knew where it came from and who Eva was. She had been my grandfather Juhani Naakka's first wife, who left her children, husband, and the Naakka home. Eva was your grandma's real mother.

According to the parish records, Eva Kuppari and Juhani Naakka were married in 1917. Two children were born to the family. One was my mother, Elli Naakka, and the other my uncle, Erik, who died in the Winter War. The marriage was annulled in the late 1920s because Eva Naakka hadn't lived with her husband for years and her location was unknown. Between the lines of the record book, the word *America* had been penciled in with a question mark after it.

Juhani Naakka later remarried, and Anna Heikkinen bore a whole swarm of children for him. I'd grown up under the impression that Anna was my grandmother. She was the one standing next to Juhani in the family portrait I took to Johansson's shop to be fixed. I called a few of my living aunts, but none of them had heard of Eva or their father's previous marriage, or so they claimed. It was understandable—the decline of the family's fortunes had begun with Juhani's worsening alcoholism, which I realized coincided with the early days of his second marriage.

Now I understood why Eva's picture was hidden in the pages of the family Bible. How it ended up there, I didn't know. But I guessed that Mother stole it from Helmi. Or that Helmi had given it to her, thinking the picture belonged to Eva's daughter more than it did to her.

June 16, 2012

Over the years my ideas about Eva's fate varied. The Finns who left for America tended to be poor, hirelings, younger children from landed families—people whose opportunities in Finland were limited. But Eva was the mistress of the large and wealthy Naakka home. When I was young, I thought she must have met the love of her life outside her marriage and left her family. That would explain my mother's reaction: Eva was a woman of sin.

After your birth, I understood Eva's choice even less. She'd been lucky enough to give birth to two healthy children, and the stench of scandal in her wake seemed to have to do with the immorality of leaving, not her hair. So if her secret was never found out, why did she abandon such a good life?

I also wondered why she'd agreed to model for a photographer. In an earlier time, someone like you could have made a safe living for herself as a muse because artists' lithographs and paintings didn't make models instantly recognizable. But photographic postcards changed the situation entirely. Collecting them became a fashionable hobby for every class of society. Even the poor could afford them because developments in technology had lowered the price of the cards so much. Suddenly the entire population began focusing on models—people began emulating their gestures and expressions, and one model complained in an interview that complete strangers would touch her hair on the street. Eva was wise to keep her face out of the erotic shots, but I recognized her even without her face, and the person who took the pictures knew who she was. What had she received in return? What did she want so much that she would take a risk like that?

I came to hate Eva. She'd been the heroine of my childhood, the most beautiful and courageous woman from our village. But in reality she was something entirely different, and I felt betrayed. I also understood my mother's rage toward Eva. My mother was tainted by scandal. She'd been abandoned, and no one ever told her why. The basis for my anger was different, though: I gave birth to you without knowing anything about the risks, which was Eva's fault. It was a miracle that Grandma succeeded in having two healthy daughters. I started to wonder whether the small number of children in our family line had something to do with this. As I understood it, my mother had a few miscarriages, as did Margit. When the first one happened, I mourned with my sister. But when Margit became pregnant again—after you were born—I began to hope that she wouldn't go to term. And that's what happened. As she grew older, she lamented her lost opportunity, but I felt only relief. I'd lived in constant fear that the same thing would happen to her as to me.

Four

For a long time, I didn't want to think about Eva at all. Then I understood that the only way to leave you a history of your own would be to tell her story. You have a right to know what kind of life a person like you can have, and you have a right to know all the dangers associated with it. I wasn't going to repeat Eva's mistakes.

Ophelia and *Regina Cordium,* Norma's mother's favorite paintings, still hung in the entryway. Snatching them off the wall, Norma inspected the back of each. No picture, no Eva. She removed the glass from the frames. Nothing. Of course not. Her mother couldn't have known that Norma would forget to put her favorite paintings in the casket. She definitely would have wanted them with her if she'd decided to end her life voluntarily, even though that was seeming less likely all the time.

Her mother had always hunted for women who might be like Norma, and her home was plastered with images of various Rapunzels. The shelves sagged under the weight of their stories. She had wanted to assure Norma, who often felt down because of her hair, that the beauty of women who looked like this had been admired and immortalized. The apartment was a mausoleum to the Goldilockses of times past, which is why it made little sense that her mother had concealed Eva's existence. Her mother had continued her search even after Norma made peace with her hair and refused to keep sitting in her mother's private hair school. But her mother still wanted a solution, an answer that could help them understand what was going on—that was why she couldn't end her hunt. She continued sharing information with Norma whether Norma wanted it or not. So why hadn't her mother told her about Eva face-to-face? Why only in a video? Why hadn't she hung pictures of Eva on her walls? The idea that there had been another woman like Norma in their family was earth-shattering.

Norma dropped the paintings onto the floor and walked over them. The glass crunched, her neck cracked, and the guilty feeling for having forgotten to put the pictures in the casket moved to her hair. She grabbed a pair of scissors off her mother's shelf, and after snipping off the guilt, began flipping through the biographies of Elizabeth Siddal and Rossetti's other muses. The cutting would help for a while—she was calmer now, and her hands were steady again. She couldn't think of a better place to look for clues than in these books and paintings. The model for *Ophelia* and *Regina Cordium,* Elizabeth Siddal, was her mother's favorite muse. She was the angel of the Pre-Raphaelites whose face and stately shock of hair everyone has seen on a card, on a poster, or in a book, yet her secret had remained hidden. She'd been just like Norma.

Elizabeth's husband, the artist Dante Gabriel Rossetti, opened his wife's grave six years after her fatal overdose of laudanum. Rossetti wanted to retrieve the collection of poetry he'd buried with her while playing the romantic mourning widower. His career had been in a downturn at the time, and the buried verses were exactly what he needed to elevate his star again. Norma easily found the section in Siddal's biography since the page was dog-eared. No message, no picture, not even any underlining. The same thing repeated in the other books about Siddal. A folded page or a bookmark but nothing else.

Elizabeth Siddal's story had shaken all the self-destructiveness out of Norma. It made her understand that accidents and suicides weren't for their kind, not even in the deepest moments of despair, because when Rossetti opened the coffin, Elizabeth's copper locks had cascaded out. Unlike the collection of poetry, they had withstood the ravages of time. Completely uncorrupted, they had filled the casket. If Norma died under conditions that left her body for someone else to find, the same thing would happen to her. What followed would be blaring headlines, paparazzi crawling through the windows, and the gawking doctors who had reduced the mystery of bearded women to hypotrichosis and a genetic defect. She didn't want that. She didn't want to be cut up in a laboratory. That was why she always carried a small piece of paper with instructions to contact Anita Ross immediately if anything happened to her. That was why she kept her apartment tidy, to allow for surprise visits by the building superintendent or the police. The building was scheduled for window renovation, but that kind of traffic through her apartment didn't worry Norma. Her home gave no indication that anyone out of the ordinary lived there.

Her mother's bookshelves yielded no results. Norma grew bored and decided to continue later. The wave in her ends was either from her fascinating new relative or from the construction worker banging around the building. She glanced around the apartment, where everything looked normal, then went to collect the hair she'd left on the bathroom floor. As she slipped her feet back into her ballet flats, her gaze landed on a pile of newspapers. A moment passed before she realized the papers were untouched. Her mother hadn't put her deliveries on hold during her trip to Thailand as she usually did. The only papers and magazines in the "read" basket were from Margit, from the weeks after the funeral. Norma's mother had been a systematic person; the objects on the shelves, on the tables, and in the cabinets were arranged by height or in symmetrical patterns, and she never left the day's newspaper unread. Norma had been looking in the wrong place again. She should be looking for flaws, not for a message. Flaws like a pile of unread newspapers.

Her mother's mail consisted mostly of bills and advertisements. None of this told Norma anything, and she decided to start over from the beginning. She would go through her mother's purse one more time, without the surge of emotion from before. Back at her own apartment, she spread the contents of the purse on the floor and carefully examined the pens, receipts, and business cards. Nothing jumped out at her until she picked up the keys. There were two key chains. One had a house key, the other a small pendant that read "Attic," with Elizabeth Siddal's picture as Ophelia. Her mother's storage locker in the attic was number twenty—the same as her apartment—but the number written on the reverse of the Ophelia pendant was twelve. Norma hadn't been up to the attic storage area for years—she didn't store her own things and couldn't remember her mother ever taking anything there. The key hooks in her mother's entryway held a slew of less commonly used keys, including the key to locker number twenty.

The attic fire door was hard to open. The sun had made the whole floor hot, and the rafters shimmered. At first Norma thought she felt faint from the heat or from the air oxidized by rat poison and dust, but then she realized she was wrong. A familiar smell wafted through the chicken wire enclosures and grew stronger as she approached storage locker number twelve.

Behind a jumble of junk was a box with an unmistakable scent. Still, Norma hoped she was mistaken, hoping so hard she forgot to breathe.

She moved the box out to the middle of the walkway.

It was full of her hair, all bundled neatly.

The family meeting would be pure hell. Marion prayed that her name wouldn't be on the list. Over the past few weeks, Lambert had been assembling all his enemies—potential, imaginary, or real—and it was a long list, still growing, which he kept concealed from view in his breast pocket.

"What if we're looking in the wrong direction?" Lambert said. "What if Anita wanted to take revenge on me? Was it really a coincidence that she ran into you in Kuopio, Alvar?"

The glowering furrow of Lambert's brow deepened. He grabbed a strawberry out of the bowl and pulled the stem off so violently that it crushed the berry. In addition to mapping out their ongoing turf war, today's agenda was also supposed to include the Nigerian water bottle factory and preparations for a trip to Vietnam, but Lambert spoke of nothing but Anita. Alvar poured a cup of coffee and tried to steer the discussion back on track. They had to get a sense for the overall picture instead of allowing Lambert to lead them toward paranoia. Anita was just one pawn.

"Anita wouldn't be able to cover her tracks this professionally. Not alone," Alla pointed out.

"And Anita wouldn't have harbored a grudge for thirty years, not even on Helena's behalf," Alvar continued.

"Wouldn't she?" Lambert said. "Are you sure Anita didn't want to finish what Helena failed at? That woman wormed herself in here on purpose. What could this be about if not revenge?"

"Dad," Alvar said, "someone got to Anita and made her infiltrate our ranks. We have to find that someone."

Lambert pulled out his list again. Apparently he'd thought of a new name who might be carrying a grudge. Someone who would be ready to make an alliance with Anita or hire her to do his dirty work and dig into the clan's secrets.

"Dad, we're at war. Remember?"

Alvar spread out his own list on the table, this one of all the organization's employees. He would go through the entire staff himself. Somewhere there was a leak. Someone had told Anita that she should go to the closed ward of that clinic in Bangkok.

"Who did Anita give the camera to?" Alvar asked.

Marion's hand went to her right pocket again, the one where she'd kept the burner phone she and Anita used to communicate. They had called it their "project phone." But the pocket was empty. Marion had destroyed it immediately after Anita's death. She had no one to talk to, and no one to ask for advice.

Marion focused on massaging Ljuba's scalp and staring at the wood grain of the sauna walls. Lambert had exploded over her nonexistent results until Alvar encouraged their father to focus on more important things. *Dad*—Alvar used that word skillfully, deliberately. That was why he received bonuses, like his villa. One of his bonuses had certainly been that they hired Anita after he brought her in, or maybe that was in recompense for Albino. No one reproached Alvar for anything. Or Alla, even though Ukraine was her responsibility.

Only Marion was blamed for mistakes, always Marion, and now she was sent away from the table whenever the discussion turned to future strategies. She was good enough to treat Ljuba's hair, nothing more.

Upstairs Lambert's fist pounded the table again. Ljuba flinched and raised a hand to her belly. No one in the neighborhood wondered about the Russian nanny. But soon her pregnancy would show, and Ljuba would have to leave. The parents of the child she was carrying were getting divorced, and neither wanted children anymore. In all likelihood the baby would be dropped off at a St. Petersburg orphanage, or maybe Alla had found a buyer for it. Marion and Ljuba were equally as dispensable when they became dead weight.

"Everything is fine," Marion said. "It just might not turn out that way for us."

Ljuba returned Marion's smile without understanding a word. If they had a common language, Marion would try to get Ljuba to talk about what Alla and Lambert discussed in private, but now all she could do was apply dye to Ljuba's hair and a relaxing mask to her face, then point to the clock to indicate how long the treatment would take.

From the bar cabinet in the sauna lounge, Marion chose a thirty-year-old Highland Park, Lambert's most expensive bottle, which had been a gift from a grateful customer of the agency, and poured glasses for herself and Ljuba. The map was still above the cabinet, and the growing number of pushpins in its surface told of the progress of Lambert and Alla's world conquest. Silver pins for hair wholesale, colored for the agency, each year with its own color. Ten colors. There was one red pin. Thailand. That was where it all started. Lambert had realized the country was full of illegal Vietnamese immigrants, who were poor, easy, cheap. The next year the operation expanded to Vietnam itself, which quickly became Lambert's favorite child, and a blue pin appeared on the map.

The clan had good relationships with local producers. Just one farm delivered fifty to sixty tons of raw hair to the Chinese hair factories—the hair moguls became millionaires, and 80 percent of the population of the surrounding villages supported themselves selling hair. The only problem was that hair grew slower than demand. Once all the village women had been sheared, the boys had to make increasingly long motorcycle journeys to far-flung areas. Russia and Ukraine—Alla's territories—were marked with green pins. Then they had expanded into Georgia. After that office opened, agency revenue exploded. They'd also succeeded in landing American customers through Mexico. Americans had begun to stream into Cancún from any state where the laws were difficult, or just looking for cheaper prices. Clients also flooded in from Scandinavia, Great Britain, Australia, and now Japan.

The pin in Nigeria might be removed once this meeting was over. They'd already decided to pull out of the country, but then Anita and her magical skeins of hair appeared. That shook up everything, and Lambert decided to give the country one more chance because their hair industry was growing by leaps and bounds. Marion could guess what Lambert was saying upstairs. He would compare Nigeria to Thailand and Georgia and Ukraine and Russia. Each area had its own difficulties, but challenges were meant to be conquered. Cowards might shit their pants and accept defeat without complaint, but Lambert never did.

Marion shouldn't have taken a picture of the map and shown it to Anita. The scope of the clan's operation had come as a shock to Anita, and after she recovered, she became reckless. There were only two days remaining of the week Lambert had given Marion, and the girl still hadn't responded to any of her messages. In two days, the clan would proceed by its own methods.

When the scopolamine patches eased the nausea and Norma could stand steadily again, Eva's blue eyes seemed to follow her. The contents of the boxes of hair still covered the living room floor, but the bundles no longer writhed like a nest of snakes, and the air from the open window had dissipated their concentrated smell. In the middle of the bundles rested Eva's picture. Her poise was majestic, and she eyed Norma reproachfully like a mother with a tantruming child, her mouth pursed like the bud of a rose. Norma pressed a hand to her solar plexus. Restless hoofbeats pounded her chest: *There's someone besides me. You are like me*. Eva seemed to shake her head. The most important thing now was to figure out what Norma's mother had gotten her involved in. Eva's business could wait.

In the attic locker she had found two boxes. One was overflowing with hair, and the other contained miscellaneous papers. Eva's pictures lay on top. One of them was the postcard Antero had sent from America. The stack also included the photo Norma's mother had found in Stockholm of Eva as an *adelita*. The face was missing. It had been used as a graphic for a book named *Confessions of Rapunzel*, and Norma's mother had printed the cover.

Norma gathered the pile of papers in her lap, closed the living room door to keep the stench of hair in one room, and spread the collection on the entryway rug. It was comprised of old newspaper clippings, notes written in an unfamiliar hand, black and white photos of women with long tresses, Sutherland sisters hair elixir advertisements, a few English-language articles about Nigerian baby farms, hotel brochures from Tbilisi and Cancún, and a relatively recent article from the *Helsingin Sanomat* monthly insert about a couple who rented a uterus in St. Petersburg. An article about Victorian wet nurses who had turned out to be the worst serial killers in history had been read carefully. It contained notes from two different pens, one in handwriting that wasn't Norma's mother's: exclamation points, angry underlining, and circled words. The article about Dr. Conde's baby farm had been ripped in two and taped back together. A New York society lady revealed in an interview in 1921 that all three of her daughters were adopted. Her husband hadn't known a thing about it. Ultimately the woman came forward out of a desire to proclaim to all the world the good tidings of motherhood made possible by adoption. Taken together, the collection made no sense, but the hair in the other box did.

Norma remembered clearly the evening preceding her mother's vacation. She had already packed and came to cut Norma's hair before going to sleep. She fretted over the single strands of gray as she plucked them out. There was no indication that she was in an abnormal frame of mind or excessively worried. Her mother had been in a good mood and seemed to look forward to her vacation. She had filled Norma's pill dispenser and reminded her not to forget to take her vitamin supplements every day. She harped on the dangers of osteoporosis, possible blood vessel issues, and all that yet again. She was only a mother thinking of what was best for her daughter, and her words left a guilty feeling in Norma's chest.

Nutritional supplements and sample packages had begun appearing in the house as soon as Norma's mother started at Shear Magic. In her opinion, the possibility of a slight increase in hair growth was a small price to pay for better health. Norma would have more energy, the gray hairs would disappear completely, and her nails would grow normally. Reassured by her mother, Norma began popping pills of trace elements. The spice shelf grew crowded with bottles of orthosilicic acid, lycopene, sea protein, and horsetail capsules. One morning Norma found a pill dispenser filled with manganese, copper, calcium, zinc, and folic acid on the table. Her hair continued to gray, but her hangnails disappeared.

The employee benefits at the salon might explain the easy and inexpensive access to hair nutrient products but not the steak that started showing up on the table in the middle of the week. While before they mostly ate tenderloin only on holidays, that spring they began roasting it on Wednesdays and weekends. Norma remembered the plastic bag from the market, the receipt at the bottom she'd found and was using to write her own shopping list, when she noticed the total on the reverse side. At first she thought it must have belonged to someone else. However, the items on the receipt matched the contents of the refrigerator—ingredients for that week's dinners—so she asked whether her mother had scratched a winning lottery ticket without telling her. Her mother replied that her pay was better than at the post office, and she'd been working long days at the salon. But her income couldn't be high enough to explain a vacation to Thailand or the trip to Africa early the previous winter. Her mother had also visited Georgia just before Easter. Where had the money for all that come from? Norma hadn't thought about it at the time. Instead she spent their evenings together lamenting her own troubles, complaining about her gray hairs, which had begun to appear during the labor negotiations at work, and devouring the beef without a thought for the cost.

83

When Norma looked at the remnants of the boxes she had torn open, it was clear that her mother had been going through her garbage.

Washing hadn't completely removed the smell of coffee grounds, composting avocado pits, and banana peels from the bundles of hair. The artificial briskness of shampoo hanging over them only made the smell worse. Airing out the apartment would take at least a day. The bundles were packed in cellophane with gold elastics holding them closed. The crackling of the packets was like birthday presents.

The careful sorting of loose hairs told its own story: at first her mother had bunched them together any old way but then later realized the value of virgin Remy quality hair. It was the best, the most expensive, and it required cutting the whole bundle of hair in the direction of growth. The early bundles weren't Remy, but the more recent ones were. Norma remembered the moment when her mother had started cutting her hair a new way, putting it up in a ponytail first. According to her mother, it made tidying up easier.

When the wind chimes jingled, Marion nearly dropped the extension iron. She counted to ten, letting the wave of relief fade, and suggested to the client that they take a break. Once the woman in her cape rustled out to the smoking spot in the backyard, Marion approached the girl and extended her hand.

"We didn't have a chance to talk at the funeral," Marion said.

The girl was frozen at the threshold, shifting her weight uneasily from one foot to the other. The rough skin of her palm was clammy, the bones clearly visible, and her grip was weak. Sunglasses concealed her eyes, and her nose twitched like that of an animal. She seemed on the verge of tears.

"Your mother was the best hairdresser I've ever had."

The girl still didn't reply. Marion would have to take the reins. First she had to figure out how to talk to the girl. At the church, the girl had kept her attention focused on pulling loose hairs from her ponytail, one after another, out of time with the hymns, and Marion had wondered how the girl's hair could be so thick if she was always pulling it out when she was anxious. Lambert's mongrels followed the girl the whole time, and she hadn't met with anyone. No men, no friends. Not even Margit. Surely no one that age could be so antisocial. She returned bags of bottles for recycling, but no drinking companions ever showed up. Alvar suspected the dealer had gone underground, and the girl was keeping a low profile. But there was no real evidence that the girl knew about her mother's business activities.

Marion opened Anita's workstation cabinet and stepped aside. The girl didn't make any move to take anything. She looked spindly from behind and had a complicated turban wrapped around her hair. The hair wasn't tinted, so the girl wouldn't be interested in a free dye job—Marion couldn't even offer that. She couldn't find any point of contact. The girl obviously hadn't come to cut a deal or to ask about Anita's fate or to discuss hair orders. Maybe she believed the suicide story. But then why didn't she ask anything about Anita's state of mind before the accident? That's what Marion would have done.

Marion made her decision quickly and hugged the girl tightly. There were customers who came to the salon only because they wanted someone to touch them, even if it was just a scalp massage. You noticed the same longing for touch in some children, and the girl had been wearing that expression.

"I'm going to make a little cocoa with a splash of something stronger," Marion said.

The girl leaned limply on Marion's shoulder. Her sunglasses had fallen to the floor. The client peeked through the crack in the door and then, after seeing the situation, returned to the backyard with a few women's magazines under her arm.

Marion sat the girl on the sofa. "How's work? Anita said you're going through some difficult times."

"Difficult enough that I don't have a job anymore."

The girl spoke. That was progress. Marion switched on the electric teakettle and nodded at an empty styling chair.

"What would you say to coming to help me every once in a while? Until you find something else. The wedding season is about to really heat up. To tell the truth, I'm in a bind. I can't even handle all the messages I have to deal with."

The ringing of the desk phone underlined her words.

"I'm not a hairstylist."

"Anyone can answer the phone and take reservations. You should have seen Anita in action. She loved her work," Marion said, grabbing a keratin glue stick. "This magic wand can make dreams come true. We are priests and midwives and therapists and doctors. We officiate at rites of passage. We wrap women in strips of foil and towels and capes to wash away their old lives and send them toward the future. Turning points in life depend on the success of our work. And best of all, once women develop a taste for good hair, they're willing to pay anything for it."

The girl's wandering gaze stopped for a moment, just long enough.

"The hair business has gone completely crazy over the past few years. Did Anita talk about it? Things aren't quite as wild here as in South America, though. In Colombia hair bandits have started running around, and in Venezuela the women of Maracaibo keep their hair concealed in public places. Otherwise a piranha will come and steal it."

Marion illustrated her words by making a swift swipe with her styling razor. The girl flinched but didn't respond to Marion's probing gaze.

"Ask any stylist you want. Business has gone bananas. The situation in America is really hot because of a wave of thefts. In Atlanta a friend I know just lost her whole stock. The robbers left new flat-screen TVs and cash. All they wanted was the virgin Remy."

The girl's expression was incredulous.

"You just have to work with reliable partners. So you don't end up in dangerous situations. Take your time thinking about it. The career opportunities are excellent."

When Marion went back to her client's hot fusion extensions, Norma poured more rum into her hot chocolate and pulled an antinausea pill out of her pocket. The hair dust had assaulted her at the doorway, and there was evidence of her hair everywhere: in the chinks in the floor tiles, the wheels of the tool cart, the bin overflowing with bags of hairpins. Through the smells she relived the past six months of her life. The casual sex, the hangover she had after May Day—she could even sense the changes in the structure of her hair caused by the vitamin supplements. Her working environment had made the quality of her hair uneven, but from March on, you could hardly tell anymore. Her mother had known what she was doing. Norma had become a carefully bred leghorn hybrid, the changes to her nutrition leading to flawless hair production.

She waited on the cool clinker floor for the pills to take effect and added another splash of rum to her cup. Lambert's scent trail was also all over the salon. Marion hadn't mentioned him, but Norma hadn't sensed any avoidance of the subject either, which would have smelled almost the same as lying. Marion's hug had contained only sorrow and longing. The farrago of hair scents that clung to her skin and clothing was just as unpleasant as Norma had guessed it would be, and Marion's own hair smelled of insomnia, wine, and slapdash meals. But her high stress level could be caused by anything. It wasn't insanity or instability on a par with Helena's.

Anita's cabinet was full of unimportant junk: spare keys, including her own and Norma's, a brush, lipstick, a stack of customer loyalty cards, safety pins, pepper spray, two pairs of work shoes, a scarf, and a sweater. The smells of the brush made tears well in Norma's eyes: their last meal of lamb, garam masala, almonds, and apricots. Her mother had visited the salon afterward. Norma struggled against the longing. The vitamins at the back of the cabinet could go into the trash. Norma's days as her mother's fatted piglet were over.

Norma put off opening the drawers next to the cabinet. Their contents were obvious even before she pulled the first one open. Wearing extensions made of this hair, women would proceed to the altar. They would travel with cavaliers, fiancés, lovers, husbands, and the fathers of their children to family reunions and festivals. They would dash among birch trees toward the lake on Midsummer Eve. They would preen and, during arguments late at night around the bonfire, think that at least their hair looked nice. Norma's hair would make for countless happy holidays and conjure enchantments from new love to June babies. It would float in fans on the surface of lakes in the unfurling midnight sun and twirl in fields of ripening grain. Wearing her hair, those women would receive everything she never would. At any moment she might walk past one of them, even near her own home. Maybe she already had but far enough off that she hadn't smelled her own locks on a stranger's head. Why had her mother taken a risk like that?

Suddenly her mother's unexplained interest in new apartments made sense. Norma had wondered at the energy her mother had devoted to tracking real estate listings and attending open houses since February. Norma wasn't at all excited by the prospect and caused a minor fight after saying so. She enjoyed living in Kallio, despite the seedy reputation, because the neighborhood accepted everyone as they were and allowed anyone to be anonymous. No one watched you here. Perhaps Marion's salon was located in the neighborhood for precisely that reason. Just then it occurred to Norma that her mother hadn't had any documentation of the origin of the goods she was selling unless she had forged it herself.

On the salon side, the client inspected her new hair in the mirror with a professional air. Empty packages of Great Lengths lay on the tool cart. The woman's careful diet and enthusiasm for protein products made it seem likely she was a bodybuilder.

"Next time reserve Ukrainian for me!"

"You're first in line," Marion assured her.

"I need it for the finals. I hear it doesn't tangle at all."

When Marion popped into the back room to look for product for her client, she pointed to the drawers lying open in front of Norma.

"That Ukrainian has been driving our clients nuts. What on earth are those women eating? We women in rich countries ruin our hair eating processed food and then have to spend all our money on treatments to fix it. Whereas women in the Romanian countryside just wash with soap at most and maybe use some herbs, but they eat tomatoes from their own gardens. No wonder Romanian hair is on the rise. But this Ukrainian stock is in a class by itself."

Alvar handed Marion a list of potential clients in addition to a new prepaid phone, then turned back to the company computer screen. Her brother had no intention of leaving. The mistrust was reflected everywhere, from the double-checking of the accounting to Alla's constant pecking and the way Alvar always glanced at the reservation book. Apparently Marion wasn't even going to be allowed to handle agency client calls alone anymore. If there weren't cameras in the salon, it was probably only because Marion would have found them and ripped them out of the wall like the last time there was a trust issue in the organization. That had been caused by Albino, who worked here as an eyelash technician. Still, Marion and her salon had ended up under the magnifying glass.

"Hello," Alvar said over the screen.

Marion grabbed the list and pretended to read it.

"It's from Lasse," Alvar said.

Marion nodded. All the nurses handled their duties differently. Kristian's patient lists were a particular mess, but Lasse, a dedicated marriage equality activist, made everyone else's work easier by doing an initial screening himself. The agency had sent brochures to the fifteen names on the list, and seven of them had made inquiries. Marion decided to concentrate on the Finns; the foreigners would have to wait. If she could hook three, Lambert would be happy.

"How did it go with that Down syndrome woman?" Alvar asked.

Marion had forgotten all about her.

"You're slipping. Call her right now."

"Why can't Alla handle it? Alla was with us in Lviv," Marion replied.

Alla and Marion had traveled with this particular client to Lviv, Ukraine, to audition surrogates. After reviewing the agency's brochures, the woman chose a few prospects, who were then dressed up and taken to a salon before the meeting to give their hair that healthy shine that made them seem more reliable to Western women. The nail technician removed their pink acrylic nails, which had been done before shooting the promo videos, but the Donetsk women had already returned to their old style.

The visit had gone well, although they could tell from the woman's expression that the facade and interior of the clinic hadn't lived up to the image created by the website. However, Marion had previously noted the woman's weakness for sweets. That was why they'd timed the visit to coincide with the Lviv Chocolate Festival. By evening, the woman had surrendered herself to the new life Lviv promised her. After the baby was born, it turned out to have Down syndrome, and the woman refused to take him. She began bombarding the agency with tears and curses and threats of bankruptcy and the police. Finally Lambert showed mercy by offering the child at a discount rate. The woman was still being difficult, though, and she might have new demands. If she did, Marion couldn't pass them on to Lambert, not in this situation.

Alvar set the phone on the table and pushed Lasse's list into

Marion's hand again. "Fine," he said. "I'll handle the Down syndrome case. You do the list."

Marion took a sip of water and keyed in the first phone number. Lasse had written a short summary below the name: "35-year-old unmarried woman from Lahti searching online for surrogate for one year. Sales director for export company, several rounds of IVF without success. Credit checks out. Owns her own home. Unable to adopt due to probation judgment related to assault and slander case."

But when the woman answered, Marion couldn't get a word out.

At the third *hello?* Alvar grabbed the phone from her hand. "Good evening. This is Alvar Lambert from the Source Agency," he said in his most trust-inspiring sales voice. "Perhaps you've already seen our brochure."

Marion stared into the yard as the girls from the nail studio brought out their garbage and, as always, left it unsorted. Anita had tacked instructions in English onto the shed where the trash cans were kept and installed some sorting bins. That had amused Lambert, but he stopped laughing when Anita pointed out there was no point attracting attention by breaking trivial laws. Alvar ended the call by warmly wishing the woman a good evening, assuring her that the christening dress handed down from her grandmother would be seeing some use before she knew it, and saying he looked forward to their meeting.

The phone banged on the table, and Alvar's face came close. "What the hell is wrong with you?"

"Don't tell Lambert," Marion said.

"You're putting everything at risk."

"I'm trying!"

"That isn't enough now."

Alvar could still cut her some slack because they were siblings, but Lambert wouldn't. Marion should be thankful she hadn't already been flown to Vietnam, Thailand, or Nigeria for a suitable vacation accident. Or Colombia.

"Do you need a vacation?"

Marion shook her head.

"You got Anita's daughter to agree to work here. That's a good start but only a start."

"I need more time."

"You're past your deadline."

Marion focused on the window, on the name Shear Magic sparkling in the glass. This was the first salon she had run. There would be others, many more. She just had to endure. She just had to find a solution. In the first days after Anita's death, she had kept expecting the wind chime to jingle like normal and Anita to appear bringing the lemon scent of her perfume and suggestions for what they should do next. But Marion wasn't waiting anymore, even though sometimes she thought she glimpsed a familiar profile outside the window. *Chin up, move forward.* That was what Anita would say now, too. *Move forward. Focus on priorities. You have to go on. You can't give up.* A pair of twins in the front of a cargo bike zipped past the window. A retired woman from the building across the way sat on her walker drinking beer. A couple walked by briskly. The winos. The customers still walking in and out of the nail studio.

Marion grabbed the phone and dialed the next number. People always trusted women more in these matters. That was why she made most of the domestic customer calls. Her Finnish was perfect, even though she'd grown up in Sweden, and she was used to soothing women. Clients trusted her, both at the agency and at the salon.

After five minutes on the phone, the couple from Vantaa was

ready to put the future of their family in her hands, and for a moment Marion felt joy. She was still good at this, even after everything. Just two more, and Lambert would be satisfied, and Marion would dare to visit Lasse. Since Anita's death, she had become more careful about where she went and how often. She had to be more cautious than before. She had one more day left and didn't think it would be enough.

Norma walked from the salon to the patio at the Playful Pike Pub and ordered a large glass of wine. What Marion had said about the hair industry sounded unreal. She'd noticed some of the growth, of course, and the change on the street. Near her apartment, a business had appeared specializing in Afro hair extensions, the Angel Hair Saloon, and next to it was an import company. She always turned her head away as she passed, but she still knew what the windows said: "Virgin hair donors! Our agents find the best virgin hair donors in the world. Also Caucasian donors! Be like Beyoncé."

When her mother had told Norma about her new job, Norma slammed the door on the way out and then came in a huff to this same pub and ordered the same house wine. Her days were so saturated by trouble with hair that her mother's news disgusted her. "So this hell isn't enough for you?" Norma had said. "You want to spend all day every day on it? I don't want to hear any more." She had sat in a window seat, staring into the winter darkness and trying to use alcohol to drive away the image of her mother bringing a cloud of filth from the salon into her home every day. Nightmare pictures throbbed in her head: women with a morbid fear of balding, dandruff from all over Helsinki, seeping sores, dermatitis, fungus, ringworm, necrotic flesh hidden with dye, keratin glue, micro rings, and hair products, their artificial fragrances masquerading as life. After becoming sufficiently drunk, she had sent her mother a text ordering her to shower before coming to visit after work. Now she could admit to herself that her reaction might also have contained a nugget of jealousy. Her mother's hands had only ever belonged to her hair.

Accepting Marion's offer was the only way to learn what had happened. Norma intended to reconstruct the final months of her mother's life, just as she'd tried to recreate her mother's final moments on the metro platform. It had to lead somewhere. If she couldn't find a reason for what her mother had done, at least she might be able to better understand her mother's betrayal.

Norma peeked into her handbag. Eva nodded back at her.

Five

Every day this spring I've been confronted with evidence of what these people would be prepared to do if they could get their hands on someone like you. And the world is full of people like them. If I didn't have Eva, I wouldn't be able to bear the things I've seen. I can talk about them only with her. I don't have anyone else.

Norma left for work at the same time her mother would have and walked on the same side of the street her mother had, passing the same Angel Hair Saloon, the same street food joint, the same massage parlors, the same bars. On her way to work, she saw the same scaffolding, the same wino crew, the tattoo parlor and the sex shop, the parolee support center. And outside the same Chinese restaurant, she spotted the dated fonts of the window decals at Shear Magic that her mother would have seen. The layout of the display window was clumsy, but it blended well with its environment, the year-round holiday lights of the massage parlors and the stardom promised by the advertisements at the nail shops. The golden locks glued in the upper-right corner brought to mind a shampoo bottle from the 1980s. It wasn't a salon where her mother would have wanted to be a client, but she had still gone there eagerly every morning, always on time. Norma tried to mimic her mother's verve as she walked through the door. Despite the exhaustion hanging in the bags under her eyes, Marion greeted her cheerfully and asked her to take the Viennese chairs outside. She had a meeting, but she would be back in the afternoon.

After Marion left, Norma sat in the sun for a moment to take a deep breath. She'd left off the scopolamine patches because they dulled her senses. If she felt overwhelmed, she could turn to her pills. The stockpile of human hair was especially troublesome even though the chemicals had destroyed almost everything her brain could deduce from it. July was approaching, and that frightened her. Summer was heating up, and the more humid the weather became, the more she would have to confront people's vitamin deficiencies and hormone imbalances, not to mention the black avalanche. She had lost her first job during one such hot spell. She'd been an assistant at a clothing store in a mall in east Helsinki and realized that one customer who was trying on dresses would die within six months. There was nothing to do. Going to a doctor would be a waste. She hid her head behind the curtain of a fitting stall just before the vomit came. The woman had been a black cloud. Norma didn't know how she would survive if customers like that came into the salon.

The ringing of the landline forced Norma to dive back inside. The woman murmuring on the other end wanted her problem solved before she left for her summer cabin. Getting away for emergencies like this would be difficult, and the tangles troubled her dreams and kept her awake.

"Anita said I should try some Ukrainian. What do you think? Should I switch?"

One of her mother's clients. Marion hadn't instructed her how to react to questions like this. Norma scrolled to Marion's personal cell phone number on her own phone. It was for problem situations, and only for her. Not for clients, not under any circumstances. Women with hair emergencies called anytime they pleased and never gave up until you answered—this woman seemed to belong to that exact group. Norma had to solve this issue herself. She had to show Marion she could handle it.

"Hello? Did we get cut off?"

"I agree," Norma said. "I think the Ukrainian would be a good fit for you. Virgin Remy, the highest quality."

After the call ended, she remained standing where she was. The words had escaped her lips unremarked. The turban carelessly tied around her head didn't feel tight, and the lock that had fallen loose by her ear didn't react in any way. It had only its normal wave. Would she hold up as well with her mother's next client? And what if someone started asking for news of Anita? The salon's clientele was sure to include plenty of women who took pleasure in the misfortunes of others. Their kind dwelled endlessly on a tragedy until all the blood and marrow had been sucked out of it, gnawing at possible underlying factors with the same devotion as dieters who try to lose weight with gimmicks like slow chewing. But the salon was an oasis of dreams, not of anxiety. Norma decided to tell anyone who asked that her mother had quit and moved abroad.

The flower smelled like a tulip, but it wasn't a tulip, and her clothing smelled like a damp cellar. Marion opened her eyes. The pillowcase was soaked with sweat and stank like a suitcase in Cartagena—used, like a towel left in the corner. She had fallen asleep and returned in her dreams to Albino's side by the swimming pool. Albino removed a rubber tree twig from Marion's hair and told her to relax and order a margarita. In the evening, they would celebrate. And just as Albino hadn't known then that that would be the last day of her old life, Marion couldn't know whether today would turn out the same for her. Her week had passed.

As she rose from her bed, Marion repeated to herself that they couldn't do the same thing to her. Not even Lambert would go that far. Although as she watched the coffee drip, Marion knew that Lambert definitely would. She rubbed her ears, which rang with the sound of Cartagenan tree frogs. It wouldn't go away. It always came back.

Marion was no more important than Albino. On the contrary. She was too old, and Albino had been young. Unlike Albino, she would be worthless. They wouldn't ship her from Colombia to Maracaibo, where the hair thieves offered a variety of services, or to Cancún, where a troop of doctors interested in her would be waiting. Maybe they'd just throw her into the sea.

When she and Alla had returned to the hotel, the staff walked the halls dressed in white like angels, just as spotless as before. The cleaner's cart already stood at Albino's door. Marion had walked by as if all were well. She didn't even slow down. Instead she hurried to her own room and its grave-chilled dampness. Albino's studio apartment in Helsinki was emptied immediately, and a new tenant moved in within a month. Would the same thing happen to Marion's home? Who would clean it, who would pack her things? Would they call her clients and cancel all their appointments, or would they look for someone to continue at the salon? Someone must have gone to Anita's apartment to get her work clothes so that the person they were trying to lure out wouldn't suspect anything when they saw her in front of the salon. When she was caught, Anita was carrying only dresses appropriate to the weather in Thailand. Maybe the same person, one of the mongrels, had also gone to Anita's to drop off her suitcase and phone. It couldn't have been Alvar. Even though Alvar had sent a message to Norma from Anita's phone so she wouldn't wonder about her mother's disappearance immediately after her trip, it was difficult to imagine Alvar wanting to show his face anywhere near Anita's home at that stage. Later Alvar had regretted the message, which didn't sound like something a woman contemplating suicide would send. At the time, the clan had believed Anita would come to her senses and cooperate. The situation went south so quickly that arranging a suicide note was no longer an option. In Marion's case, they wouldn't make the same mistake. It would be easy. They would need only to hint at Helena, and no one would suspect anything.

As she dressed and applied mascara, Marion kept an eye on her phone, glancing outside every now and then as she had that night in Cartagena when she'd hoped Alvar would call. She would have liked to hear a familiar voice after returning to the hotel without Albino, a voice that would say everything would work out. But Alvar hadn't answered her calls. The entire night was punctuated by power outages, and Marion spent it alone listening to the tree frogs and water dripping from her hotel room air conditioner. The palm trees rustled like dead leaves. When they returned to Finland, Alvar hadn't asked anything other than whether they had managed to visit Cancún as well.

When she stepped out into the stairwell, Marion listened carefully for strange noises. As she walked down the stairs, she felt certain that one of Lambert's mongrels would lunge at her as soon as she stepped outside. They had surprised Anita at the door to the baggage claim, and they could take Marion the same way, in broad daylight when she least expected it, as she had just sent off another happy bride overjoyed at the results of her test styling before the big day. Or not. The Lamberts were precise. When the clock struck indicating that a week had passed, she would go on vacation. They had monitored Albino for a month before the decision. Exactly one month. Marion had been given one week.

No one was at the downstairs door. She didn't see any guard dogs on the street, or suspicious cars in the parking lot. On her way to the salon, the asphalt lurched under Marion's feet like the deck of a ship, and she felt rigor mortis in her limbs, but nothing happened. An hour later Alvar came to fetch her as agreed for a client meeting and chose a route that went where he said it would.

"Is something wrong?" he asked in front of the Palace Hotel.

"No, nothing," Marion replied with a smile.

In the elevator, she was her old self. No one was going to come take her for a "vacation" in the middle of a client meeting. Perhaps Lambert's way of punishing her was to make her imagine the worst.

Her hair had started hissing in the elevator, and when Norma pulled her turban off, she saw that it had become a mass of curling tentacles. She snapped that yes, she'd noticed the stray hair on the mat in the entryway. It belonged to the same man she had seen in the stairwell before, and there was nothing strange about it. It was part of the window remodeling. She needed help for her real problems, not for imaginary ones, and threw the scarf into the laundry basket with such force that it fell over with a bang. Hearing her own cry, she pressed her hand to her mouth. She didn't act this way. She didn't talk to her hair. Her nerves were giving out.

Her curls relaxed as she drank a glass of box wine. Norma poured another glass as she waited for them to calm down enough that she could start with the scissors. Her head felt leaden. Over the day she had accumulated an unusual amount of gray, and it was the salon's fault.

Her mother had gone unhinged after finding Norma's first gray hair, and Norma had thought her mother's reaction had to do with Norma's age. Steel gray stood out so glaringly on a woman as young as she was, and dyeing wouldn't help because her roots would show almost immediately. She wouldn't be able to conceal her abnormality anymore. She comforted her mother by saying that the situation would go back to normal once the labor negotiations and the anxiety surrounding them passed, but personally she saw her graying as a sign of premature aging. That was a problem for many freaks of nature and was why her home was always ready to greet the police and paramedics. She kept her mother's videos and the boxes of hair in chicken wire locker number twelve just in case.

As she stared at the ball of hair she would soon discard, a coincidence occurred to her: the gray had made its first appearance after her mother began work at Shear Magic. What if the reason wasn't the labor negotiations or unhealthy living but rather her mother's betrayal? What if her hair had been trying to communicate that to her? What if it didn't want to adorn the heads of strangers?

Norma rushed to the computer. Thanks to her mother, she already knew all there was to know about dyeing aging hair. Even so, she looked it up again. All the familiar instructions about preventing gray with green tea and garlic, the ginger Indians rubbed onto their scalps, and the nutritional importance of manganese, calcium, folic acid, and copper.

Norma read the instructions as if they were a mantra she could chant to calm her mind and place her problems in proper perspective. Or maybe she hoped she would find a trick she had missed, some magic spell that had slipped between the lines. But she didn't find any magic spell. And the mantra didn't calm her mind. Her time at the salon would be limited.

Her mother had probably thought the same. She had seen the gray hairs as dwindling cash flow, and that was what had caused her distress.

The couple from Espoo held their coffee cups with both hands as if warming them. This private room at the Palace was a deliberate ploy for meetings with clients who were easily impressed by the patriotic atmosphere, the view of the sea, and the Finnish modernist design. But instead of admiring the view, the couple stared at the white wall. Their hands remained up, elbows to stomachs, cups huddled in hands. They were significantly early, as people like them always were.

"Alvar will be here soon," Marion said, keeping her voice low and reassuring. She noticed her fists were clenched tight, her knuckles white just like the couple's, although for different reasons, so she hid them in her lap. Clients often overinterpreted things. Even the sight of a handkerchief could cause a stream of tears, and just after remembering that, Marion realized she'd left her handbag open with a large packet of tissues visible. She surreptitiously pushed the bag under the table. This meeting was set to be the easiest of the week, with no reason for tears. Everything had gone well. The first round of IVF had been successful, and upon hearing the news, the couple joked that they'd been prepared to pay for at least ten rounds after all the rumors they'd heard about fraud in the industry. The quick results came as a surprise, as did the reasonable cost. Thirty thousand dollars was a small price to pay to fulfill a lifelong dream—the man had laughed that his boat was more expensive.

Marion had now handled four agency clients since her deadline expired. The uncertainty hadn't completely eased, but the tree frogs ringing in her ears had gone silent and some hope had rekindled. Norma was working at the salon, and Marion made a good start befriending the girl. As she looked at the couple, she couldn't help thinking that the woman represented precisely the customer profile she and Anita had hoped to attract at their new salon. Her feathered bob cut had summer highlights obviously applied by a skilled hand, and she had her own hair, her own eyelashes, and her own nails. This was a customer who would never be late, would never beg for an installment plan, and whose credit card would never turn up missing, Marion thought as she wrote out the bill. The idea of hair extensions would be unfamiliar to her at first, so Marion would have to figure out whom the woman might admire. She would be shocked and refuse to believe that her idols were hooked on extensions. That was why Marion would suggest volumizing first. That sounded more natural, and no one would even notice a few keratin bonds in her hair. Visit by visit, she would gain the courage to take more radical steps. The younger generation was easier since Beyoncé, Rihanna, and Victoria Beckham's daily changing lengths had already done the work. In Finland, *Big Brother* had the same effect: the audience watched every day as girls removed their hair to sleep and reapplied it in the morning. Soon nothing felt so natural as to do the same themselves. Before long, they began to tire of constantly fussing with low-quality clip-ins, and then they went to a stylist for a permanent solution.

Alvar walked through the door at precisely two o'clock. The couple's heads turned, and their faces relaxed in bleary smiles as Alvar placed the ultrasound images in front of them. Marion looked at the clock. In two minutes, Alvar would turn on his computer and begin delivering news from the clinic. That would be followed by a video chat with the woman carrying the couple's child, with the aid of an interpreter, after which they would review legal details and travel plans. Couples like this were the best because they began building the story of their future child's origin early on. The woman had told her friends she was undergoing fertility treatments. The trips to Georgia were vacations, and the man's work carried him abroad anyway. This time his wife was just accompanying him. In six months, they would return to Finland with their biological child, and the birth certificate would list their names as the parents. In addition to the easy legal environment, the choice of country had also been influenced by the fact that Finns knew next to nothing about it, so no one would connect the couple's trips to Tbilisi with fertility tourism. Georgia didn't have a reputation as a baby factory, and there hadn't been scandals, at least not any that passed the bar for international news coverage. The Georgian War was already a memory, along with the other disturbances in the area—no one would think about how these things had resulted in widespread poverty and many single women with families to support.

The couple wanted to watch the video again. Alvar restarted it and handed them the latest test results for the woman carrying their child, an updated dietary report, and a brochure of housing options in Tbilisi if the future parents wished to rent a cozy family apartment rather than stay in a hotel as the due date approached. Alvar's moves were cunning. When the woman heard the word *family apartment*, a beatific expression spread across her face.

"Of course, Marion or I will come along to make sure everything goes as planned. Just last week we had a happy family return to Sweden. They didn't even bother getting a passport at the embassy. They simply headed home with the birth certificate."

Alvar flashed a family portrait of a couple holding two children, one an infant in a christening dress, the other two or three years older.

"The boy looks just like his father."

"Of course. He is his biological offspring," Alvar said.

"Of course." The woman's relief was evident. Many believed that some signs of the woman who gave birth to the child would remain, something in the skin tone or hair color, or perhaps the shape of the eyes, even though there was no logical foundation for such worries. To those people, Alvar showed pictures of a surrogate holding a child who looked completely different from herself. That reassured them.

The man cleared his throat. "There was a third woman we considered, too," he said. "This little gal could use some company. What do you think? Could we do it?"

"She could begin the medication immediately. The eggs and sperm are still on ice."

"And since your first is going to be a girl, you could also consider whether you'd like the next one to be a boy," Marion added.

The couple turned to look at her. "Is that possible?"

"These days anything is possible," Marion continued. "For that we just need to move to Ukraine, which is a shorter flight anyway. We can easily move the genetic material there from Georgia. That isn't a problem, and you won't need to go through the donation process again."

The man was first to show interest; the woman hesitated. They glanced at each other.

"Any child would be welcome in our home," the woman said, but the man was clearly already imagining the hockey practices. The possibility of choosing the sex always upended clients' thoughts. Sometimes it was clear they'd already argued about it at home. One had visions of pedal cars and video games while the other dreamed of flowing dresses and hair bows.

Marion liked asking this question most, throwing it casually into the air. It made her feel like a good fairy. The parents' frozen expressions lasted for a moment, and then their imaginations galloped off, and nothing could hold them back anymore.

Alvar produced his Ukraine binder from his briefcase and handed it to the man.

"Take your time. We can choose an appropriate candidate when it feels right. Are you ready for the call?"

The couple shifted in front of Alvar's computer. Marion guessed she could already begin making travel plans for Lviv. Ukraine was one of the clan's strongest areas. The border to Russia was open, and you could trade in anything. The surrogate business was growing steadily, the paperwork was a breeze, and the law wasn't an issue. And even if it was, you could deal with that easily enough. Not one single international surrogacy scandal had sullied the country's reputation, and that made it reliable in the eyes of prospective parents. At most, they were concerned about the lingering effects of the Chernobyl nuclear disaster on the food chain, which was why agency brochures emphasized the cleanliness of the Western diet in Ukraine. Lviv had been an excellent choice of location for the clinic. Despite the Cyrillic letters, the city looked European.

After the couple left, Alvar remained sitting at the table fiddling with his phone. "That went well. Do you feel better?"

Marion nodded, even though she hadn't been sleeping much. Her deadline had passed, yet she was still sitting here. The salon was still hers, and she was being allowed to handle agency business. That was a victory in itself.

Her relationship with Norma was warming, and that had bought her more time with Lambert. Anita would say she had to keep going. She had a goal, and she couldn't let anyone stop her. This afternoon she'd be back in the salon unraveling tangles, but soon her clientele would be different. At the new salon, there wouldn't be a single girl who spent her vacation taking selfies of her bikini butt in the mirror of a stranger's Ferrari, by a yacht in Marbella, or at the door of a Versace shop. None of the hair studio's clients would show her such pictures as if they were some great accomplishment. Her new customers would have real merits, the kind you didn't even need to brag about, and it would show in the way they carried themselves. They wouldn't think that if they managed to get their face in the same picture as some expensive brand logo, they were someone. The new customers wouldn't think that posing in front of a nightclub frequented by stars made them stars too and moved them closer to Hollywood, fairy-tale weddings, cinematic love stories, and wealthy men. The new customers wouldn't scramble after VIP club passes, certain they were in the fast lane to better hunting grounds where they could end up on the arms of men who knew important people. They wouldn't think that was the way to find their prince. They would know that that road led only to one kind of pimp or another, a Lambert who took everything there was to take from talentless bimbos and then threw the husks to the crows.

For just a little longer, she had to maintain the energy to admire these simpletons' tapping on their phones. She had to keep pretending to be fooled by their pirated handbags, keep lying that they had the makings of a model or Madonna, that stardom and Hollywood were waiting around the corner, and that all you needed to get into a *Playboy* audition was good hair and big tits.

There was hardly a break in the stream of customers. Norma was horrified. The Ukrainian stockpile was supposed to be reserved for the best clients, but today the situation had gotten out of hand. She'd given appointment times to a stay-at-home mom complaining about her fibers tangling, a woman suffering from spot baldness, a sobbing nursing mother who was shedding hair, and a fashion blogger. She'd promised the Ukrainian to a dance troupe on their way to stardom and a fitness fanatic going through a fat-cutting phase. She'd found the right words even though she didn't have her mother's self-assurance, and to her this hair was trash. The feeling had been like a mild buzz, and her turban still wasn't tight. Had it been this easy for her mother? She hadn't been able to help her daughter, but here she'd been able to help everyone, and her hands had transformed mice into princesses. Norma was beginning to understand her mother's buoyancy after work. Now she felt the same. The whole stock was reserved before she even realized what she'd done.

She spent the whole day adding entries to the reservation book alongside her mother's, and her fingers holding the pen had remained steady. She was starting to see her mother's handwriting as if it were anyone's instead of reading those appointments as if they were obituaries. Her mother's pen had begun writing on the pages of this book after Christmas, and from February on women had streamed onto the streets of Helsinki wearing Norma's hair, just like the ones she had spoken with today. Not one of them asked where the hair came from. They wanted to know only the price and that the hair being taped or glued to their heads was Ukrainian.

Norma had imagined the customers would be like Plan sponsors who knew exactly who and what their money was going to and hoped the children they supported in Africa would send drawings from school and letters about their successes. But no. For these women, the hair being glued to their heads was an impersonal, faceless mass of strands, and they didn't want to know who had owned it before they did. They didn't want to know that someone else had worn these same locks as they made love. As they went off on a rant. As they hoped and cried and dreamed. At most, they were concerned about lice and disease. Marion had stressed this as she taught Norma the secrets of customer service. Norma was floored. No creature could survive the processing the hair underwent, which forced the factory workers handling the hair to wear respirators, and still the customers were concerned only about lice, not the source of the hair. But the same women used only free-range eggs for their omelets and scrutinized product labels. Norma didn't understand the logic, and she was tempted to respond in kind when the first customer expressed her concerns about hygiene. It had felt like a personal insult that required self-discipline to swallow, and Norma considered overcoming it a victory. She could do this. Whenever asked, she simply followed Marion's instructions and stated that Shear Magic purchased raw materials only from vendors who could offer hygiene certificates.

Norma was also no longer startled by the women whose gazes

became transfixed by the salon display window. Marion had set out a Ukrainian sample, and each girl who stopped to size it up could already picture herself as the hottest young thing in the nightclub, her social media exploding with new followers and likes. The ecstatic expressions began to tickle Norma. She kept a count of how many passersby her hair trapped each day and was disappointed when the breaks in the stream of admirers were too long. Maybe Elizabeth Siddal had felt the same as she posed in the midst of a crowd of artists competing for her. Before her career as a model, she had worked at Mary Totzer's hat shop. Mrs. Totzer wanted salesgirls who would be attractive to her customers, and Elizabeth undoubtedly was with her copper locks.

Alvar's phone rang. His face remained impassive, but he answered immediately, then stood up and walked to the window. Marion continued packing and tried to listen, but Alvar's muttering betrayed nothing. He ended the call with a grin, looking like a dog that had caught the scent of a hare and was waiting for permission to attack its prey.

"We found something in Norma's apartment," Alvar said.

Marion put the folders back on the table. The mongrels had already checked the girl's apartment before, and it had been a waste of time. That's what she guessed, anyway. They didn't tell her everything anymore, and they wouldn't reveal such an important detail without ulterior motives. Either the clan didn't care how credible she was in the girl's eyes, how well she could lie to her, or they hoped this news would make her nervous, and the girl would sense it and grow nervous herself. Nervous people made mistakes.

"You didn't tell me what they found last time."

"Nothing relevant to this mess."

"How am I supposed to achieve anything if I'm always kept in the dark?"

The seascape in the window rocked before Marion's eyes. She had lost. The knowledge began spreading through her limbs like the water that splashed on her cuffs. She picked up the glass she'd knocked over. She had ironed this blouse in the morning, but now it looked and felt like dirty, melting snow. One of the mongrels must have laid his grubby fingers on something she should have found first, and only because she had lulled herself into the belief that Norma's home was the same dead end as Anita's. She should have stolen the girl's keys herself during work and gone to search the apartment. She could have grabbed the spare keys from Anita's workstation right after her death. She'd had numerous opportunities to handle this, and then she would have been a step ahead of everyone else. She hadn't done that, though, because she feared being caught. The girl could have come home unexpectedly, or she could have missed her keys in the middle of the day. One of the mongrels could have been inside just as Marion tried to slip through the door. She was a depressing novice and shouldn't be doing any of this.

"The apartment is cheaply furnished and clean," said Alvar. "Too clean. Scoured. There's bleach in the cupboards and not much else. It's the opposite of Anita's house. Plus she has a huge pile of Scopoderm patches and Marzine. Marzies. Scopolamine."

The last word hit Marion in the diaphragm.

"The girl's pill collection probably doesn't have much significance to the Ukrainian catastrophe. They're unique choices for recreational use, or she must really mix her drugs. But it gives us more ammunition."

"Is it all over-the-counter?"

"Yeah, mostly for motion sickness. It's not the same as Devil's Breath from the borrachero tree, even if it is related. That's why I didn't say anything. I was only thinking of you."

They hadn't talked about Albino after the Cartagena trip or even after the meeting where Albino's fate had been decided. Alla had been in charge of putting the plan into action, and Marion followed her instructions. She wasn't even sure whether Alvar had been aware of the details, but now she knew he had. Lambert thought the Devil's Breath was a stroke of genius. It transformed a person into a helpless zombie, willing to carry out any command but still looking completely sober. When Albino left her margarita on the table in the middle of the negotiations and went away with a man she didn't recognize, Marion hadn't understood what was happening. Albino walked on her own legs, apparently of her own volition. But of course, the pills in Norma's apartment had nothing to do with Albino. She should forget about Albino entirely. Her weakness and her inability to forget had made Alvar conceal things from her. Her brother thought the strange coincidence would make her imagine that Alvar had become like Lambert, a sly, taunting brute.

"I'm sure they can also be used as sedatives," Alvar said. "Anything will knock you out if you take enough of it. But why would Norma want to drug anyone? Or Anita, if they were hers? Why wouldn't they have chosen something more normal? There are plenty of options. Can you think of a reason?"

Marion filled her water glass again. The water had a strange aftertaste. Blood. She had bit her tongue.

"You're not concentrating. Lambert is satisfied for now that you've created a connection with the girl. All our options have to be open, all the traps set, all the hooks under the surface. She'll take the bait eventually. We just don't know which way she'll go. That's why you still have time. Borrowed time. You have to be aware of what's going on because we've made a breakthrough. Guess what we found in the girl's compost? Half a bundle of matted hair. Ukrainian. The length and color match, and the quality."

The tree frogs chirped in Marion's ears so loudly, she could barely hear Alvar's voice. The girl knew about Anita's business. She must know where the hair came from.

Six

We met Reijo and Lambert at a dance. Helena had just finished singing and was coming down off the stage when Lambert swung in front of her. Peonies bloomed on Helena's cheeks, and Lambert called her a star. Lambert called her a star until Marion was born. Then it ended, as did Helena's performing.

March 2, 2013

In Sweden we didn't have the courage to leave the factory or the Finnish immigrant community, even though we should have. The same lack of courage made us throw ourselves into Reijo's and Lambert's arms. They were from the same parish as us, and they remembered Helena's parents and our house, but at home we'd never noticed them because they were the children of an impoverished drunk. Meanwhile they had transformed into exciting businessmen out to conquer the world. Markku Lambert had even changed his name to Max to make it more international. The world was laid out before them, and it would be for us too if we joined up with them.

Our weddings were small affairs, as was the custom at the time, and without any relatives. Our parents didn't approve of our choice in men any more than our decision to go to Sweden. For Helena and me, these were huge steps that helped us break away from our village. We didn't understand that our new husbands' businesses were so shady. We were starry-eyed in love. When we finally began to learn what kind of work they were involved with, Helena was already the mother of a small child. And we believed Reijo and Lambert had just made some mistakes, listened to the wrong advice. We blamed their hustler friends. We would lead our husbands back to the straight and narrow, and building families would help our efforts. That's how it seemed. A few years later Helena had a second child on the way, and Lambert started talking about returning to Finland. He wanted a new direction in his life, and Helena believed him. For a while Lambert behaved like a model father. He got Helena and the kids an apartment in Laajasalo in Helsinki, helped with the move, and promised to follow soon. Lambert's talk also rubbed off on Reijo. Both of them convinced us of the risks of raising children in an environment where Finns had a bad reputation, where even speaking Finnish was an embarrassment. Thinking back on it, that was nonsense. They probably just had business problems in Sweden, creditors breathing down their necks, and wanted to handle things without complaining wives and whining children around. We were slowing them down.

Helena seemed content with life in Helsinki and encouraged me to follow her. The idea was appealing—settling down in more peaceful surroundings, without Reijo and Lambert's dodgy circle of acquaintances—and I planned to look at a couple of apartments when I visited Helena. Suddenly in the middle of the trip, I found out you were coming.

March 4, 2013

By the time you were born, it was clear I needed to get away from Reijo Ross. I called Helena from the hospital and made up a story about Reijo having a new mistress. That was enough. Helena brought money, escorted us to the train station, and promised not to reveal our destination to anyone. Going home was my only option. I showed up penniless, with a bundle in my arms and no husband. My mother greeted us by asking if I was the return of the family curse.

Over the years, I tried to leave so many times. I even saved money for it but always chickened out. We were at least safe in the village, tucked away in the forest, and I could take care of you during the day. No one other than my mother paid us any attention, and time had already begun to gnaw away at her alertness. I didn't dare to plan our move in earnest until you were in high school—I decided that you were strong enough then and knew how to take precautions. You would understand the dangers of the world better than I had when I moved to Sweden. I made bad choices because I was stupid and inexperienced—Reijo was one of them. I hope you won't do the same.

Reijo died about ten years ago in Thailand in a boating accident, and after I heard, I breathed a sigh of relief. Even if something happened to me, you could never go looking for him now. That would have been the beginning of the end for you. Reijo was too similar to the Sutherland sisters' father, who came up with the idea to market his daughters' musical performances. They became an immediate sensation in the States, not because of the music but because of the hair. Everyone wanted them and the "Niagara Falls," as their hair was called, to perform in their theaters, to tour with their circuses, or to lie in their department store windows. Hurrahs, applause, admiration, the cover of *Cosmopolitan*, and the front page of the *New York Times*.

I'm not sure you'd be able to withstand the ecstasy, the sudden riches, and the associated side effects experienced by the Sutherlands. When one of my clients sighs in rhapsody as she looks at her new hair—your hair—those sisters always come to mind. Their childhood reminded me of our years living with your grandmother. The girls' mother rubbed their scalps with disgusting smelling liniment imagining that it might slow the growth of their hair, and the girls were teased because of the bad smell. Maybe that was what inspired their father to invent an expensive snake oil elixir, which he sold with the girls' picture. It broke the bank. Seven Sutherland Sisters' Hair Grower and Scalp Cleaner built the family a mansion, complete with marbled bathrooms and furniture imported from Europe.

When they toured, they kept to themselves and did a good job concealing their oddity except for occasional small slips. Mary Sutherland had fits of madness—caused by her hair, I suspect—that occasionally drove the family to lock her up. After Naomi Sutherland died, the sisters wanted to store the body at home, claiming the reason was the slow progress of construction on their family mausoleum, but that attracted the attention of the authorities. Only two of them married, both past their peak age of fertility. That was wise, though their choice in men was appalling—morphine addicts, adventurers, and circus performers—and they paved the girls' road to ruination. The Sutherlands spent their final years as impoverished hermits in their decaying mansion, weeping over their many heartbreaks. They would have been happier if they'd stayed in their log cabin. Elizabeth Siddal's fate wasn't much rosier, although the artists who supported her as their muse weren't nearly the con men that the knaves who hounded the sisters were. No one like you can assume love is sincere.

Men took advantage of Elizabeth and the Sutherlands for their hair, and that's why I'm so shocked by everything Marion has told me about the hair trade. Evolution hasn't improved women at all. The Sutherland sisters lived during a time when women's authority was limited to the home. They needed the men who ran the circuses and the entertainment industry in order to succeed. Now women have the same rights and opportunities, but we still don't take home the profits even though we provide all the material and all the labor for the beauty industry. Century after century we've given our faces, our hair, our wombs, our breasts, and still the money ends up in men's pockets. They're the leaders.

Every business Lambert and Reijo have ever run has been based on women's sweat and tears. In Sweden they brought starlets to the stage and later continued the same thing in the Canaries. In Thailand they started selling bachelor vacations and cheap impotence pills. After Reijo's boat accident, Lambert must have gotten bored in Thailand and moved to the growing markets of Russia. That's where he found Alla and a new industry based on dreams. It's ironic that I was the one to have a daughter like you and that Lambert would become my gateway into the hair trade.

March 6, 2013

Helena considered leaving Lambert many times, and I supported her as best I could, but whenever she made up her mind, Lambert would come to Finland, play the role of model father and husband for a while, swear he would return permanently soon, and then disappear again. As Alvar approached school age, Lambert decided there might be opportunities in the Canary Islands. Finnish tourists had started pouring south, so bars were popping up to cater to them, and demand for entertainment was growing. This was Lambert's area of expertise, and he decided to set up a restaurant with the very best stage on the island. It would be reserved for Helena alone. The children just had to get a little bigger. Then Helena could follow him and spend every night singing.

Helena swallowed Lambert's lines until she received a call from an old acquaintance from Sweden, who had been vacationing in the Canaries and stopped at Lambert's bar. Lambert had a new starlet, and her stage name was Ann-Helen. According to this acquaintance, Ann-Helen and Lambert seemed quite intimate. Helena broke down completely.

March 9, 2013

I usually disposed of your hair by burning it and thought that was harmless until one morning you seemed ill and your grandmother suspected carbon monoxide poisoning. Grandma was feeling poorly too, and my own head hurt. I'd thrown some of your hair in the oven just the night before, and it occurred to me that the two things might be connected. Your hair was growing stronger and had started expressing its own will. If you happened to be angry, cutting it required strength, and at night you woke up with strange nightmares. You told stories of adventures in a place you called Amuli and described landscapes you recognized from Charlie Chaplin films. Once you tried to explain that you had been playing in your dreams with a woman we saw in a television documentary about Chicago and the Great Depression.

I stopped burning your hair, and your bad dreams went away immediately. Later Grandma caught you trying to light it on fire yourself. You got a beating, but that was also when I started experimenting with smoking it in a pipe.

Life in my mother's house was difficult, and she was extremely strict when it came to alcohol. The salesperson at the state liquor store was a friend of hers, and I knew word would get back to her if I bought so much as a bottle of wine. Smoking was an easier solution. It calmed my nerves. Things felt like they would work out. I felt more confident, and that was what Helena needed too after that fateful phone call. I heard about Lambert's betrayal from Marion, who called me in a panic and asked me to come visit. Helena cried incessantly, and the neighbors were complaining about the howling at night.

The situation in Helena's home was even worse than I expected. So I gave her my pipe. She fell asleep instantly.

I called on Helena as often as possible, even though arranging visits was complicated. I couldn't leave you with your grandmother. If she learned our secret, you probably would have drowned in the well. That was how our village handled abnormalities. We didn't have the money for hotels, and I didn't dare take you to Helena's because I was afraid she would recognize that your hair was what she'd been smoking. During my visits, I would send you to a park or the zoo with a babysitter.

I mailed Helena regular doses of your hair between visits, and it clearly helped. The children didn't ask any questions about Helena's new habit. For them, all that mattered was she could sleep and the constant weeping stopped. I should have remembered that one glass of wine was enough to put Helena under the table, but I didn't know any other way to help, and no one talked about therapy back then.

Marion kept me up-to-date on Helena's health. She was a teenager and old enough to take care of Alvar and the house on her own for the most part. They didn't hear much from Lambert anymore. Sometimes he would send a telegram, sometimes a card, sometimes money. After Helena smashed the telephone, Marion would call me from a phone booth. That was around the same time Helena started to wander. Once the police brought her home after she snatched someone's baby out of a carriage and hummed lullabies to it. Finally Marion had enough. She didn't want to waste her youth watching over her family, and after meeting her future fiancé, Bergman, she moved in with him. I visited Marion's new home once and assumed that tiny feet would soon be toddling on the rug they had just bought.

Six months later Lambert's new flame wanted to get married, so Lambert needed to divorce Helena. She didn't take it well. Marion called and told me that Helena was talking to herself, knocking her pipe on the table, and constantly looking for something. She would angrily shake the envelopes I had sent her. I realized immediately what was happening. She was in withdrawal. I arranged a trip to see her. Beforehand I sent a batch, though, and it was a big one.

That was the greatest mistake of my life.

When the first reporter drove up to our house, your grandmother was weeding the carrot bed, and the photographer began snapping pictures before she had any idea what was going on. Through the crack in the kitchen window, I saw her mouth hang open and heard her denials. No, it isn't possible, she kept repeating. The reporter knew he had reached us before anyone else and tried to hide his excitement as he launched into his questions. The neighbors in Helsinki had talked about Helena's best friend with whom she'd lived in Gothenburg. The phone started ringing off the hook. Acquaintances from Sweden tried to call, wanting to reminisce about situations they claimed made them suspect something was off. Even Reijo tried to reach us, but Grandma pulled the phone out of the wall.

Still she ended up in the tabloids as "Elli Naakka, horrified villager." That was just the beginning. The press attacked with such fury that nothing was ever the same. But no one caught Grandma off guard again—she and the dog drove away all comers. I avoided going into the village. I was afraid someone would realize Helena's behavior was really a withdrawal symptom, the police would search her apartment, and I would get caught. Then I'd lose you, and you'd be found out. My nightmares were coming true in spite of my precautions. I never put a return address on the envelopes, and I tried to make my handwriting as different as I could when I wrote her address. I even wore gloves. I imagine I had sensed something would happen.

Religious as they were, Helena's family blamed the devil, not drugs or mental illness. Preachers visited the village; even an exorcist showed up. Helena's entire family tree was suspect: each unfortunate death, whether from hanging or drowning or alcohol, was seen as evidence of the demonic possession dwelling in the line. Helena's old teacher was interviewed, and he said there had always been something odd about her. All her school friends had a story to tell about a strange encounter with Helena. Children no longer dared to go to school alone because Crazy Helena supposedly prowled the road. The rumor mill ground away, and then came the name calling. Bitch. Slut. Whore. Lambert became an object of pity and compassion, and someone began saying that Helena had been giving herself to men behind the co-op building since she was a child.

After Helena went to prison, Alvar was taken to his grandparents' house, where he slept behind lock and key. They were constantly on the lookout for signs of Helena in him, and he would get into fights in the village. I went to see him a few times. I'll never forget how he clung to my legs and kept repeating, "Call Daddy." But I couldn't, not that man. Later Alvar managed to escape and got to Sweden on his own. He didn't return to Finland until Lambert's business brought him here.

When I ran into Alvar in Kuopio, I felt all those years of worry wash away. He'd grown into a sensible young man, and I'm grateful for that. On our way back to Helsinki, we talked through everything that had happened. Alvar told me how Helena waited for the mail night and day, lying in front of the mail slot and licking the last wisps from the envelopes. In her most desperate moments, she'd cut her own hair and try to smoke it. Alvar knew she was high. He thanked me for giving him his first weed, grinning and asking what variety I'd been sending. It didn't resemble anything he'd found since.

Apparently, since the tragedy, Marion had found time for several long relationships, a cat, and gallivanting in Stockholm. She came back to Finland when Lambert bought her a salon. I got the impression she had finally found balance, her own place in the world. I hesitated to ask about children, but I plucked up my courage. Alvar was silent for a long time. Then he said Marion thought Helena had been right about one thing: Marion wasn't meant to be a mother. Once when she was drunk, Marion had even said she could stand anything except having one of her children turn out like Helena. She would never take that risk. And that was my fault, too. I had pushed Helena over the edge. Everything that happened as a result was my responsibility and mine alone.

March 10, 2013

You still hear about the Laajasalo Balcony Murder when the gutter press does scandal retrospectives. People haven't forgotten. One of the customers at the salon brought up Helena while browsing posts on a true-crime website. I noticed how Marion blanched, and I whispered to her that I would finish the color job.

The woman was a typical murder fan, the kind who thinks she's the only person who knows the truth, and she considered herself an expert on this particular case because she had lived in the same building as Helena. She'd heard Helena singing and knew people who had seen her walk out onto the balcony that last time. The balcony itself became a murder-tourism destination, which affected property values in the building. The woman whispered that she had managed to sell her apartment only to an immigrant family who hadn't heard about the case. I wanted to slap her in the mouth. Instead I had to listen to her for more than an hour, enduring her musings about the children and how there had been talk of a divorce and womanizing, which would make any woman go crazy. She was sure the real target had been Lambert.

I thought it was more likely that Helena wanted to ensure the end of her family line. What she did was her way of arranging that. Eva has told me about similar tragedies, and her opinion is clear: no one should ever risk passing insanity on to their children. Even though the chance of inheriting schizophrenia is only 10 percent, I can see that Marion worries about it.

The same thing could happen to you as Helena if your secret is discovered or you have children. Children like you. The risks you face in life aren't just about getting caught and becoming a slave to the beauty industry. It isn't just the businessmen, the investors, the researchers, and the doctors who would chase you. The real threat is the unpredictable behavior of your hair. If its effects become known, you wouldn't be fit for hair dye advertisements or fashion magazine covers. You wouldn't be the face of a new line of hair products as the Sutherland sisters were. You wouldn't become a muse like Elizabeth, and you wouldn't just become a fallen star like all those women. You would end up in a prison, an asylum, or some other institution designed for dangerous people. The photographers would show up on your doorstep and at your windows, and the vultures would descend on your grandmother's house once again. Freak-show producers would flood in from every corner of the world to film their exposés against traditional Finnish scenery on a birch-lined road, in the yard of a country cottage. The whole gang of researchers would come to investigate the Naakka family genome. The only people in the villages now are the old folks, but they would tell stories of the strange Naakka clan and the overprotective mother who never let her daughter run around by herself, never let her go on class field trips or to summer camp or confirmation school. Everyone would have some story to tell again, and no one would object to their fifteen minutes of fame.

Seven

I put Helena's family through all the things I dreaded. It's Eva's fault. If only I'd known how powerful your hair can be, Helena might not have gotten sick. At most, she would have had a nervous breakdown because of Lambert, recovered, and started a new life. Marion would have a family and be rushing between work and her children's hobbies. And I wouldn't be like a drunk driver after an accident who goes and spies on her victim's family to see how they're doing and hopes not to get caught.

When Norma arrived at the salon in the morning, a man she didn't recognize was leaning in the doorway to the back room, smiling as if he had been expecting her. She froze on the stairs. Marion hadn't said anything about a visitor.

"You must be Anita's daughter," the man said, and raised a steaming cup of coffee in greeting.

Norma closed her eyes for a moment. The man was tall, slender, and dangerous. Instead of fading, that impression only grew, and the hair inside her turban began to tingle. That could also have been caused by the boxes of hair that had strangely reappeared on the desk. She'd brought the boxes to Marion the night before and watched as she unpacked them, took the hair to the back room, and threw away the packaging. Someone had dug the cardboard and cellophane out of the garbage and repacked the hair. Perhaps this man.

"Beautiful name. Rare for a Finn."

"When my father proposed to my mother, an opera with the same name was playing on the radio," Norma replied, and then she realized: *This must be Alvar, Marion's brother. Crazy Helena's son*. There was always something similar about siblings, or maybe the man's hair had been on Norma's mother's or Marion's clothing. That was why the scent was familiar. Instinctively she'd associated him with Helena. The tone when people talked about her never went away. The tone, the gossip, the knowing glances—the feeling of danger came from them, not from him. Her tongue stuck in her mouth with shame. If Helena were her mother, she would never want to see anyone who remembered Helena's case, even less someone complicit in her fate. It was of little comfort that Alvar knew nothing about Norma's role in the tragedy. She knew, and that was enough.

"I'm sorry. We all liked Anita," Alvar said, and led Norma to sit as if she were a lady suffering a fainting spell and needed the nearest park bench or exit. A glass of water appeared in front of her, along with a packet of tissues and some fresh coffee. Alvar's pomade was TIGI Rockaholic Punk Out, and his aftershave was Burberry, which she could tell from the notes of sandalwood and cedar. He had been drinking the previous night, but not to excess. He had eaten something Asian—kaffir lime, ginger, cinnamon—plus apples and multivitamins. Traces of diazepam, from perhaps two weeks ago, but no other pharmaceuticals, no drugs, no testosterone products. A dog. He had a German shepherd.

"Has Marion told you about her name?" Alvar said. "Helena listened to Marion Rung when she was homesick. In Sweden. Do you know that singer? She was on the Finnhits albums. You might have heard 'Tipi-tii' or 'El Bimbo.' I forgot to introduce myself. Alvar, Marion's brother. I've heard a lot of good things about you. You left the funeral before I could express my condolences."

Norma's sweaty palm disappeared in Alvar's assertive grip, limply, guiltily. At the funeral, her nose had been stuffed up, and she had been high on benzos and scopolamine thinking the combination would help her endure the ordeal. She didn't remember seeing him and took the cup of coffee to avoid responding.

"We were hoping for a little help from you with these boxes. Marion said you found a package slip in Anita's mail and decided it must belong to us when you picked it up."

Norma felt her turban loosen. Her hair cuticles opened, and ants began running across her skin. She hadn't thought this through far enough. When Marion took the boxes, her roots had throbbed with excitement, and a smile had flashed on her face, but no uncomfortable questions followed. Marion accepted the vague explanation about the mysterious package as if it weren't even necessary. Norma expected to deal with the issue later with Marion, whose tact was silky smooth when it came to anything related to Norma's mother. Norma hadn't anticipated that someone would jump on her about it the very next morning. Marion was Helena's daughter, and she must have suffered the same rumors and curious glances as Alvar had—yet she lacked the same prickly aura.

"Anita said her sister's or cousin's mother-in-law lived in Ukraine," Alvar said. "Or something like that. So these boxes came from there?"

"Yes."

"The original box is missing, though, and the package slip."

"I threw them away."

"We just want their contact information."

"I don't have it."

Norma managed to catch the grin that flickered at the corner of Alvar's mouth.

"How about this: you help us by giving us their contact information, and you get a cut of all future sales."

Alvar took some hair out of the box. Norma's stomach did a somersault, and a lock that had escaped her turban twisted and undulated. As Alvar's fingers lifted the hair from the box, brushing it in long strokes, she felt his touch on her spine. When he wrapped the bundle around his wrist, it was as if he had placed his hand on Norma's neck, his fingertips on her skin. It was an illusion, an illusion brought on by shock, but it didn't feel constrictive. It resembled a caress.

"Twenty percent. For Anita's sake."

Norma leaned against the wall, and the rough feeling of the plaster on her back calmed her. She pulled her cigarettes out of the pocket of her dress. Alvar offered a light. He was one of those men who opened doors, offered chairs and drinks, and took care of women's coats. Still, the sense of danger lingered. But though that lingered, the smell of criminality was absent. His dopamine levels weren't those of a man prone to violence. Nothing in him smelled of insanity. He didn't act confused. He wasn't pulling an ax out of his coat. Maybe she just read danger in him because during the night she had learned about the pipe smoking and her own role in what happened to Helena. If it weren't for Norma's hair, Helena wouldn't have tumbled over the edge. She would have recovered from her divorce and eventually might have been able to put her life back together. Helena would have had her children, and her children would have had their mother. Marion would have had a family. Norma now understood her mother's words from the video in a different way. Her mother had been visiting Helena all these years out of guilt, not friendship, and she had lived with that guilt for decades.

Alvar stepped closer and apologized that he had to bother her with business like this so soon after Anita's departure. Norma tried to return his gaze. She couldn't. Her face burned, her blood flow concentrated in her scalp and nose, and she was sure Alvar would notice she was thinking of him as Crazy Helena's son. He was an expert in that field just as Norma was with hair, and her eyes wandered up to the sky, the balconies and fire escape ladders of the building across the courtyard, and back to the asphalt, the rug-beating rack, the car tires, the back windows, and the nail studio technicians and their ankles. She had prepared poorly for her lies.

"Can you hear me? You look like a deer in headlights."

Alvar snapped his fingers. Norma jumped.

"We can help you look for the contact information. Did Anita have any other phones?"

Alvar's voice, his ordinary, rational tone, felt like a cold spring on a hot day and cleared Norma's head. Her wandering gaze stopped on a piece of gum stuck to the asphalt. He thought her mother might have had more than one phone. But why? Had her mother hidden one somewhere, as she had concealed her videos as a spare key left with her florist? Norma didn't understand what was going on. The Ukrainians' contact information couldn't be important enough to make Lambert follow her around and Alvar ambush her at the salon, unless they sensed the real situation, and that wasn't possible.

"Everything will be fine if we can just get that address. Shall we talk about this again tomorrow? I'll stop by in the evening," Alvar said, and glanced at his watch. When he led Norma back inside with a light grip on her elbow, she realized that he was used to handling people as a stylist handled hair.

The female voice on the GPS gave driving directions, and the radio channels changed constantly, with news, weather reports, commercials, and music mingling in a confused carpet of sound that made Marion's eyes twitch. They wouldn't be back in Helsinki until morning and weren't going to get much sleep in the meantime. Marion wished Lambert would concentrate on driving instead of channel surfing on the radio.

"Alvar seems to have made some sort of connection with the girl," Lambert said. "Sometimes he has a magic touch with these things."

"Norma hasn't stolen anything. There's no need to treat her like a thief."

"Like Albino, you mean? Let's not talk about that anymore. For the sake of your nerves."

Marion concentrated on staring at the dead bee on the dashboard. Lambert's car was parked near Hämeenlinna, where his mongrels had left another car for them to continue in. Usually Lambert let his men take care of the dirty work, but he wanted to handle this himself, and the only person he wanted along was Marion. For the educational value, he had said. One of Lambert's principles was that sometimes a good leader picks up a shovel himself. That was the only way to avoid forgetting the price and value of success.

"We'll make you some coffee when we get there. That should perk you up," Lambert said, and started humming. He was in a good mood. Too good.

The Midsummer vacation week had drawn people away, and the neighborhood seemed deserted. Between the homes built during the boom were an equal number of lots that would never be filled. The old building stock was represented by a former grocery store with peeling decals in the window, hearkening back to a time before chain stores and hypermarkets made the village shops extinct.

Lambert parked the car behind a shuttered convenience store. The parking lot was overrun by willow herb, and plywood had been nailed over the windows. Marion got out to stretch her legs and listened. The silence was unbroken. She and Lambert melted into the summer gloaming like fish in weed-choked water; no one would see them.

"Lasse did good work again. I have new lists," Lambert said as they walked across two overgrown building lots. He stopped to inspect Kristian's garden, then grabbed a stem of chives and put it in his mouth. Something was stuck in the bird netting. Perhaps a thrush, perhaps a hedgehog. Marion turned her gaze to the trampoline and hot tub. She didn't remember what people who owned their own homes had in their yards. When she was young, they didn't have friends who played in little houses built by their parents on manicured lawns. Instead, Marion had run the blow-dryer in the evenings to cover the sounds of fighting and practiced for her future profession by cutting Alvar's and Helena's hair because they didn't have money to go to a salon.

Marion held the hem of her skirt in her hands. Nettles stung her ankles. She lacked Lambert's self-assurance and glanced nervously at the neighboring houses—their windows remained black, and no motion was visible.

"Taste the strawberries." Lambert wiped his mouth with a handkerchief. "Such a delicate berry. They don't travel well. Otherwise we could pick some and take them back with us. What do you think? Should we give Lasse a little Midsummer bonus?"

Lambert tried the back door. It was open. He shook his head and laughed.

Kristian had fallen asleep in front of the TV. On the coffee table was a half-eaten sausage and an empty beer bottle. As Lambert woke the man of the house, Marion went to check the bedrooms, even though she knew his wife and children were visiting grandparents. The mongrels had verified the family's schedule. The sounds of a commotion came from downstairs. The bottle clattered off the table, and a chair leg screeched across the floor, but Kristian didn't utter a word. Marion peered around half of the double door. Lambert had turned on the lights and closed the curtains.

"Could you make me something to eat?" Lambert asked.

Marion went looking for coffee filters in the kitchen. She found a tube of hydrocortisone in front of the radio and applied a layer to the nettle stings on her ankles. A note on the refrigerator listed the week's menu, and inside were servings of potato salad, meatballs, and diced pork in plastic containers, all untouched. On the counter loomed a pile of empty sausage wrappers and a line of beer bottles, which Kristian had probably intended to dispose of before his wife and children came home. Beyond the table, she could see into the utility room. Marion felt sorry for the family when she looked at the dryer and the children's soccer cleats all in a row, but she couldn't change the course of events. Kristian worked for the clan because he was in debt to Lambert. Kristian wasn't a volunteer like Lasse, but still he had become difficult. Marion turned on the radio and closed her ears.

On the way home, Lambert smiled. "Did you remember to bring snacks?"

"I made sandwiches."

"Good. Any coffee?"

"In the thermos."

"I didn't get anything new out of Kristian. Anita paid him well."

Marion didn't understand. She'd thought they'd gone to see Kristian because he wanted to quit.

"Alvar has been showing Anita's picture to all the agency's employees. Kristian recognized her even though he tried to deny it at first. They shouldn't have had any connection."

"Why didn't anyone tell me?"

"Because of your nerves."

Marion glanced at Lambert, but his expression revealed nothing. If Anita had gone off on her own with Kristian, had she contacted other employees? What about dissatisfied clients from the agency? Anita had money for bribes. She could have found any number of surrogates, donors, or staff members. Marion would have to visit Lasse as soon as possible and make sure everything was still okay. The metal box would be safe with Lasse as long as no one suspected him.

"How could she have known to go to Kristian in the first place?" fumed Lambert. "Who told her about the agency? And why?"

"Did you find out anything else?"

Marion didn't recognize her own voice. It was thin, like a streak of salt on a winter boot, and rippled unevenly, but Lambert didn't seem to notice. Lost in his own thoughts, he hummed the same song Helena used to on car trips. Marion remembered sitting in the backseat with Alvar, scraping frost from the windows of the Volvo. Salami sandwiches wrapped in plastic. That song. Fights.

"Kristian didn't know who Anita was working for. We'll have to see what happens. If anything. Maybe the message will get across."

Marion closed her eyes and pretended to sleep. Two dead bodies sent a powerful enough message as far as she was concerned. The song wouldn't leave her ears. Kristian's case would look like suicide, an overdose, or both. When Lambert said he was ready to leave, Marion hadn't turned her eyes toward the living room; she knew to keep them where they belonged. She didn't even remember how her fiancé, Bergman, had looked that night, a knife in his chest. The memories were missing. There were only fragments, the smell of blood and the feeling that her teeth were coming out. The open balcony door, the white curtains billowing, the paralysis. She couldn't remember any sounds. Helena's hands she remembered, her hands groping for the pipe, and her mouth, which had moved as if talking, probably to the same voices as before—to Dr. Jackson, to Alma, to the child she had left waiting somewhere, always waiting. Lambert hadn't resisted when Alvar dragged Helena toward the door. He just stood like a statue, then pulled a flask out of the pocket of his linen jacket and handed the jacket to Marion. Milk had come through her blouse. Lights flashed blue and red. Only blue and red. The tunnel leading into the night swallowed everything else like a hole expanding in the ice on a lake.

Later she had visited Alvar at their grandparents' house. Alvar tried to prevent her from leaving by hiding her ankle boots, but Crazy Helena's daughter, wearing her grandmother's church shoes, attracted even more attention in a small town. A kid on a bike yelled at her as he passed. Every glance contained an accusation.

On that village street, she decided she would never give anyone her heart. She would never let Helena's disease be passed down. She didn't want more Lamberts in the world. For her, this family was done.

Norma didn't understand the sheet of paper on the table, even though this had to be the "unpleasant business" Lambert had wanted to talk about at the cemetery. She recognized her mother's handwriting and signature. Next to it was the name Max Lambert. Norma had inherited her mother's debts.

"Have you decided what payment system would be best?" Alvar asked.

"My mother didn't even borrow sugar from the neighbors. What would she have done with this much money?"

"Bought a new kidney for your grandmother."

Norma put her hand to her mouth. The laugh was unintentional and inappropriate for the situation. The zeros still danced in her eyes. Alvar put a glass of red wine in Norma's hand and offered her a match. Norma had forgotten to light her cigarette. Because she had to play the role of a person who didn't have anything to hide, she didn't resist when Alvar invited himself over. She would have preferred to meet with him in a public place, but now she understood the reason for the house call. Alvar had thought this might agitate her, and news like this was best to deliver away from prying eyes. The turban choked her head like the hoop on a barrel.

"Apparently there wasn't much time, and Anita wanted to speed up the process."

"Where could she have gotten a kidney?"

"Anita visited Romania to buy hair for Alla. Maybe from there. At least she saw how easily poor women will sell their hair or their kidneys or anything else anyone wants to buy."

"This is illegal."

"Necessity knows no law. Do you intend to go ahead with the operation?"

"For the kidney? No!"

"Not even for your beloved grandmother?"

Alvar cocked his head, and Norma instinctively took a step back. The windowsill got in the way. Her mother had lied to Lambert again. There was nothing wrong with her grandmother's kidneys, and her mother wouldn't have sullied herself like this for her anyway. Every word about Elli Naakka in the videos—including the bitterness in her mother's voice, the wrinkle in her brow—was evidence of that. She would have taken such a crazy loan only for Norma or Helena, not for anyone else.

"As you can see from the contract, the first payment comes due in July," Alvar said.

The wind blowing through the open window didn't clear Norma's head. The fans she had placed strategically around the apartment before Alvar's visit weren't helping, either, and the wine and tobacco didn't make her feel any better. There was no solution. There wasn't enough time to scrape anything together. The estate inventory coming up in August would give her only worthless personal effects. Her mother's apartment deposit was too small, and you couldn't get a payday loan that large. Asking for a loan from a bank would be pointless. Her wildcat years were over, and Norma had a terrible credit rating, from a time when her life had been more reckless and she thought she deserved everything because she was unique. She preferred not to remember those days, but this was the price. Lambert probably already knew she wasn't credit-worthy. Where did desperate people get loans?

From men like Lambert.

"Why do I get the feeling you aren't really listening?" Alvar said.

Norma lit another cigarette. According to Alvar, her mother had been getting one hundred euros per bundle of hair. They were delivered to the salon every two weeks, twenty ponytails at a time. That was four thousand euros a month, tax free. That was a lot but not enough. Her mother had agreed to utterly unreasonable loan terms and payment amounts.

"You can get a kidney for fifteen thousand euros. But Anita borrowed a hundred. I thought she must want to help her relatives who were in trouble, too. Originally Anita started dealing hair because of them."

"My mother didn't tell me anything."

"Maybe your relatives need more money if you don't think the loan was just for the kidney. You don't seem to believe that."

Alvar had come close. Too close. Norma's nervous laugh died, and ash fell onto the rug. Alvar bent to wipe it up with a handkerchief he produced from his pocket. He wasn't lying, and Norma realized she was afraid. The roots of her hair squirmed like worms on hot asphalt, and she felt her carefully maintained restraint cracking.

"If Anita didn't use all the money, enough should be left over to cover the immediate emergency. Do you know where it is?"

"No. Her account is empty."

"Lambert would probably be satisfied with the Ukrainians' contact information," Alvar said. "After that, all this will go away and you can still have the twenty percent. That's an unusually generous offer, for Anita's sake. I wouldn't advise looking at last-minute airline tickets. You have that look on your face. Next you'll try crying or suggest we go to bed."

The blush spread over Norma's face before he finished his sentence.

"And let this be the last time you try to pull a fast one," Alvar added. "I doubt Anita logged into social media from the other side. What were you doing there? Were you looking for the money or warning your Ukrainian relatives? You know where to find them, don't you?"

Norma had been caught. Email. Messenger. Skype. Those pings from the inbox. Investigating the salon's Facebook page and her mother's overflowing email account. She had turned off the network after looking, but she had still been caught. She wasn't going to beat these people. They knew what they were doing, and she didn't.

Her hand went to the knot on her turban. It was holding. "I don't know anything about any Ukrainians," Norma said. "I only know the password to my mother's computer. I had to look to see if she'd left any messages for me."

Alvar grinned. His canine teeth were sharp. He had one day of stubble and summer in his pores. They breathed the same air in the same rhythm for a moment, and Norma heard her pulse in her ears, which also fell into the same pace.

"Not a bad performance," Alvar said, and wiped a bead of sweat from Norma's nose.

Norma drew a breath and took a step back. The moment passed. She had been on the verge of confessing. What was wrong with her?

Alvar took a business card out of his pocket. "Call me if anything happens."

"Like what?"

"Anything. Or if you change your mind."

After Alvar left, the apartment felt as if all the air had been sucked out, and the walls closed in. Norma had to go outside. The girls at the nail studio on the ground floor were finishing their day. They never greeted each other.

The girls made eye contact only with the asphalt. They wouldn't see her sniffing, and even if they did, they wouldn't react. She pressed her forehead to the cool stair railing in the shade of the backyard, steadied her breath, and pressed her hand over her mouth. Nail studios had started showing up on the street at about the same time as the extension salons, and they were all full of Vietnamese nail technicians. They were easy to recognize, as was the bitter aroma of fear. They feared their madams, just as Norma feared her creditors. They were all in the same position, and no one was going to help them.

The trash bins had already been emptied, and the nutritional supplements Norma had thrown away were gone. She would buy more from the pharmacy. She would buy everything possible. She had promised to deliver hair to Alvar on the same schedule her mother had.

According to Alvar, that was enough for the interest but no more. Only the Ukrainians' contact information would bring complete forgiveness.

Lambert wiped raspberry jam from the corner of his mouth. Before reaching the beltway, he had wanted a freshly baked doughnut, and his expectations were rewarded at the counter of an ABC station, which was still quiet so early in the morning. Lambert dropped his crumpled napkin onto his plate and smiled. Raspberry seeds stuck between his teeth.

"Hard work gives a man an appetite. You should have one, too."

Marion rotated her coffee cup and shook her head. After getting home, she would check the balance again. That would calm her nerves. At least she could get away and start over. A good stylist can always find work, although without Ukrainian virgin Remy, there was no chance of a place as glamorous as she deserved. That was why she held back, hoping that she might still find the importer before Lambert.

Lambert began to collect his things but then seemed to remember something and took his phone out of his pocket. He started scrolling. "That was sent from the Bangkok clinic."

Marion didn't dare look at the screen, but Lambert pushed it in front of her. Maybe the gesture was a hint. Maybe she was reading too much into it. Maybe it didn't mean anything. Lately messages from the Bangkok clinic had meant only bad news for Marion.

She still didn't understand how Anita had managed to slip into the closed ward and why she had taken off her sunglasses and hat, making herself vulnerable to the security cameras. Maybe she'd wanted to show her face to the girl she had questioned, to seem more trustworthy.

"Look now," Lambert demanded. "For Christ's sake, Marion. It doesn't show Anita."

Marion took the phone. On the screen was a copy of a Japanese passport.

"What do you think? Mr. Shiguto wants a white child, preferably several. Shiguto's representative, a woman I might add, made the order."

"If it's suspicious, don't take it."

"He's already been to Bangkok to donate sperm."

"So?"

"He's already paid."

"What's the problem?"

"Nothing, yet. He's just young. Twenty-two. How many clients that age have we had? Alvar reminded me about that American pedophile."

"He wasn't at any of our clinics."

"No, and no one would have even noticed him if his sister hadn't started calling around and alerting people about his background."

Marion remembered the incident. After growing tired of the indifference of the authorities and the clinics, the man's sister contacted the news. After that, the media caught the scent. A Swedish journalist managed to infiltrate a Nigerian baby farm as a customer and documented everything with a hidden backpack camera. The story rocked Sweden, and it was only a matter of time before someone else tried again. That was why Lambert's partners delivered detailed reports of anything even the slightest bit suspicious. That was why Anita got caught. Everything would have gone fine if the Bangkok clinic hadn't sent that security footage to Lambert. Everything would have gone fine if Anita hadn't been sold an old security camera map. She had been cheated.

"Marion, take a picture of the girl, without that scarf she wears. And try to make her look presentable."

Lambert grabbed his phone and stood up. A line of sugar still glittered on his lower lip.

"For what?"

"We don't have any pictures of her."

Marion couldn't swallow the coffee she had just sipped. Lambert was looking for a buyer for Norma and wanted Marion to know.

As she lay down on the eyelash bed, Norma refused to take her turban off, and Marion nearly lost her temper. The trust between them was still delicate and she couldn't crush it even though she was fighting against time. This was the first evening they'd spent together without any clients around, and for once the phone was quiet. Every day Marion had suggested going out after work, but the girl always complained of being in some vague rush.

"Think about that lash technician training," Marion said, and dripped glue on a jade stone. "It only takes a day, and I'm a certified trainer. If you handled the eyelashes, I'd have more time for hair clients."

Norma drew in short, rapid breaths. She was so different from Albino. She wasn't tempted by the assurances that there were only a few pages of theory, let alone by the free eyelash treatment. She had agreed to extensions only after Marion fluttered her own and reminded her that you had to keep up appearances when you worked in a salon.

"These are exactly the kinds of industries women retrain for when jobs are hard to come by," Marion said. "Hair, nails, eyelashes. Even during a recession, the market stays good. It's the sort of simple luxury people give up last. Alvar said you're going to start delivering hair just like Anita. That's great. The customers have been clamoring for more."

No reply, just a tremor in her eyelids. Occasionally a hand rose to check the turban.

"We only use artificial fibers and real hair for eyelash extensions, never mink. Remember that. Animal rights activists ask questions about that sort of thing."

"Why isn't anyone that strict about hair?"

"Because it's not related to animal rights. Quality and country of origin are enough," Marion replied. "And if someone does ask, just say something about Hindu princesses."

The few customers who demonstrated interest in the source of their new hair had always seen a documentary about temple hair or read about it in the news. That's why they were willing to pay such outrageous prices for their Great Lengths extensions, and they thought they were actually doing a good deed. To justify the price, the company appealed to their ethical approach, which was sourcing hair only from Tirupati, from pilgrims who sacrificed their hair without compensation. The idea of a sacred sacrifice had just the right romantic ring to enlarge the company's halo. Of course no one talked about what the Temple of Tirupati did with its income or how much the pilgrims had to fork over to the barbers. With the money they made from free hair, Tirupati had long ago surpassed the Vatican in wealth, and the middle managers took what they could on the sly. You'd have to look long and hard for a more corrupt road to the gods.

After the job was done, Norma inspected the results, and as she batted her eyes, Marion took a series of pictures in the mirror.

"You have the same expression Anita had. Really, no one cares where the hair comes from. Anita couldn't understand that either," Marion said.

Anita had tried to draw customers into asking about the source of the hair and started selling hair only once she was sure no uncomfortable questions would follow. Maybe Norma was wondering the same thing. It was time to get to the point.

"Lambert is willing to pay handsomely for the Ukrainians' contact information. You could quit work. You could travel. You could do anything."

"I promised Alvar I'd deliver the hair."

"That isn't going to be enough. Anita borrowed a lot of money."

"Why?"

Norma's mouth snapped shut, and Marion was left wondering whether the girl had actually asked or if that was just Marion's wishful thinking. If Norma didn't believe Lambert's explanation for the loan, that meant she knew something. Or at least suspected. Marion sought Norma's gaze. She remained mute. Why wasn't money enough? Did Alvar and Lambert seem like the kind of men it was a good idea to be in debt to? Was someone paying her to keep quiet, or was she giving hair to someone else? Norma's clothes were cheap Swedish fast fashion—sometimes she looked like she lived on the street—yet money didn't have any effect on her. Marion decided to open a bottle of sparkling wine.

"Let's talk seriously," Marion said, and handed Norma a glass. "The beauty industry has always been women's territory. It's made up of microbusinesses that people can run out of their homes if they have to. It takes almost no capital, but whenever it becomes profitable, someone swoops in and takes over. Every time it's the same, whether it's women or colored people. We can be consumers but not owners, and we never get rich. The multinationals are controlled by whites, and they consume everything, the Unilevers and L'Oréals. Africa has already been taken over, and China and India are next. Anita hated that."

Norma took a glass. She was listening, her attention had focused. "That sounds like Mom."

"That was why Anita couldn't stand the idea that Lambert was benefiting from all of this."

"I never understood why Mom came to work for him."

"Middle-aged women don't have very many options, and without start-up money, it's hard to do anything. This was supposed to be temporary. We had other plans for the future."

Norma was clearly interested, and she sniffed again. For a fleeting moment, Marion wondered whether Norma could be her new partner. Would she be interested? Was she like Marion, who had needed a friend like Anita in order to take her life in a new direction, to see the world through new eyes? Maybe. But did the girl have the nerve for it? Marion decided to take the smallest risk she could. She would tell only part of the story.

"We were supposed to open our own salon. That was what Anita needed the loan for. The Ukrainian hair would have gotten us off to a running start."

The girl fluttered her new lashes as if something were in her eye. "Where's the money?"

"In London. Anita took it to a bank there and paid cash for a storefront. Of course it was a secret. Lambert never lets anyone leave easily."

Marion called up a picture on her phone: Bond Street, where they would have opened their salon. The girl didn't seem curious about how Anita could have deposited such a large amount of cash. She clearly didn't understand business or banking. Marion sighed.

"We could open it together, you and me."

"I have to repay the loan to Lambert."

"We'll handle that once we get the salon open."

"The first payment—"

"Don't worry about that. I'll figure something out."

Marion grabbed Norma's hand and squeezed.

"Anita never would have given the Ukrainian to Lambert, never. And you shouldn't either. You did the right thing. Promise me you won't tell anyone about this, or—"

"Or what?"

"Or what happened to Anita will happen to me."

Norma leaned her forehead on the cool tile of the bathroom. Her head was heavy—it had been more than four hours since her last haircut. She took out the scissors and untied her turban. The smell clinging to the fabric was so bitter that something had to be wrong. Her hairline was full of kinks. Marion had spoken of her mother with a warmth reserved for friends, and she didn't believe in her mother's suicide either. Maybe Marion knew the murderer and was afraid of him. She had told the truth about the business but lied about Bond Street. Norma just didn't know why. Maybe the money was there, maybe not. Maybe Marion didn't know where it was, or she wanted to keep it.

Norma turned the water on to cover the sound of the cutting, then grabbed a hank of hair and fixed rubber bands around it. Opening a salon didn't make any sense, even though it would explain the need for the loan. Her mother had known about Norma's multiplying grays. She must have lied to Marion about the purpose of the loan.

After folding the bundles into bags, Norma was ready to continue the evening and get more information. She stepped out of the bathroom. However, Marion no longer sat on the couch sipping sparkling wine. Instead she was digging through the cellophane packages delivered earlier in the day—Star Locks, Glamour and Dream Hair, Hair Gl'Amour, Simply Natural, Long Beyond, Delightful Hair—and piling them in a jumble.

Apparently a customer was having an emergency, and she had to leave. "We'll pick up tomorrow where we left off."

Marion's voice was different now, and the sweat on her forehead had gone cold. She wasn't afraid of Norma, but she was of the bald man waiting outside.

As the car pulled away, Norma picked up the brush that had fallen out of Marion's handbag and sniffed. Her mother, in her final days, never emitted the kind of intense fear that now poured out of Marion constantly. Not even Marion's old hair, which Norma found in her mother's apartment, smelled of anything more than everyday stress. Had Lambert discovered that the women at his salon were planning to open their own shop? But would he be ready to take extreme measures just because someone wanted to leave the business? The security cameras in the metro showed clearly that her mother had jumped onto the tracks herself.

After noting the bank and credit cards Lambert was turning over in his hands, Marion focused her gaze on her coffee cup and the gold filigree of Alla's Russian porcelain. She had thought the emergency had to do with one of the agency's clients.

"Did you ever see either of these women with Anita? Were they customers at the salon?" Alvar placed two photographs in front of Marion.

"Do they look like customers to you?"

Lambert flicked Marion in the forehead with a finger, and coffee splashed in her lap. She started wiping her skirt with her napkin, focusing on that and hoping that everyone would assume her pallor was a result of Lambert's bullying.

"This isn't a good time to be fresh. Look at the pictures."

Both women were about Anita's age and blond like she was. Marion had seen them for the first time ages ago when prostitutes walked the streets openly in the Kallio neighborhood and the johns' cruising kept the area busy through the night. The blondes' lunch break must have fallen around the same time Marion finished with her last client, so she often saw them at the diner. The two disappeared suddenly at one point, and after they showed up on the street again, Marion overheard a conversation that made her think the women had been behind bars. That's when it occurred to her they could provide the perfect cover.

Marion and Anita had made the decision in haste. Lambert had put off his answer on the loan for so long that they were on the verge of missing out on the possibilities offered by the Lagos trip. The clan knew people who could provide new identities, but Marion didn't. These two ladies of the night were a quick solution. For an appropriate sum, they agreed to open accounts in Marion and Anita's names and deposit the loan money in small amounts.

"Do they have something to do with Anita?" Marion asked. "I've never seen them before."

"Anita had bank cards in her pocket with these women's names on them. And they recognized her photo," Alla replied.

"Why didn't you tell me earlier?"

Lambert snorted.

"I don't believe they played any role other than allowing their names to be used," Alvar said. "We let them go. The accounts have a good amount of money in them, presumably ours."

"Are you going to use it to offset Norma's debt?" Marion asked.

Alla laughed so hard, she had to stop filing her nails.

After Anita died, Marion saw one of the prostitutes on the street. She told her that now would be a good time to clear off and gave her all the money she had in her purse. Marion had managed to transfer most of the money from the accounts to her own new straw men, and she'd thought everything was fine. The clan shouldn't have had any connection to the two women, since drug running and prostitution weren't in their line of work. But still this happened. One of Lambert's mongrels had found the women in Copenhagen, and now the ice was cracking beneath Marion's feet.

A gang of immigrant boys was hanging around near the halal butcher shop. Marion didn't see any familiar faces, but she still stopped and pretended to search for something in her purse while she registered each face in turn and then inspected the flow of customers at the international call café and braiding salon next door. Since Anita's death, she flinched every time she saw darker-skinned young people, even though she realized that no one would connect her to the attack. Lambert's mongrels didn't remember anything about their attackers other than the color of their skin.

Folake was straightening a little girl's hair, but no other customers were in the shop. Occasionally the little girl's nose wrinkled at the smell of the sodium hydroxide, but the smile stayed on her face and she waved at Marion. Now she was going to be beautiful. Now she would have good hair. She proudly reported that she was turning six soon. One day, after she'd burned her scalp enough times, she could be Marion's customer, too.

Marion handed Folake the box of hair and asked, as if in passing, whether anyone had stopped in and asked about her or the boys.

Folake cocked her head. "Are you in trouble? You need help?"

Marion shook her head and waved to the girl as she left.

On the street Marion instinctively tried her left pants pocket again. She was used to calling Anita whenever she got nervous or whenever she learned something about the clan's operation that Anita would want to know. Anita was always ready with a solution, and fast. Now Marion had to decide everything herself. She even had to arrange the ambush that freed Anita on her last morning alive.

When her project phone had beeped after Anita was captured, Marion guessed that the message came not from Anita but from Lambert, who was trying to lure out Anita's co-conspirators. Marion answered the message as if suspecting nothing and suggested a meeting in front of the salon. Lambert responded that some other place would be better. No, we shouldn't change the routine, Marion replied. Then she called Folake to ask whether she knew the right boys for a little job. When the first baseball bat hit the windshield, the minion driving Anita jumped out of the car, and by the third blow, Anita was off and running, reaching the protection of the crowds around the metro station before the mongrels farther off could catch up with her.

Anita's project phone was probably still with Lambert. As far as Marion knew, it hadn't been taken to Anita's apartment with her regular phone. Marion could still keep up the game. She could still pretend to be Anita's boss and maybe even blackmail the clan. She could suggest a trade and try to get more money. The thought was tempting. But the plan was more important. She wouldn't take risks. Not anymore.

Later they grilled her about what she had seen through the window of the salon. Four black boys and a baseball bat. Or three. No, she didn't think she recognized the boys. No, she hadn't ever seen them before, or at least she didn't think so. Everything had happened so fast. She'd noticed the car parked in front of the salon and Anita sitting inside, and the baseball bat hitting the windshield and the boys who continued pummeling the car. No, Anita didn't usually meet friends at the salon. No, she didn't have any idea whom Anita intended to meet that morning. She was just as surprised by the turn of events as everyone else. She certainly didn't know how Anita's boss had learned so quickly that Anita had been found out.

She had reserved a baseball bat and money for Anita in the closet in the back room and assumed that Anita would run into the salon after the boys attacked the car. She was prepared to defend Anita, to stall the mongrels and help Anita escape through the back door of the salon. Anita could have taken a taxi, maybe rushed to the harbor and left for Stockholm or Tallinn, wherever she could without a passport, and Marion could have followed. But no. Anita had run to the metro station for reasons Marion didn't understand—unless her purpose was to protect Marion until the bitter end.

Eight

Ever since Eva told me about her fate, I've wondered what I would do if I received a call that you had been arrested. Flashing lights, police, paparazzi. The whole circus. Dear God. I couldn't handle it. I wouldn't be able to visit you in the same kind of institution where Helena is now. The idea that you could be locked up in a place like that for decades is unbearable.

March 14, 2013

I visited Laajasalo a couple of weeks before the tragedy. Easter was coming, and because Helena wasn't up to holiday preparations, I decided to bake Alvar a cheesecake. I was just about to grate the lemon rind when Helena suddenly grabbed my arm and asked where the sugar was. She wanted to help. Her grip was strong, her voice higher than normal, and it had a strange tone to it. Her eyes were completely clear. She said she missed birch trees and the horizon when she was in New York. Eva spoke to me, through Helena.

At first I thought Helena was hallucinating. We had talked about Eva so much that it wouldn't be any wonder if her world had become confused with the other voices in Helena's head. But she was acting like someone completely different. Even her expressions weren't the same, let alone her voice, and she pulled her hair the same way you do and claimed she'd visited us in the hospital after your birth. She had come to greet one of her kind. I had thought the scent of lemon and bergamot in the air was from a stranger, but really it was Eva! Eva left the smell of Shalimar in the room! She had started using it in America when she needed something that would give her faith in the future, just as lemon rind and the colonial goods store in Finland had smelled of hope and possibilities, like riches across the sea ripe for the taking. In New York the same smells had been different, and her new life had turned out to be something else. Money was in short supply, and America felt oppressive. Originally created as an antidote to the Great Depression, Shalimar had given Eva precisely the joy she needed. It still smelled of distant lands, unknown continents, and roads she could take if she met a dead end in America.

After Helena was locked up, I didn't hear Eva's voice for years. I stopped sending pipe hair to Helena and stopped using it myself.

When I realized Grandma wouldn't be any help with Eva, I pilfered Eva's picture from the Bible and took a copy of it to Helena in the hospital. She was overjoyed. She had missed Eva. The next visit I took a risk and let Helena smoke. I didn't do so lightly. But no repeat of the tragedy was possible. Helena was under careful watch, and I would have stopped if her condition worsened. However, it worked immediately, and her mood improved. Helena had talked about Alma and Juhani before, and about a lot of other people, but she also said plenty of things that made no sense. Only regular smoking made her words comprehensible and gave shape to the confusion of sounds coming out of her mouth. Through Helena, Eva told me everything.

We started getting her out during the day and visiting as far away as Kuopio with Alvar, walking the square and visiting the bank. The purpose was to get Helena used to living outside the hospital. I was optimistic. I still believe she'll get free someday, maybe as soon as we return from Bangkok. Eva is excited for that, too. Sometimes I get the feeling she likes Helena more than me.

Eva didn't talk to Norma, she talked to her mother. That could mean only one thing: during the spring, her mother's mind had crumbled like a sand castle baked by the sun, and Norma hadn't noticed anything. Not her mother's betrayal, not her descent toward madness. Maybe they were one and the same. Norma prodded the photograph next to the computer. It fell on the table with Eva's face down, and Norma pressed her hand to her pounding chest as if trying to stanch a hemorrhage. These videos weren't going to help her with her debt problem, tell her where the loan money was, or explain Marion's fear or Lambert's strange behavior. All she would get was her own long journey into insanity.

Some of the videos had been filmed in her mother's apartment, and some in hotel rooms that could have been anywhere in the world. In one place, a blackout shade flashed between dark brown curtains that matched the décor; in another place, a ceiling fan rotated. Sometimes it was late and the staff had turned down the bed, set an evening chocolate on the pillow, a water bottle on the nightstand, and a cotton cloth on the floor next to the bed with slippers on it. Sometimes the bed had been slept in, and her mother was applying day cream while she talked to the camera. In some shots she smiled at someone even though she was definitely in the room alone and looked like a completely different person. But nothing in her behavior or environment was confused. Only her conversations with Eva revealed the break in her mind. Every word her mother uttered increased Norma's distress, and every excited explanation amplified her despair until panic dried all the saliva in her mouth. As spring arrived, the change that had happened in her mother was obvious: her voice had become more determined, and it had lost the exhaustion that had been apparent since her visit to her own mother's house. She was a woman on a mission, and that mission blazed in her eyes. She faced it like a soldier, her bearing full of energy. But she didn't say anything about the money.

March 15, 2013

Last winter Eva told me to visit the asylum at the same time as Alvar, but it needed to look like a coincidence. At first I didn't understand what was going on, and after Eva told me her plan, I didn't think it would work, but she understood more about Lambert's businesses than I did. She had smelled the clan's source of livelihood on Alvar, and she knew how to take advantage of them. Alvar helped with this unwittingly, because when he visited his mother in the secure facility, he thought he saw Helena moving toward a clearer state of mind. Once Eva hugged Alvar as an experiment and shocked him out of his wits. Alvar asked the doctor if they had changed Helena's medication. The smoking was what was doing it. And Eva.

Alvar started talking to Helena more the better she seemed to feel, and gradually they moved from general topics of conversation to matters of the heart. His girl had been fired from Marion's salon after getting caught stealing, and Alvar was angry and sad in a self-medicated haze of alcohol and amphetamines. He needed a listener, and this gave Eva more faith that our plan was worth all the risks. We had to seize the moment. Both Marion and Alvar would be happy to take on someone at the salon whom they could trust—an old friend, someone discreet. I doubted my abilities as a stylist, and I was afraid of meeting Alvar. I didn't know what he had turned into. But Eva assured me that Alvar would be sympathetic to me, as would Marion. Through the clan's network, I would be able to find what you needed, and we could avoid the mistakes Eva had made in her life. She had dealt with men like this before. Nothing about it was new to her, but it was to me. She dispelled my doubts by telling how she got her own children.

Eva was born in Amuri, a working-class neighborhood of Tampere, the daughter of a factory worker. Her mother abandoned her after the birth and ordered the sauna cupper, Kaisu, a folk healer who had helped during the postpartum period, to take the baby to the poorhouse. Unlike the child's mother, Kaisu was not troubled by Eva's strange qualities and believed that she possessed magical powers. She wanted to keep the baby herself, and it was Eva's good fortune that Kaisu turned out to be a good foster mother who knew how to appreciate Eva's gifts, but after Kaisu died, Eva was utterly alone. She couldn't take over Kaisu's profession because she had a poor tolerance for the sauna and sweaty backs, and factory work would have meant living with the other workers and long days of toil. She needed fresh air and a more flexible schedule.

In the moment of her despair, one Sunday at church Eva happened to meet the master of the Naakka holdings at the time and could smell the scents of a rich household—mace and lemon rind, crystal sugar and imported goods—and decided to use all her wiles to win Juhani Naakka's devotion. And she succeeded—Juhani led Eva to the altar despite his family's opposition. The match was seen with disapproval because the foster child of a cupper born in a nest of Red agitators was not considered appropriate material for the lady of a White home. But Juhani ignored all such talk. He cared only about Eva and was eagerly anticipating little towheads running around the yard. That was a problem for Eva. Reproducing was not for freaks of nature, and she kept her cycle under strict control using methods learned from her foster mother. The clock in her loins ticked away.

The solution to her problem came from an unexpected direction. After the Civil War, Eva received a letter from her sister, Alma, who wrote in despair—starvation had come to the working neighborhoods of Tampere, and word that Eva had married into a rich household had reached them there. Eva wept until Juhani Naakka relented and gave her permission to go to Tampere to tend to her bedridden relatives. What Eva left unsaid was that the letter also explained that her sister had been widowed in the war and was expecting a child.

Alma and her mother didn't recognize Eva when she entered their room. The communal kitchen behind her stank of dandelion root, and the diseases seemed to have soaked into the walls of the building. Looking at the women in their beds, it was clear their time was short. They exuded only blackness. Eva would have to do everything in her power to keep Alma alive until the child was born. The situation was bad enough she wasn't sure she would succeed. She needed a backup plan.

Eva sought out a horse cabbie who knew the way to a sugar bootlegger, and after a visit there, she asked the cabbie to take her to an angel-maker. She arranged the price with the old woman and placed sugar, lard, and flour on the table—the gifts she had brought for her sick relations. On the way to Amuri, in addition to the corpses, Eva had noticed the smell of child-bearing. Despite the poor nutrition, the war had caused the city to breed, and there were plenty of extra children around. She could get a boy even if Alma's child died or was a girl or a freak.

For the following months, she fed Alma with a rag soaked in milk, heated porridge in a hay box, and numbed her nose with camphor cream, breathed in lemon rind, and fetched more morphine and creolin soap from the pharmacy. Her efforts were rewarded, and Alma gave birth to a girl, healthy and normal. That girl was your grandmother. A week-old baby acquired from the angel-maker became her brother, and Eva could begin to arrange burials for her mother and Alma. She wrote to Juhani that he should send a farmhand to fetch her after the funerals and that their house would be welcoming twins, the future master of the house and a beautiful girl. The children had been born prematurely, which could be blamed on the stress of living in a den of Communists.

Norma turned off the computer and fetched her mother's cardboard box. She stored the hair and her mother's videos in attic storage locker number twelve, but she kept this box at home. Other than Eva's picture, the contents didn't seem important. Still, Norma decided to go through the pile once more with fresh eyes. It might be more evidence of her mother's mental breakdown, like the videos with their stories of complicated family histories and Eva's ghost made flesh. Norma had begun to suspect that her mother had started smoking again. It had earned Helena a sentence in an insane asylum, and long-term use had probably affected her mother as well.

The papers in the box had one common thread: all of them had something to do with procuring children. Her mother said as much in the videos, even though she'd never seemed particularly fond of children. But would she have told Norma if she'd dreamed of a larger brood? What if Norma's birth had meant the end of her mother's baby dreams?

The number of women undergoing fertility treatment had grown over the past decade, as had their age. At the salon, Norma had come across a woman who was taking injections of clomiphene and hCG and complained the medications were ruining her hair. She was doing her treatments in Estonia, where you didn't have to explain why you wanted a child if you were single. She also praised the Estonians' prices and customer service. Plenty of women considered even cheaper countries. Norma turned on her laptop and looked up the Finnish rules for infertility treatment. Her mother was too old. She would have had to go abroad.

Or had her mother hoped for a child for Norma? At first the idea seemed insane. Norma had accepted long ago that family and relationships were not part of her future. But what if her mother wanted something else? Perhaps Eva had planted the idea in her head that Norma could become pregnant with someone else's egg. On the videos, her mother was always saying that her plan would bring some kind of improvement to Norma's life, not her own.

Norma had always preferred going to bed with people who were already spoken for, because they made no demands. Their skin brought a moment of joy and forgetfulness. That was enough. She wasn't built for family life and long-term relationships. She had tried dating once, and it didn't end well. Eventually she grew tired of sleepless nights, and he got fed up that Norma wouldn't try to cure what she claimed was insomnia but was really her hair waking her whenever it needed to be cut. Her mother had mourned the breakup more than she did, just like every job she lost. For vacations, her mother booked them trips to places that wouldn't remind Norma of what she was missing.

Making the call was a mistake, and Norma knew it as soon as she picked up the business card. But she had to. There was no address under the name. While she waited for a reply, she looked up the number online. It was either blocked or a prepaid account.

The silence in Alvar's car stank of discomfort and loneliness, and Norma didn't know where to start even though she had already thought through all her questions. She could hear noises from the SUV parked next to them, which came from a family of four enjoying their Happy Meals. A golden retriever claimed its portion of the children's food. The meeting spot had been Norma's suggestion. She had wanted to meet in a public place without extra people listening in, but she already regretted her choice. The children in the SUV were focused on the toys that had come with their meals. The girl's figurine looked like a golden-haired princess, and the girl herself like a future Saint Lucy's Day procession leader.

"Was it ever like that for you?" Alvar asked, nodding at the family.

"No."

"We didn't have a car. Helena didn't like buses, so we walked regardless of the weather. She threw the radio away. The television started to talk, so it had to go, too. Lambert was mad when he came to visit and saw both were missing. I told him they were stolen and got a beating. You wanted to hear about Helena, right? People don't usually know how to talk about her. Or they find the topic uncomfortable. Didn't Anita tell you?"

"No, never."

"When I was a kid, I thought I'd be able to control Helena's voices. I hoped so, anyway. It didn't go that way, though, ever. I was always someone different to her. If I was Juhani, she liked me. If I was Jackson, it was best to disappear. But if I was Alma, she wanted to know what the news was from Tampere and whether people still hated the Reds. Sometimes I was Juhani, and Alma was there with us, and we discussed the Civil War, which was educational at least. Sometimes she had an amazing accent. She could have been a great actress, a better actress than a singer. Anita blamed Lambert when Helena stopped singing, but she was wrong. Helena's symptoms had already started in Sweden. Once Helena thought the water at a venue was poisoned with henbane and that the microphone was reproducing someone else's voice. Lambert had no way of knowing what would happen onstage."

"Who was my mother? One of the voices?"

"No, Anita was always Anita. Helena remembered her, even though she hasn't recognized me in ages. Well, she recognizes me, but not as me. To her, I don't exist. To her, I'm whatever she imagines I am, and I play along. Before, that was the only way to keep her calm and get food. When I reminded her of Alma when she was starving, she would buy milk, lemons, sugar, and bread and complain that the store didn't have any lard. We stored our food on the windowsill instead of in the refrigerator. My first memories are from a bright summer night. Seagulls were screeching, the apartment was full of flies, and there were boxes of strawberries that had started to mold sitting in front of the window. The summer was hot, and I was sleeping under the open window. Luckily. Helena thought Dr. Jackson was sleeping in my bed. She stabbed my pillow and mattress. With a bread knife."

Norma blinked. The new lashes felt like heavy windshield wipers, and she squeezed her eyes shut after realizing that Alvar had shoved his arm in front of her. She guessed what she would see before Alvar rolled up his sleeve. No more questions were necessary. Alvar had grown up surrounded by madness. He lacked any fear of the things other people feared, and Norma's nose had interpreted that as danger.

"Anything else?" Alvar asked.

"Did my mother ever act the way Helena did?"

Alvar rolled down his sleeve. "Why do you ask?"

"For the last six months . . ."

"You think Helena stabbed Marion's fiancé and threw their baby off a balcony because voices told her to? And you want to know whether Anita jumped onto the tracks for the same reason?"

Norma waited.

Alvar turned to shake ash onto the asphalt. "Helena was so quick, there was nothing anyone could do. Marion had given her the baby, and at first Helena rocked it as usual. Did I notice anything strange? No, Helena was always strange. Could I have prevented it? No. Or, well, maybe. I could have stopped Lambert from coming inside. He was visiting Finland and gave Marion's family a ride to Laajasalo. Would that have changed anything? Should I have read the signs better? Maybe. If I had been more discerning, would Marion still have a family now? Probably. Should we all have watched Helena more closely? Yes. Yes, we're all guilty, but so what? Maybe she would have killed someone else. Or herself. Or maybe it's Anita who's to blame. Why didn't she intervene? She was an adult. Maybe she killed herself because she couldn't bear the guilt anymore. What would you say to that? Maybe she didn't like how Marion and I turned out. Maybe she saw us as monsters of her own creation. Would she be alive if Marion had a house and a husband and spent her days driving kids to ballet and hockey practices? If I—"

"Stop it."

"You're wasting your time thinking about all this. It won't change anything. Do you want some coffee?"

Without waiting for a response, Alvar stood up and walked toward the McDonald's. Norma pressed her hands to her nose. She had been on the verge of saying that she would give up the Ukrainians' contact information, that she would give everything, anything, just so long as Alvar told her that killing herself was a logical thing for her mother to do. Or that it had happened during a moment of clarity when her mother had understood the severity of her condition and wanted to interrupt the cycle of madness before she ended up like Helena. Norma wanted to hear that her mother was just disturbed. The crisis hotline cards in her handbag were probably for moments of desperation like this. Following the accident, she regarded them with derision, but now she wasn't laughing. Of all those business cards, she had chosen Alvar's, even though she knew she shouldn't let him know about her weaknesses and the strange manifestations of her mother's broken mind. Alvar was the last person she wanted to see her cry.

Norma opened the glove compartment to look for a tissue. What she found was a brush. Two women had used it, both of them Vietnamese, both pregnant, both young. Alvar's lovers? No, Norma would have smelled them on his clothes.

Alvar stepped out of the fast-food restaurant. Norma shoved the brush back into the glove compartment and felt around inside. Nothing. She pushed her fingers into the side pockets and between the seat cushions. A hairpin. She tucked it away just as Alvar opened the car door and handed her a coffee.

"Was my mother going crazy?"

"Would you feel better if you heard that Anita was so screwed up, she wanted to die? Do you think that will take away the pain?" Alvar asked.

"Does it?"

"No."

Taking her chin, Alvar turned Norma's head. He wasn't lying. Norma was sure of that. Her senses had failed her before, but this time she was sure.

"Your mother was not crazy. Your mother was not Helena, and your mother was not going senile like your grandmother. Your mother was mixed up with unpleasant people. That's why she jumped onto the tracks. Of her own free will. I'm sure she thought she was protecting you, even if she ended up leaving the whole mess on your shoulders."

Norma remained standing in the parking lot after Alvar left for another meeting. She took out of her pocket the hairpin she'd found in the car. It too had belonged to a young woman whose hair blossomed with expectation. Maybe a Russian. Her stress level was abnormally high. Something was wrong, but what? Twins? Triplets? Quintuplets? Surely not.

A knock came at her mother's door. Norma froze, her hand fumbling for a can of tuna fish on the top shelf in the kitchen, and the stool under her wobbled. The knocking came again. She set the can on the counter and went to the entryway. She couldn't see anything through the peephole, and the stairwell was dark. When she put her ear to the door and listened to the breathing of the person on the other side, her hair started curling.

Quickly swinging the door open, Norma caught a glimpse of eyes shining in the dark and a flash of a strange woman, before she bounded down the stairs, and succeeded in catching hold of the woman's shirt. The woman grabbed her hair and tumbled them both onto the landing. For a second, pain clouded her vision, but Norma didn't release her grip. Thirty years old, a few children, pasta, rye bread and Edam, healthy living, the smell of a hospital.

"Where is Anita?" the woman panted.

"That depends who's asking."

"None of your business."

"Now it is."

Teeth sank into Norma's arm, and the woman got away, only to trip on Norma's loose ponytail, which wrapped around the woman's ankles and held her in place until Norma could sit on her chest. Upstairs someone opened a door. The woman clearly didn't want to attract attention, so she kept quiet and held her breath.

"I'm handling Anita's business now," Norma whispered.

"So give me more money."

"Why should I help you?"

"Kristian is dead. They're coming for me next. Where is Anita?"

"On her way home. How about we go inside and talk while we wait for her?"

Under different circumstances, the woman sitting on Norma's mother's couch could have been anyone: middle class, normal height, average income. But the blood in her veins seemed to have jelled. She shuddered, and her voice swelled with sorrow and fear. Still, she was a real person, not a phantom channeled by an addled mind like the ones on the videos, and therefore Norma had to find out what she knew. The woman looked at her with suspicion and refused to say anything other than that Norma's mother had promised to help if any problems arose. She was a nurse, and she needed a job. She was just as good as her husband Kristian, if not better, and she was willing to travel anywhere.

"A nurse?"

"Specialized. I've been at Felicitas for more than ten years. Anita should know that."

Norma pretended to know what the woman was talking about, although the name Felicitas meant nothing to her. As she waited for the water to boil for tea, she glanced at the Felicitas website on her phone. It was a fertility clinic.

"Kristian told Anita everything she wanted to know, and now this is the price he paid. When will Anita get back? Don't they know what happened to Kristian? Why are you handling things for Anita now?"

"So you want a job?" Norma asked.

"Felicitas has the best rate of positives, and I've done work for Lambert's clinics before, too. I also have experience with multiples. I'm highly qualified, and I love my work. Anita knows how good I am."

"She may still want something more."

"I have these."

The woman waved a stack of papers in her hand.

"Kristian was always lax with client lists, but I'm not. I already did some weeding. And this. You'll want this."

The woman brought up a picture and showed her phone screen.

"Kristian was supposed to bring Anita video, but we haven't heard from her."

The screen showed a room, a screen, rusty hospital beds, and an IV bottle. Paint peeled from the wall, and a bowl of something red sat on the nightstand, perhaps tomato salad or peppers. Three girls, all of them pregnant. One of the girls wailed and held her belly. The other two stared indifferently at the whimpering girl, spreading butter on white bread and sprinkling some sort of spice on it. In the corner of the picture was a worn plastic bag with Cyrillic lettering. Norma didn't recognize the language. A blond woman dressed in a tight-fitting white suit looked on in boredom and lit a cigarette. A man with dark hair standing next to her ran to the girl who was in pain. Mouths moved, but no words were audible.

"One of the girls went into labor just as I showed up. Without me, she would have lost the babies. Twins. The situation was confused, and they forgot to check me. They're so careful nowadays."

"Anita didn't say what your duties were."

"Didn't she?" the woman said. "I'm the surrogate coordinator for the agency. We were supposed to be there picking two new girls. We never use anyone we haven't examined ourselves. All these hospitals will definitely start working with your boss once you get rid of Lambert. Girls are so cheap in Romania and Bulgaria. The only payment they want is a passport, a set of papers to get out of the country. Lambert's clinics are decent. We take good care of the girls, and they're happy to come to us."

The woman's voice was defensive, as if she were trying to make a case for the respectability of her actions. Because Norma didn't come across as a professional. The woman was reacting instinctively to that, but soon the realization would dawn on her and the ruse would be up. As she set the tea out on the table, Norma looked around trying to provide a distraction. Her mother stocked her house with all kinds of food for her perpetually hungry daughter. The upper shelves in the kitchen were full of seeds and tuna fish, and on the bookshelf was a dusty bowl of nuts. Norma grabbed it, offered it, and took a few walnuts herself.

The woman didn't take the bowl. Casting Norma a stern look, she stopped the video. "Wait, you've never seen something like this before. What line of work are you really in?" She slipped the phone into her pocket. Her movements were slow, and she lifted her teacup with exaggerated calmness. "Do you work for Lambert?" she asked. "Where is Anita?"

Norma barely managed to dodge the hot water. As she ran to the door, the woman overturned a table with a potted fern. Slipping on the broken pieces, Norma shouted after her, "How did it happen? How did Kristian die? Was it a suicide? Did it look like a suicide? Did Anita pay in cash?"

But the woman was gone.

Norma went back inside, pushed the pot shards and clumps of

dirt and fern into a corner, and opened a can of tuna fish. Now she understood. These people owned baby factories, and her mother had wanted to buy a child either for herself or for Norma, maybe using a surrogate. Or maybe she had just wanted an egg. And she really couldn't have found anyone else? Were these the only people who didn't ask any questions? In Finland surrogacy was illegal, and doctors would want to know why a fertile woman wanted to use someone else's eggs. Unless her mother wanted twins, triplets, or God only knows. Norma remembered the hairs she found in Alvar's car. Her mother might have been afraid of all the tests, since her smoking would have shown up in her blood or urine. Or maybe she was thinking of Norma, not herself. Either way, she had hankered so blindly for a child that she was willing to risk getting involved with criminals. In a state of madness, this might have seemed like logical behavior. That was why her mother had told her on the video how Eva got her two healthy children. All it took was money and lies. She had wanted to remind Norma that those were the only options for people like them.

When Norma returned from picking up lunch, a German shepherd sat on the steps of the salon. It caught her scent from a distance, of course, and when her steps slowed, it watched her all the more closely. Alvar came to open the door before she could go around back, and she had to stop to let the dog sniff her ankle thoroughly before she went inside.

She felt the dog's wet nose on her skin, and Alvar's watchful gaze bothered her, even though she didn't realize at first what was wrong. The dizziness grew worse. First she registered her hair. Her hair on a strange woman's head, the woman whose locks Marion was currently blow-drying. Then Norma recognized the woman, and saliva filled her mouth. She dropped the takeout containers. Unable to remain in the salon, she pushed Alvar out of the way, running outside and across the street, ignoring the honking horns and screeching brakes. She stumbled down the stairs into the park and rushed to the trees. The woman was the same one as on Kristian's wife's phone, the same blond in the white suit, and that woman had Norma's hair.

After her retching subsided, Norma sat down in the shade where the grass was still cool. Fumbling for the scopolamine patches in her pocket, she slapped them behind her ears under her turban.

She heard dog paws on the gravel, and soon Alvar shoved a water bottle into her hand.

"Heat doesn't always agree with me," Norma said. "Who is that blonde?"

"Alla. Lambert's wife. What about her?"

Norma's field of vision began to return as the fog faded from the edges. She realized she had spoken too hastily. It was a mistake to ask anything about the woman. She could still smell the scent of her hair mixed with the woman's own, with her scalp oils, last night's champagne, and a low-carb diet. Her hair on the woman's head was dead. It didn't recognize her. It was fused with the woman's life, and despite her higher-than-average stress level, the woman smelled as if she were in love. Lambert and the woman were happy. They walked the world hand in hand spreading joy to some couples and sorrow to others. Storks to the right, scythes to the left. Still, Norma didn't understand what her mother had needed with a video of Alla examining possible surrogates. Why hadn't her mother just bought a child? Why had she been prepared to pay Kristian for that footage?

Alvar snapped his fingers in front of her face. "Should I call for help?"

Norma opened her eyes. "Did she come to demand money?"

"She came to have her hair styled. Are you having problems with the people you're getting the hair from? Did someone show you Alla's picture?"

"No."

"What about mine? Or Marion's? Or Lambert's?"

"Why would someone do that?"

"You recognized Alla, and now you're denying it."

"I must have run into her on the street."

"Do you vomit every time that happens?"

Norma discovered she was scratching the dog, to keep her hands occupied. Though she was always suspicious of animals: they sensed she was different from other people and spent more time sniffing and investigating her.

"Who was Anita working with, and who was her boss?"

"Marion was her only boss."

"I don't know what kind of game you think you're playing, but you're about to run out of time. Right now Alla is calculating your value just as Anita's boss is, and if you think you should be more afraid of whoever that is than the blonde sitting in that salon, you're wrong."

Alvar stood up to leave and ordered the dog to follow. "Call me."

Norma couldn't return to Shear Magic, not now. She would go home and continue with the videos. There must be some logic to them. She had wanted to reconstruct her mother's final moments in order to understand what happened to her, and now that also meant finding the common thread through her mother's incoherence.

The meeting invitation came as a complete surprise. The message was terse, just the sort that might indicate a desire to make a deal: the girl wanted to talk, preferably immediately. When Marion arrived at the Playful Pike, Norma was already sitting and waiting. The envelope resting on the table increased Marion's optimism.

"What did my mother talk about during her last few days?" Norma asked.

"About our future business. She was excited," Marion replied. "It was our dream."

"So why did she jump in front of a metro train?"

Marion couldn't catch Norma's eye, but still she was sure this would be the moment. To cover the sound of the tree frogs, she jingled the ice cubes in her glass of water, lifted one out, and squeezing it in her hand, decided to forge ahead.

"Lambert learned about our plan and wanted to get rid of Anita. He wouldn't have approved of us leaving, let alone that our new salon would have exclusive rights to the Ukrainian hair, as Anita was planning."

"But my mother jumped onto the tracks herself."

"Lambert is a master of these things."

Norma frowned and rubbed her eyes, her nose moving.

Marion had just revealed a significant fact and was expecting questions. None came. The sound of the tree frogs intensified, and the ice in her hand melted into a puddle on the table. Maybe Norma would understand the situation if Marion gave more detail, but she couldn't. She hadn't told Anita either. Even if Marion had left out the one part of the story that proved her complicity, Anita would have seen through her: Marion had lied to Albino in Cartagena. After the drug wars, Colombia wanted to be like Venezuela, a factory that endlessly pumped out international beauty queens; Marion pretended they were traveling to a business meeting so Albino could get acquainted with the growing hair business in Colombia, a step up for her. Marion had been convincing and Albino's eyes trusting. But Marion wouldn't have been able to look Anita in the eye. Instead she told her that Albino had run off with a new lover and broken Alvar's heart.

"Lambert murdered Anita," Marion said emphatically. "I'm sure of it. And that's also Lambert's way of dealing with people who don't pay their debts."

Marion repeated herself to make sure the girl understood what she said. No one would pass up an opportunity to take revenge on her own mother's murderer, and Norma could get retribution most easily by giving Marion the Ukrainian connection. But Norma remained mute.

"We can go anytime and leave all this behind," Marion continued.

"And Lambert wouldn't follow? What about the loan?"

The girl had opened her mouth. That was a start.

"That's a question of planning. I have ways to keep Lambert in check."

"You should have used them when my mother was alive."

"We didn't have time," Marion said. "The money is waiting in London. After we open the salon, we can take care of the rest of the payments. All we need for success is the Ukrainian hair. If you don't believe me, I'll get you an account statement and all the papers. We both want a new life. Let's create it together. You just have to trust me."

Norma pursed her lips and pushed the envelope to Marion between the drinking glasses. Now Marion was sure of success. "I started to pack my mother's things and found these. I thought they would go well on the walls of the salon."

Marion opened the envelope, then immediately dropped it on the table. Disappointment flashed across her face, and she rubbed her arms as if warding off a chill. Norma shook the pictures out of the envelope. She had chosen a random selection of blond women from her mother's collection, leaving out Eva.

"My mother's calendar had an entry about taking old photos to Johannes," Norma said. "Does that name mean anything to you? Maybe he's a photographer. I don't know anyone named Johannes."

Marion grabbed her bag and stood but then sat back down just as suddenly, managing to knock over her glass. Her handbag thudded to the floor, and she began to dry the table without saying a word, fetching more napkins from the counter and prodding the ice cubes back into the glass. Her reaction surprised Norma. When she accused Lambert of murder, Marion's voice had been steady and self-assured, but now she was acting erratically. Had Marion really thought Norma would believe her story that easily?

"Maybe Anita was taking them to Helena in the hospital," said Marion. "Johannes was one of Helena's voices." She didn't look at Norma, instead waving to the waitress to bring more napkins.

"Tell me."

"There isn't anything to tell," said Marion. "Lambert is not a good man, and Helena had to invent something to help her bear it all. When he suggested divorce, she fell apart completely. She was pregnant at the time, and miscarried. She never recovered. You should leave that in the past, though. None of it matters anymore. What we should talk about is how to escape Lambert to get out of the mess we're in now."

"I'd rather hear about Johannes first."

Marion grabbed a napkin and started picking at it.

"Why would my mother have taken pictures like this to Helena? I just want to understand."

"Maybe Anita wanted to keep Helena in a good mood," Marion said. "Helena had an obsession with old photos and a fantasy about a traveling photographer. Supposedly he was her lover who was going to take her to America." She picked up another napkin after shredding the previous one. "Whenever Helena saw old pictures in the newspaper, she would cut them out and save them because she believed Johannes took them. They were everywhere. Sometimes she cut out the faces. We couldn't bring visitors to the apartment because Helena would want to tell them how Johannes was saving money for their journey. He took pictures of hookers to satisfy the tastes of his customers, some of whom were important officials who could arrange travel papers: passports, certificates of nonimpediment for marriage, birth certificates. Helena was always going on about that. Johannes was arranging the documents she'd need to run away with him. She just had to be careful their romance wasn't exposed."

Marion's explanation was identical to the story her mother had told on the videos. The fantasy about Johannes was Helena's way of defending herself. Helena's move from Sweden back to Finland had also played a part in her deteriorating condition and further fueled these delusions about emigrating. Marion thought it might have had something to do with the bad reputation of Finns in Sweden, although Helena was always talking about America, not Sweden. She was especially concerned about the Italian Hall Disaster, a tragedy that occurred in Michigan. It was real—Alvar checked. Finnish immigrants had been involved in organizing mining strikes, which turned bloody, and in 1913 American officials began deporting them. Then at a Christmas party at a union hall in Calumet, someone yelled "fire," and dozens of people were crushed to death. Alvar tried to find some sense in their mother's interest in the event. Maybe she had read about it and identified with the Finns in America. In the legal proceedings after the disaster, the prosecutor demanded answers from all witnesses in English, even though none of them knew the language. The witnesses who eventually appeared before the court gave testimony in English—but they hadn't seen a thing.

Once she'd worked through the entire packet of tissues, Marion said she was finished and left. On the table were a puddle of melted ice cubes and a pile of shredded paper, heaped up like snow. Norma put the photos back in her bag. Marion hadn't wanted them.

April 2, 2013

At the market when Eva walked past the photographer's stand and swung her braid, the photographer jumped as if from the crack of a whip. The next morning he appeared with his camera at the Naakka property and said he wanted to photograph the farm's prize cows. Eva was sent to show him the way, and Johannes's camera fell in love with her, not the cows. He was leaving for America, the land of opportunity, and he began seducing Eva, trying to persuade her to come with him. At first Eva wasn't interested. Then she noticed the purr of her hair and the new sweetness of its scent. It rippled as if ready for an ocean voyage and gravitated toward Johannes as if he were made of barley sugar.

Eva's situation in the Naakka home was not easy. The heirs romping around the yard had not eased her mother-in-law's suspicion of her, and good living had made her overly fertile. Despite constant drinking of nettle and juniper tea, she had already missed her cycle twice and she knew a day would come when neither wild rosemary nor angelica root would help.

Before long she would be caught, either because of her nightly haircutting or by having the wrong kind of children. Better to leave before then.

The reality in America turned out to be different from what Eva had imagined. Her compass broke immediately after they arrived in the New World. It didn't help that Johannes had arranged for living quarters in a Finnish boardinghouse in Harlem. There were no other white people living there, and her blond hair stood out. Some openly stared. The children would try to touch her hair without being seen, and Eva was constantly afraid that she'd hear the sound of scissors at the base of her ear and be sheared like a sheep. Straightening irons heated in the ovens of the salons day and night, and the stench of singed hair hung in the air. Black women wore wigs made of white women's hair. Within a week Eva saw her first wig theft in the middle of the street. A legal case ensued, which was solved when the police found the stolen hair concealed in the robber's mattress.

The Finns' poor reputation in America also provided good reason to fear the immigration officials. Some believed that Finnish independence would improve the situation, and they rejoiced that Finns were no longer marked as Russians on their papers. For Eva, this progress was still too slow. Suspicion of Communists was rampant, and there were plenty of them among the Finns. The bloodbath at Calumet cast a long shadow. Eva feared the boardinghouse would be the target of a raid sooner or later. She had to get to a better area, somewhere where she would be less conspicuous. But all their savings had gone to travel expenses.

The hair business was experiencing a revolution: short hair for women was all the rage, but exposed necks were blamed for the economic downturn in the industry, and curlers arranged demonstrations against bob cuts. A French innovation, a lightweight wig cap, brought a glimmer of light to the predicament. It allowed a woman to have short hair during the day and then at night a long mass of curls appropriate for evening dress. Eva could have solved her money problems by selling her hair. She didn't do that, though.

Later Eva met numerous hair salon matrons, hair culturalists as they were called, and businesswomen who built fortunes with hair products regardless of their skin color. She read about the Harperists who set up salons under a franchising agreement with Martha Matilda Harper, and the opportunities Harper offered poor women by giving them jobs and training. The Harperists' clientele came to include such legendary women as Jacqueline Kennedy. Success would have been guaranteed for Eva if only she'd known how to take advantage of her uniqueness.

So when Eva presented her plan to me, she knew what she was talking about. We guessed you would object to selling your hair, which was why we thought it best not to tell you. Plus, the more I familiarized myself with the industry, the more I doubted your hair would have an overwhelming competitive advantage. Chinese factories put out twenty thousand kilos of bulk Remy quality hair every week; from Russia there were thirty thousand kilos every month. I didn't understand why Lambert's clan would go crazy for your hair if the supplies were already at that level. But Eva laughed at my concerns. I just needed to trust it, and your hair would be unstoppable.

Some of Norma's mother's videos showed just grass or flower beds, with talking in the background. Sometimes her mother and Helena sat in the apple orchard at the mental hospital or walked in the park, passing piles of thinned wood on paths lined by pine trees. The administration building flashed in the background, its classical symmetry strange in contrast to the otherwise unbalanced content. When a shirtless man looking haggard from too much medication appeared on the screen, Norma realized her mother must have been doing something unauthorized. That explained the strange angles and the recording stopping in midsentence so often. Sometimes Helena and Norma's mother sat in a garden swing, and the creaking of the swing mingled with the voices of the healthcare staff. A chain-link fence that curved in at the top surrounded the buildings visible in the background. It was a reminder that despite the surroundings, the area was not a museum or a beautifully restored mansion with a garden shop for tourists and well-kept canna lilies in the flower beds.

During the first videos, the apples were green. In the autumn recordings, her mother walked past the same trees and plucked a ripe piece of fruit. Sounds of chewing mixed with her words. In the winter, snow covered the grass of the park. Her mother turned up the collar of her recently purchased winter coat and stroked it like a new cat. Surrounded by an idyllic eastern Finnish winter landscape, she once again extolled the effects on Helena of smoking Norma's hair.

A line of fir trees stood in the background like a mocking, toothy grin, and her breath condensed like speech bubbles. This was around the time she had announced to Norma the good news about her new job.

In some frames, Norma saw the Kuopio market square in the background. On Helena's days outside the hospital, she dressed normally, and no one would have guessed she was an inmate at an asylum for the criminally insane. Her conversation focused on her departure for America and how Johannes, whom she had in her snare, had agreed to a first-class cabin and a private room at the port in Hanko. The dorm room at the emigrant hostel would have been impossible, Helena said, smoothing her hair, inspecting it for split ends, and lighting her pipe. The doctor's physical required before the journey had made her nervous, but she sailed through it.

When Helena spoke as Eva, the effect of the medications disappeared from her eyes—her gaze was like that of a mouse, focused and keen. Sometimes Finnglish crept into her speech, and her accent was strong. Norma's mother called her Eva. Maybe the purpose of the recordings was to convince Norma that Helena really was channeling Eva. Some of Eva's story might be true, such as being born in Tampere and abandoned to Kaisu the cupper. Eva's ability to read hair would have burnished Kaisu's reputation. But Norma's mother and Helena also might have made it all up. Her mother knew how Norma's hair worked, so she and Helena could have crafted stories that Norma would find credible. Her mother could whisper Norma's secret into Helena's ear without concern: if she let something slip, no one would believe her anyway. At most, they would increase her medication.

But Norma hadn't told her mother everything. She hadn't revealed that she could read death, cancer, and disease from people's hair. She recognized the darkness the first time as a child—the cashier at the store was terminally ill—and even then had known that the ability to predict death would have been too much for her mother. Her mother wouldn't have been able to walk past these people without caring, without trying to take them to the doctor. So how was it possible that her mother and Helena were talking about that on the video?

Marion put the phone back in Norma's bag. She stood behind women playing with their screens all day every day and had never seen such an underused phone, not from someone that age. She'd expected to find communication about her murder accusations, but Norma hadn't tried to contact anyone since their conversation at the Playful Pike. Maybe she should see that as good luck. If the girl had rushed to Lambert to accuse him of murder and told him who put that idea in her head, Marion wouldn't be sitting here. She wouldn't have spent the morning waiting for a moment when Norma left her phone on the counter before it locked, and she wouldn't be searching her handbag now, the contents of which seemed just as trivial as the phone's: a couple of bags of walnuts and seeds, a pair of scissors, a stack of crisis line business cards.

This wasn't Marion's first time searching here. When she'd been looking for clues about the Ukrainian hair, she had set her hopes on the girl's phone, but in vain. All she'd come up with were Anita's funeral arrangements and a few updates from the women at Norma's former job. The only spice came in the form of a few suggestive texts from men who were clearly short-term interests. Anita's old messages were about everyday things, and the more recent ones were neutral vacation updates. Norma didn't use social media apps either. The camera had only a handful of pictures: except for one of Anita, they were all from parties at her old office. Everyone had at least a few pictures of themselves on their phone, but not Norma. This was the phone of a person with something to hide. It was the phone of a criminal. Only the model was wrong.

Marion heard the girl get back to removing extensions out in the salon. Marion's hand instinctively went to her pants pocket again, the one where she had kept her project phone, as if she wished she could call Anita to ask why Norma hadn't reacted to Marion handing her a murder suspect on a silver platter. The morning after their conversation, Norma had arrived at the normal time and immediately started arranging the hair for their first client. She seemed the same as always, down to her evasive gaze. Maybe she was still out of sorts after losing her mother. That would explain the strange questions about Helena's voices. She clearly didn't understand the stakes.

Only one interesting thing had turned up on the phone, though it wasn't what Marion had expected: the day before she'd seen Marion at the Playful Pike, the girl had texted Alvar an invitation to meet. Could it be that Alvar had reached her first? Did Alvar promise her evidence that Anita's death wasn't a suicide? Did Alvar realize he could get the Ukrainian connection that way, and probably all the other information the girl had? He hadn't mentioned anything about it.

Nine

The Lamberts are megalomaniacs. They want the whole world, and they chose the right professions for their crusade. He who controls dreams, controls the world. He who controls hair, controls women. He who controls women's reproduction, controls men. He who keeps women satisfied, also satisfies men, and he who seduces people with fever dreams of hair and babies is their king.

This wasn't the first time Marion waited for Alvar outside the fence of Villa Helena. Even though she hated it, she always did it when her calls went unanswered, when she realized she hadn't been told everything: she came here, sat on the lid of the same closed well, and waited. She'd come because of Albino, she'd come because of the ones she already wanted to forget, and on the day Lambert removed Anita, she'd come for Anita, praying she would find her here. This time she came for herself and hoped that once again her doubts would turn out to be groundless worrying. But as Alvar approached the gate, his steps slowed, and Marion guessed that she had reason for concern.

"Is there anything new?" Marion asked.

Alvar didn't respond. He stopped to light a cigarette.

"Norma's going on vacation either way, is that it?"

Marion couldn't make out Alvar's expression in the summer evening light under the rowan trees. But she still recognized his old tells, such as how he concentrated on the dog to avoid answering. He wouldn't tell her what had happened at his meeting with the girl.

"Even if she gives up the Ukrainians and even if she makes a deal," Marion said. "Even if she finds the money Anita borrowed."

Marion fell silent. After Norma's attack of nausea, Alla had asked Marion about Norma's private life, about whether she had any old boyfriends, whether there might have been an accident, and quipped that fertility was a good sign. The clan was just waiting to get what they needed first. Then she would go on her vacation. It was an unusually simple case. No friends, no family. No one would miss her, and no one would look for her. Revenge on the daughter for the mother's betrayal—it was a simple settling of accounts. Norma was stupid if she had arranged something with Alvar. It wouldn't change anything. Suddenly Marion felt a chill—if the girl had in fact made a deal with Alvar, it was doubtful he would have accused his father of complicity in Anita's death. The blame would have fallen on Marion.

"Why don't you go and get some rest," Alvar said.

"I'm not tired."

"Lambert has a new client. She wants an egg from a woman like Angelina Jolie. That's your job for the night."

"Is Norma on Lambert's list? Who else?"

"Lasse isn't on the list, if that's what you're asking," Alvar said. "You can tell him we have a good surrogate for Pekka and Aaron in Thailand, two actually. One of the women needs money for college and the other one for nail technician training. Both are Vietnamese. They can choose whichever one they want. They are a registered couple, right?"

"Of course. Is the woman enrolled in a university? In case Aaron goes and checks."

"Yes."

Alvar didn't expect the sudden hug. It made them both feel awkward, and the awkwardness brought melancholy. Marion let her arms fall. They didn't suspect Lasse, that was the most important thing. As he punched in the gate code, Alvar said, "No one doubts Lasse's loyalty. Not even Lambert. Believe me."

"What about mine?"

The question slipped out and hung spinning in the wind like dry grass. The gate slammed shut.

Alvar seemed to be telling the truth. Marion would still retrieve the metal box from Lasse, though, just in case. She'd used her last weapon, her murder accusations against Lambert, and now she had to move on to the next stage. She would follow through with the plan.

Everything had started when she and Anita opened a bottle of white wine after a long day and started flipping through hair magazines and imagining their dream salon. They would call it a "hair studio," and the customers who came would understand their own worth and never ask the price. Modern fonts on the window, an espresso machine, an assistant who would walk clients' dogs while Anita wound the hot rollers. It would be in Brooklyn, on Lafayette Avenue. Or in London, on Bond Street or in Covent Garden.

When Anita brought her the first batch of Ukrainian hair, she took it to Folake, and it started to seem like their fantasy might become a reality. Folake and the other Nigerian braiders discovered how much better the Ukrainian mixed with kinky hair than the Russian they had been using. After the blond craze set off by Nicki Minaj settled down a bit, the braiders came back to the Ukrainian stock and found that it fit perfectly on any head. White-girl flow was never going out of style; black women would always want what you couldn't do with Afro locks. Folake had sent some of it to her relatives in Nigeria, and new requests began flooding in. Alla got excited, and then Marion. And then Lambert.

In Nigeria, the hair market had exploded along with the growth in the middle class. Four out of five women had extensions. A mother and daughter might drop fourteen thousand dollars on them. However, kinky hair created strict quality requirements: the hair used in extensions had to be springy. Peruvian and Chinese were too heavy, even Indian lacked the desired flexibility, but the Ukrainian flowed and also conformed naturally to curls from the roots. When Folake told a story of a woman caught out in the rain whose hairdo stayed presentable, Marion knew there was magic in this hair. When wet, the Ukrainian fluffed just enough to be natural, and the ends stayed silky and wavy.

Lambert couldn't resist a combination like that. Girls and children were so cheap in Nigeria, and the hair business created a perfect front, a credible reason to travel around the country, to meet women and enter their homes, to investigate clients' finances. Wherever Boko Haram was a threat, more and more women wanted house calls from their hairdressers.

Lambert wanted a stylist's eye on the ground, and Marion was given an opportunity to demonstrate her abilities. The Ukrainian hair had come through her, and everyone else was busy, so she received permission to go alone. Marion immediately called Anita. This would be their chance. This would be the beginning of the end for Lambert.

They took different flights, stayed in different hotels, and met up only to take a car to Lambert's water bottle factory. No one in the clan had ever visited before—everything was handled through local agents and straw men—so Anita had no trouble posing as the agency's new coordinator. Really Lambert owned the factory by accident: a doctor he knew had fled to Nigeria after being caught, and contacted Lambert with a new client requesting an egg from Scandinavia. Lambert approached Nigeria with suspicion, but because he needed to decentralize the agency's activities anyway, he decided to take a risk. The doctor would run the operation, and on paper it would look like a water bottle factory.

The place had been burned in a police raid three weeks earlier. There was no sign of cameras, only guards, old junk cars, and ashes. Marion's back hurt from the bumpy journey, and her gums were bleeding where a water bottle had jammed into them at one particularly deep pothole. Another raid shouldn't have come, at least not immediately. Yet come it did, just as they were talking to the head of the facility, a woman everyone called Mama. Chaos ensued—screaming women, wailing infants, overturned cribs—but amid it all Mama maintained her stoic calm, certain that money could quell any raid.

As soon as the hullabaloo started, Marion and Anita slipped over to the women's area and followed one girl in the final weeks of her pregnancy as she ran into the backyard. There was a gate and a rusty lock, which Marion kicked open. A police officer stood by their car. Anita pulled out a wad of dollars, and they sped off.

Anita kept her new camera running and did her best to interview the girl as they drove to a regular hospital. On the recording, the girl said she had originally gone to the hospital for an abortion, but they wouldn't let her leave, and the abortion never happened. When the baby was born, they took it away and brought some young men to her. She became pregnant again and was moved to the water bottle factory, where she'd been a prisoner ever since. She didn't even know how many babies some of the girls at the factory had borne. Some of them were surrogates, and some had ended up at the farm after getting pregnant by accident, like her. As she told of the tiny bones the dogs unearthed in the backyard, the girl wept.

That night they ate roasted plantains and *jollof* rice with Folake's family and heard about the growing popularity of salons that specialized in unstraightened natural hair. Marion wrote down everything for Lambert and Alla but also studied the market with an eye toward her new business. The beauty industry had an innocent reputation, unlike the baby trade. No one would pay any more attention to Lambert's hair trading network after her takeover than they had before. Then the Lagos elite would be hers, and she could move in on all the clan's other hair areas.

As the evening passed, Anita's gaze grew empty. They didn't have any airtight evidence against Lambert, only a baby farm that had been raided repeatedly, which would simply change location if it were exposed to the public. The pregnant girl hadn't known anything about the Source Agency, neither where the customers came from nor where the children were taken. She could say only that some of the girls were rewarded with a new phone.

As Marion toured the salons and met the hair agents, Anita pretended to be a Swedish woman hoping for a baby and tried to find any incriminating traces of Lambert. He owned the water bottle factory through a front, so acquiring evidence of ownership would be difficult, but Anita wouldn't give up. She began visiting every country where the Source Agency operated. Marion tried to hold her back. They needed only to point the police in the right direction. Anita didn't listen. She wanted to visit each clinic herself, in every country and every location.

The clan was satisfied with Marion's report about Nigeria. She was assigned more responsibility and sent on more trips alone. No one guessed that Anita was traveling with her. Anita became increasingly brazen, and it wasn't until she was preparing for that last trip to Thailand that she began to feel she had seen enough.

May 4, 2013

Lambert delayed his decision about the loan for more than a month. When I finally received the order to go speak to him, he savored the moment. He enjoyed the humiliation. At first he pretended not to notice me and made me stand in the middle of the room while he read his papers and let the torturous minutes tick by. Then he feigned surprise at finding me there and began chatting about the weather. I was sure he wasn't going to give me the money. Just then he slapped his hand on the table and said that of course he would give a loan to a friend in her time of need and ordered Alvar to bring the bag. It was full of small bills as I had requested.

After that there was no turning back. I owe Lambert, and now even the friendliest-seeming gesture is a reminder of that fact. Alla keeps suggesting we take a trip to Ukraine together. She says she wants to meet my friends and help with the problems an innocent person can so easily run into with the tax authorities there. Alla's local resources would be at my fingertips. I can't refuse directly, so I've been saying we should go in the fall.

Claiming that your hair was from Ukraine was a thoughtless move, and making up distant relatives there was even worse. I had just started at Shear Magic and thought my choice of country was a plausible basis for the high price. At the time I didn't know that Lambert had significant business interests there. I'm sure Alla is already making inquiries about the hair and probably cooing in Lambert's ear right now that this miracle will soon be in their grasp. They didn't even suggest the Ukrainians' contact information as payment for the loan, which I'd been afraid of since it would have been difficult to turn down if I'd really had relatives in dire financial straits. But no, Lambert wanted to make me dependent on him. He wanted a way to blackmail me. He understood I wouldn't have any other way to pay him back, and it won't be long before he moves beyond soft tactics.

May 10, 2013

At first, Marion thought it was an impossible dream. Then she understood it would be within reach if the clan weren't in the way. I had only to feed her bitterness and remind her how the Lamberts treated her as if she were beneath them. I just had to encourage her. So I used the clan's own playbook and plied her with visions of supplying hair for Ursula Stephen, Rihanna walking around wearing her products. Then she would land Paris Hilton's wig master, and every door would swing wide open. *Vogue, Harper's Bazaar, Elle, Cosmopolitan*—her clients would grace every cover. Not Alla's, not Lambert's—hers.

First we just had to get rid of Lambert.

Marion had the means: *Thelma and Louise* style, send the whole clan to jail. The Big Bang.

May 11, 2013

Every day for twenty years I've regretted sending Helena that batch of your hair. Maybe for the next twenty years I'll regret destroying Marion's dreams. I was the one who did it, not Lambert. I led Marion on with the intention of betraying her. I took greater advantage of her than Lambert ever did.

But it was unavoidable. I needed money and connections to people in the industry. Without Marion, I couldn't have collected evidence for the Big Bang, and without that, I couldn't get rid of my creditor—to carry out my plan, I needed money I wouldn't have to pay back. I needed to win her over, and that meant supporting her goals.

She doesn't suspect anything. She just keeps planning our wonderful future. It's hard to watch. There won't be any money left, and Marion won't get her fancy salon. I won't be selling her any more of your hair. That will end when you and I reach Bangkok and begin our new life.

Norma browsed the flights departing Helsinki-Vantaa International Airport and tried to digest what her mother had said. She still didn't know where the money was, but her mother mentioned a loan she wouldn't have to pay back. The only way to accomplish that was through blackmail, and Kristian's videos and information were the perfect bait. If her mother had already taken action, the clan would have had ample reason to get rid of her, which lined up with Marion's murder accusations. But one fact didn't fit. At the Playful Pike, as soon as Marion started talking about Lambert, the temperature of her scalp rose. She had been lying when she accused Lambert of murder. Maybe there was a reason for the lie. If Marion had discovered Norma's mother's betrayal, she must have been furious. She herself would have had a motive for murder. Maybe she was trying to shift the blame to someone else. Lambert was a credible alternative, but he was hardly the only one with the means to make a murder look like suicide.

Norma let the recordings continue to play and scrolled to Alvar's number in her phone. But she didn't call. The due date of the loan was approaching, nurses mixed up in baby trafficking were running around in her stairwell, people were dying under strange circumstances, and her mother had betrayed numerous people, including Norma. Despair surged like milk boiling over.

She should leave now. She should flee like Eva to America. This would be her last chance.

Ten

Do you remember the nightmares that would wake you when you were small? The situations changed, but one element was always the same: your secret was exposed. When you were older, you dreamed about being in an accident that left you in a monthlong coma, returning to consciousness only to find that you were a prisoner in a research institute. You had dreams about getting trapped in the middle of a desert because of a car breakdown and having to gnaw your hair off. In your dreams, you always left your scissors at home.

April 19, 2013

The traditional postcard industry landed in trouble after the war. Postage rates went up, and no one sent cards to the front anymore, so the little money Johannes could make came from landscape shots of the homeland that he sold to Finnish immigrants. That was why Johannes decided to return to his old ways after being introduced to the art bootleggers on Fourth Avenue. Because of the indecency laws, they were low on pin-up cards—finding anything up to French standards was impossible. Johannes knew he could do better, especially with an exotic model waiting at home. Counterfeiting the famous studios' marks on his cards would be easy. He had photographed Eva before, just never for public consumption. When Johannes promised to remove her face before the emulsion dried, Eva agreed to even more risqué poses.

Johannes's cards became popular, as men found the mysteriousness of the model stimulating. Sometimes Johannes sent his customers locks of Eva's hair to prove its authenticity and stir them up even more. The success Johannes enjoyed made life good: they moved into better quarters in a better area, ate lamb chops and stuffed chicken prepared by a cook for dinner, and traded bathtub gin for higher-quality bootleg whiskey.

When Eva's morning sickness began and not even jimsonweed helped, she had to admit to herself that she was in trouble. She was out of the tinctures of angelica root and wild rosemary she had brought from Finland, so she had to go to a pharmacy. She chose one from a business card that had been shoved at her by a kid working the crowd. The card's claims that the pharmacy's "French pills" were sure to restore any woman's cycle turned out to be wrong. They made Eva feel twice as bad. When Johannes grew concerned, she claimed her condition was just a case of food poisoning and forbade him from calling a doctor. In the morning, she sent the parlor maid to fetch another batch of pills and tansy oil. Betty brought the requested supplies, but in order to ensure that Eva understood the dangers of what she was attempting, she told her a story about a friend who miscalculated a dose of pennyroyal and ended up lying unconscious in her own vomit, bleeding from between her legs and from her eyes. Betty didn't want to see such a sight. She had a better suggestion.

April 20, 2013

The effects of the ether wore off, and Eva regained consciousness. She couldn't move, and she didn't understand what had happened. Betty's reassuring hand squeeze was the last thing she remembered. Now Betty was nowhere to be seen, and no one was in the room. Eva's hair was everywhere. Then she saw the doctor and the nurse. They lay on the floor, eyes staring lifelessly at the ceiling, hair wrapped around their necks. The doctor still had a curette in his hand. Eva hadn't just been exposed—she was on her way to the electric chair.

The receptionist came knocking at the door, waited, knocked again, and called for the doctor, then the nurse. Eva held her breath and tried to keep calm. Straining to reach the scissors on a nearby instrument table, she succeeded in cutting herself free and rushed to shove a chair under the door handle. Then she looked for her clothes. Her handbag was under a toppled screen, as were her shoes, jacket, and dress. Her hat was crushed under a confusion of rubber tubes and bandages. She could find only one of her lace gloves, and her choker was missing. Eva grabbed the doctor's bag and, after emptying it, began collecting her hair from around the chairs, screen, instruments, towels, and enamel basins, cursing herself for trusting an abortionist over her own abilities, for imagining she could get something for three hundred dollars that she didn't know how to do herself, for daring to hope that it would be easier, more certain, and that no accidents would happen. That choice could lead to death row now. She cursed Betty, who was the reason she had told the receptionist her real phone number. She had started with a false name, but Betty tugged her sleeve when the receptionist asked her number and looked at her so intently that Eva didn't dare lie anymore. They'd come to the clinic precisely because of its quality, and that included the doctor calling later to check on the state of the patient. That had been a mistake. She would have to get home before the police and destroy any pictures and negatives there that showed her face.

The receptionist knocked again and tried the door handle. The clock ticked. The window—this was New York—should have a fire escape. Had Betty gone that way? Or through the door? The fire escape. Betty was a black woman and would know to keep her mouth shut because no one would listen to her. Could Eva accuse Betty of the murders? Whose story would the public believe: a colored woman's or a Communist Finn's? No, it wouldn't work. Eva's position was no stronger than that of a black parlor maid.

The receptionist had come to the door again and began shoving the knob violently.

231

By that point, Eva was already at the window. On the fire escape. Outside.

~

Norma twirled her hair. Her mother claimed it was capable of murder. Maybe her mother wanted to scare her. She had always done that. While other mothers were warning their daughters about skirts that were too short and dark alleys, Norma's mother offered up horror stories about the unhappy fates of people who were different.

If she forgot cutting time, her mother lectured her about freaks forced to display themselves for money, Mengele's human experiments, or some collector's circus of curiosities, and asked whether Norma wanted a future like that.

Norma did a quick Internet search for the term *hair murders.* The results were mostly about failed dye jobs. She knew her mother was telling Norma her own kind of bogeyman story. Even so. Could her hair really do what Eva's had? Without her being able to control it?

April 21, 2013

In Harlem, Eva had walked by the place many times. In the front room was a permanent machine that looked like a milking contraption, and in the back room you could find a poker table, bookmaker, whiskey bottles, and gangsters' girlfriends selling undergarments that still had ten-dollar tags but were being sold for three. Heroin passed from hand to hand in brown paper rolls.

Eva went to the back door and flashed her basket. Once she had the money, she fled. She had just sold her hair for the first time.

The police found Eva's home and a stash of indecent cards and books, including, under the rug, one without a face. The receptionist, who was in custody, remembered the doctor's last patient and recognized her unusually heavy hair in the picture. The papers started calling Eva the Woman Without a Face. But her hair wasn't front-page news—only bob cuts made for scandal in those days, because they were considered a sign of a dangerous life. So the headlines focused instead on the mystery of the faceless woman and the cold-blooded murder of an abortionist. The police's theory about the hair left in the procedure room was that the murderer had used voodoo to try to exorcise the evil spirits from the place.

Johannes disappeared, and the police never caught up with him. Eva guessed he had gone to work for the mafia bootlegging pornography. Because Eva had presented herself as Johannes's wife in the neighborhood for the sake of propriety, only Johannes knew her real name. That was why the newspapers called her Mrs. Johannes Nieminen. That gave Eva time to get new papers.

May 7, 2013

Eva ended up in Chicago by chance. She needed a doctor who didn't mind dark alleys and wouldn't ask too many questions, and Dr. Jackson was just such a man. A few furtive inquiries in a café frequented by streetwalkers led her to him without much trouble.

———

Eva knew her hair would resist if she tried again to get rid of the fetus. In order to ensure that the episode at the abortionist's clinic wouldn't repeat, she planned to weaken herself by fasting and then shaving her head when her water broke. She had arranged with the doctor that an accident would happen to the child immediately after it was born. She could feel the hair that was growing in her womb, how it behaved the same way her own did. It reacted to people and sensed evil intentions, but still so faintly that Eva didn't believe it would be any danger to Dr. Jackson.

Eva stepped out of the doctor's office relieved. The police were still searching for the Woman Without a Face, and it was possible that one of Johannes's old photographs would pop up—a version with her face visible—and a Finnish immigrant would connect her to the mystery. There wasn't room in her life for another freak of nature.

She didn't read about the scope of Dr. Jackson's activities—the children buried in his backyard—until later. She hoped her child had ended up in Jackson's oven or in the mass graves arranged by the undertaker. Even so, she carefully studied every circus advertisement she saw, and listened to what people said about the shows and the freaks on display. She didn't hear anything indicating Jackson hadn't kept his promise, yet still she doubted and was haunted by dreams of her child calling to her, waiting and calling.

Norma shouldn't have been surprised, and yet she was. Somewhere in the world someone else like her might still exist. Someone who succeeded in concealing her strange attribute as Norma did. Someone who considered living underground as important as Norma's mother had. Although some of her mother's story must have been invented to prove a point, there was nothing impossible about the idea that Eva might have descendants.

She could find her distant relative easily if she wanted to. If she did exactly the opposite of what her mother had taught her. All it would take was putting a video of herself online. When she was younger, she could have done it. Back then she had sometimes mocked her mother's caution just as a matter of principle, claiming that the world had never been so ready to accept a new minority. Her mother thought she was childish and naïve, and observed with concern the way reality television swept the world and gave new life to the traditional freak show. Her mother watched them all: *Body Shock*, *My Shocking Body*, and any other program that masqueraded as documentary. Her mother was horrified. In the old days, the circus took the freak away and left the family alone, but not anymore. Now the media wanted all the relations, too. Norma had laughed and said her mother should relax. The TV pushed human rights for even the smallest marginal groups, and popular shows dealt with sexual minorities, vampires, and supernatural phenomena. Clairvoyants and angel whisperers posed on the covers of glossy women's magazines. All the other freaks had already come out of the closet now, so Norma could, too. She could live like everyone else. Maybe there weren't any others like her, but what did that matter?

If she exposed herself, she might hear from someone as soon as tomorrow. In a few hours, someone like her somewhere in the world could be reading an article about a strange woman and wouldn't be able to resist the temptation to get in touch. She wouldn't be alone anymore. Neither of them would be. Together they could prove all her mother's suspicions wrong, and Norma's secret dream could come true: she had always wanted to meet someone who shared her problems. Norma turned the fan toward her face. Her neck and temples were wet as if her hair were crying.

May 18, 2013

We spent your whole childhood visiting all sorts of doctors, scientists, charlatans, and snake oil salesmen. I reported vague symptoms and hinted at your abnormal hair growth, making sure that none of them saw it themselves, and hoped that along the way something in the blessings, curses, exorcisms, homeopathy, or whatever would help. I wanted to find someone who might give me the sense that there were other people like you. I hoped that someday in some office we'd run into another pair like us—a mother and daughter—and that you would recognize them even if I didn't.

I was looking for help in the wrong place. It's men like Lambert who know doctors like Jackson, and doctors like Jackson never talk. No patient records, no leaks. No real name. It isn't cheap, but it's possible, and once you're normal, you can have a family and a regular life, everything I've always wanted for you.

Finding the right man took time. I didn't arrange the date for the Big Bang with Marion until I was sure Grigori was the one. I met him on a business trip to Stockholm. Our conversation moved to hereditary hypertrichosis, its treatment with laser epilation and pulse light therapy, and he told me about his friend who specializes in excessive hair growth treatment and researches the genetic mutations that cause hypertrichosis. There were only fifty known cases, and he found the rarity of the disease fascinating. In the past, sufferers were believed to possess supernatural power and would be abducted for it.

Grigori had succeeded in curing a woman who suffered from hypertrichosis. I've seen her myself, with my own eyes. She was a client at one of Lambert's clinics. Her hair is normal now, and her children were born healthy.

Norma, dear, there are so many things I wish we'd talked about. I didn't bring them up because I wouldn't have had any answers. In these videos, I've tried to tell you everything you should know. If something goes wrong, Eva will help you find these recordings, and then you have to leave right away. Go to the airport, take the first flight anywhere, get to Bangkok. By that time, everything will be ready and paid for. I'll give you the contacts and their exact information later. I'll also get you papers under someone else's name. Marion knows people you can get a passport from. Maybe I'm worried for nothing, but Lambert has lookouts everywhere. We've met too many people, and eventually somebody's going to talk. Even Lasse and Kristian are vulnerable. Patient information leaks like a sieve, and everyone has their price. I've especially started to suspect Kristian. I'm afraid his nerve will fail, and he'll reveal everything to Lambert just to save his own skin, or he'll think he can get money for it, maybe even forgiveness for his debts to Lambert.

Helena's case and Eva's fate convinced me that we can never be sure how your hair will act. I would have been prepared to abandon my plan if these women I trust had warned me away. Instead, Norma, they approve of everything I've done.

More than the wild behavior of your hair, I've been afraid of something else that no woman has been able to resist: the enticements of the heart. Before long, you'll meet someone from whom you want more than momentary companionship. Before long, your heart will betray you the way it betrayed your ancestor. That's why this is all necessary. I trust your head but not your heart.

Eleven

The Thais prefer to use Vietnamese women, or Cambodian or Taiwanese. This isn't just about cost but also cultural differences. The Thais respect their own women more. Everyone ends up feeling this way. Using someone different from you is easier. You should remember that.

New brochures from the Source Agency were spread around the table. Alla checked the Russian version while Marion worked on the Finnish and Swedish. Source represented quality, not unsavory charlatans, so no mistakes could be allowed in its materials. They had chosen the best paper, the graphic designer had cost a fortune, and it showed. Alvar focused on reviewing the surrogate videos, which were also top-notch. Occasionally everyone glanced at the clock on the wall. Lambert had called a few hours ago and told them to put champagne on ice. It was time for a little celebration.

One of Lambert's habits was withholding good news to increase suspense. He was like a circus ringmaster. When he finally arrived, he threw open the door and strode into the room to the rhythm of the summer's hit pop song that happened to be playing on the radio. He hummed. He whistled. He grabbed the new brochures, danced across the room browsing them, then gave them his approval by tousling Alvar's hair. Producing brochures in multiple languages had been Alvar's idea. Now both the surrogates and the clients would receive materials in their own languages. That engendered trust.

"Soon we'll need to print some in Vietnamese," Lambert said

with a grin. "The government is changing its stance on surrogates. The deputy prime minister has been making beautiful statements about everyone being entitled to dreams of motherhood. Just think. Growing a good braid takes God knows how long, but a pregnancy lasts only nine months. And the girls are so healthy and natural."

Then Lambert stopped his skipping, turned off the radio, and let the silence grow. Marion felt a chill, and the skin on her forehead quivered as if she had just stepped out of the sauna into subzero temperature. Alvar shook his head at her imperceptibly. He didn't know what was going on either.

"Dimitri called from the lab. They've analyzed the hair."

Lambert banged the corner of the coffee table and blew air through his lips. The champagne glasses on the tray jingled.

"It's clean, extremely clean. No residues. Dimitri thinks it's possible it was produced in a lab after all."

"Just because of the hair's purity?" Alvar asked.

"No. It's also the DNA," Lambert said, clapping his hands. "They took samples from three different bunches, from three different deliveries. All of them have the same DNA, which is possible only if the hair came from one living creature. I think someone has invented a cheap way of quickly cloning human hair, and Anita's partners are part of the project."

Marion realized that Anita had lied. Anita's obscure relative wasn't traveling around Ukrainian villages collecting braids. The hair must come from an advanced high-tech laboratory with tremendous resources and lots of staff. Someone would talk. Someone always talked. Lambert would find that someone, and then he would find the producer.

"Dimitri is looking for parallels right now and ordering samples from around the world," Lambert said. "We'll find the source before long. The fastest way is to go through the girl. Are we making any progress there?"

"We still wouldn't know who planned it all, who has the camera, who Anita was collecting evidence for, and what they intended to do with it," Alvar said. "The girl has to pay down her debt soon. How can she afford to pay unless she tells us what she knows?"

"My son is always such a killjoy," Lambert said with a sigh. "Squeeze the information out of her."

Marion remained sitting at the table when the others went outside. When the conversation turned to the girl, Alvar's gaze had been evasive, just like with Albino. That time Marion had torn another pile of paper tissues into shreds. Lambert had sniffed the apple scent of the Calvados served with the coffee as if it were the finest perfume and presented his apologies that we had ended up in this situation. His sympathy lay with young hearts, but Albino's betrayal could not be overlooked. They had brought her into the family after Reijo's boating accident, supporting her and then giving her a job. Lambert had treated her like his own daughter. And how did she reward him? The little bitch had betrayed Alvar most of all by taking advantage of his affection. Albino's greed was evident from the beginning, Lambert had reminded them, taking them back to the moment when she'd seen a briefcase full of dollars and wanted to touch them. Just a little. She had actually salivated. It bubbled on her lower lip, which was sticky with lip gloss, and that had spawned her stupidity. She had thought she could poach on Lambert's land without getting caught.

On the bookshelf in the living room had been a picture of Lambert and Reijo Ross posing with their children: Marion, Alvar, and the offspring of Ross's new family, Albino and her brother.

After that night, the picture disappeared, and in exchange Alvar received a villa and a new car. He didn't seem to mourn Albino any more than Marion mourned Bergman. Albino had offered good companionship, Bergman a way out of the house, a connecting stop Marion had thought would lead to the beginning of her own life. Later she realized no beginning would ever come. There would be no love, no family, nothing and no one of her own, not for either of them. There would be only Lambert, in every direction. But that would end now. Determination melted the stiffness in Marion's limbs. There was every reason to believe that the girl hadn't actually made a deal with the clan. Maybe she had met with Alvar to ask about Anita's final days, just as she had with Marion. So Marion could still do the right thing and try to save the idiot. Then she wouldn't haunt her as Albino did.

Alvar drummed the steering wheel at the traffic light, then continued through intersection after intersection, swung through a roundabout, and changed lanes. He had no expression, none at all, uttering not a word the whole way from the warehouse to the salon. As they approached Kallio, Marion surfed the airwaves, which were full of cheery advertisements, promises of continuing summer weather, and weddings.

"Could it really be true?" Marion asked. "What Lambert said about the DNA of the hair?"

Alvar shut off the radio just as he had shut his mouth.

Marion tried again. "You feeling wound up? Listen, I've got a salon to run. If the girl goes on vacation, you're going to have to send someone to replace her."

"Last time I brought Anita. That didn't go very well. Talk to Alla." Alvar stared ahead over the steering wheel, his wrists relaxed but his jaw tense, and Marion hoped, hoped so hard, that he would move her way even a little bit. When she and Anita had begun planning the Big Bang, Marion had been fully prepared to sell the whole family down the river. Later she changed her mind and decided to save her brother from the avalanche that would follow. Anita had suggested that they could warn Alvar just ahead of time. Marion couldn't do anything she might regret afterward—and yet she needed to find a convincing reason to save her brother.

"Norma isn't like the others," Marion said. "She hasn't done anything. We could let her go. Lambert never forgives me for anything, but he does forgive you."

Alvar laughed. "You just tell yourself that."

"You know how to pull his strings!"

"You would too if you ever bothered."

"It wouldn't be any use. Lambert always sees Helena in me."

"You're imagining that. All Lambert sees in you is the dolt who endangered everything by believing Anita's lies. You aren't cut out for this."

Marion sniffed. Alvar handed her a handkerchief.

"Do you know where Albino is now?" she asked.

"No idea."

"You didn't try to find out?" Marion asked.

"Why would I?" Alvar sneered. "Why are you thinking about this? You didn't even like her."

"I don't want to be there for that client meeting."

With Albino, everything had progressed quickly after the decision, in just a couple of days. Alla had been juggling a lot: in addition to the problems Albino had caused, there were distribution issues in Maracaibo. Venezuela accepted all the Russian hair Alla sent, but the theft of hair from local women had led to stricter monitoring, and some wretches were still trying to smuggle cocaine alongside the hair. More bribes were needed. On the Mexican side, they needed surrogates. Alla had decided to handle everything on the same trip. She had bought three tickets to Bogotá and from there three more to Cancún.

Albino had been thrilled about the vacation and the hotel swimming pool. She thought she was living in a dream. She bought two new bikinis. Her lover had money, and she could just lie by the pool with a margarita in her hand.

Two weeks later Lambert was introducing a potential surrogate to an American couple when Albino appeared on the screen. Marion was shocked. Albino's hair was more sedate, and her fake nails had been removed, but she still had her lash extensions. Her tan from the pool in Cartagena balanced the amphetamine twitch that they hadn't been able to powder away. Lambert said she was just nervous in front of the camera. Albino was presented as a Finn who had moved to Mexico and needed financial support to start a new life after divorcing her Mexican husband. In the corner of the screen, the Planet Hospital logo wavered. Lambert had emphasized the Americans' luck: women like this were hard to find. The child would be beautiful and probably have blue eyes.

"Why did you have to pick the very worst option for Albino?" Marion asked, as Alvar continued to drive grimly. "That man in particular. Can't you find someone better this time? For Anita's sake."

Most of the couples were model parents, but Albino's case represented the other extreme. Lambert hadn't cared one bit when the future father called and explained that it would be better if his wife didn't see the surrogate anymore. Because the eggs weren't hers, she might doubt her own maternal instincts later if she focused too much on the biological mother. Then he asked if natural insemination would lower the price, and of course it would.

"What about that couple who gave up their adoption plans after the Haiti comment? Don't you remember? They went to an adoption seminar, and the lecturer said that the Haitian catastrophe improved the market but that natural catastrophes like this were rare, and dry years were coming. The couple was shocked. You remember them."

"They've already chosen a surrogate."

"Say she got sick."

"Too risky. That couple wants to see the surrogate and really get to know her."

"By that point, Norma will have realized she's out of options. She'll understand."

"Would that calm you down?"

"Yes, yes, it would."

"You were fine when it was Albino. Why all this whining about Norma?"

Marion could still feel Alla's elbow to her ribs as they watched Norma throw up in the park. She couldn't save Anita or Anita's daughter. The least she could do was arrange a slightly better situation for her. Then she would leave, it didn't matter where to, and warn Alvar a day before the Big Bang. If he would just keep his promise.

Lasse hefted the Ukrainian hair in his hand and waved at the dresses draped over the couch. He couldn't decide which to wear for the Pride Parade. Maybe he should go as the mother of all blondes, Marilyn.

"This democratization of blondness and duck lips has made me respect Marilyn more than ever," Lasse said, pouring more coffee for Marion. "Or what about Angelina Jolie? I could be a brunette for a change. Angelina's mastectomy was a big deal. Lambert must have been rubbing his hands."

Lambert had gone even further, in fact. The news had made him grab Alla and start dancing. Having a superstar remove her breasts because of a cancer gene was an astonishing boost to business, and agency employees were instructed to mention the case whenever they encountered a client with hereditary issues. Now Lambert was just waiting for news to break of a Hollywood star who turned to donated eggs due to a predisposition to Alzheimer's or schizophrenia.

"Business was hot after Nicole Kidman had her child using a surrogate," Marion added.

"And Sarah Jessica Parker. Lambert may yet become as big a name as Sarah Jessica's agent. But honey, tell me what's on your mind. Worry isn't good for a woman's skin."

"Has anyone come around asking questions?"

"About this box?" Lasse set the metal container on the table. Marion shoved it into her bag. She would sleep better if she could check on it in the middle of the night, and she wouldn't need to worry if Lasse didn't answer her messages instantly.

"About anything."

"No, nothing, no one."

Marion watched Lasse's expressions. He still believed he had been looking after Marion's rainy day fund and that she had given it to him only because Marion couldn't control her shopping habit. Anita and Marion wanted to keep the box in a safe place the clan wouldn't think to look. Lasse was one of the agency's only employees who wasn't motivated by money, which was why everyone trusted him. But distrust still flickered in her mind. If Lasse figured out what she and Anita had been up to, he might sing. Lasse wouldn't want to endanger the agency's activities. After the Big Bang, none of the male couples in his circle would get a child. Lasse's friend who was becoming a father through the Bangkok clinic would never buy a family ticket for the train or search for a family room at a hotel. Their dreams crumbled the instant Lasse handed Marion the metal box. They could go ahead and rip Elton John's family portraits off their walls because soon they wouldn't be able to stand looking at them or reading stories about how Elton John had just welcomed another angel from the gentle womb of a surrogate mother. Marion found her eyes itching again. Pollen, that was it. Currently there were ten pregnant girls at the Thailand clinic, five in Georgia, eight in Ukraine.

"Should I be worried?" Lasse asked.

"No, Lambert is just so paranoid. It makes everything difficult."

Marion noticed two phones on the table. Lasse's own and a burner he used for agency business. When there was time, she would send Lasse a message to destroy the agency phone immediately. He didn't deserve trouble. She needed to protect him, but she also needed to keep him calm. Marion herself felt at ease. Her hands weren't cold and didn't reach automatically for the pocket where she used to keep her project phone.

"Did Anita really have to steal from Lambert?" Lasse asked. "I didn't know she had money problems."

"I didn't either."

"But to throw herself under a train because of it . . ."

"Lambert doesn't forgive things like that. It was a lot of money. Anita had relatives in trouble—" Marion stopped talking. She didn't want to lie to Lasse.

"He's quite a man."

"You could say that."

"Just don't get caught like Anita, okay?" Lasse said, then raised his hand. "No, don't tell me any more. I don't want to know. This is probably goodbye, then."

Marion's jaw trembled. It hadn't occurred to her that she would never see him again.

Lasse tossed his Marilyn dress onto a chair and came over for a hug. "You deserve a fresh start," he said. "Take it and run."

Twelve

There are so many girls. I don't know what will happen to all of them after the Big Bang. Nothing will be gained by delaying, though. Business isn't slowing down. Eva said I shouldn't think about the girls who are involved. Everything has its price.

The realization hit like white lightning. Norma stopped the video. Her mother's new camera bag was visible in the image, as was a suitcase into which she was throwing something: her first digital camera. It was old enough now for thieves to ignore, so she always traveled with it. But she had taken the videos with her brand-new model, which currently sat on the bookshelf.

Norma checked her mother's final messages again. Not a word about her old camera disappearing on the trip. She sent Margit a text and received an instant reply. Margit hadn't seen the small pink camera, and she hadn't taken it. Norma grabbed her mother's roller bag and checked the contents again. Swimsuit, cotton skirts, sunscreen. Linen jacket. Souvenirs for Norma: a new silk wrap and lemongrass ointment. Her mother intended to give them to her on a night that never came. More silk. No camera.

The hotel where her mother stayed reported that nothing had been left behind. The Bangkok airport gave the same answer. At Helsinki-Vantaa, Norma's call was forwarded to the Finnair desk. Norma described the camera and gave the two dates when it could have gone missing, the departure and arrival days. On the strap it had a small charm with Rossetti's *Regina Cordium*, Elizabeth Siddal's wedding portrait, on the medallion—

Norma hadn't misheard. The camera was at the Finnair desk. The same worker had happened to be on duty when it was brought to her. Another Finn had seen the woman drop the camera, but the group had been moving so quickly she hadn't been able to catch up to them.

Norma dumped a mixture of nutritional supplements into a cup, drained it, then cut a length of her hair. She mixed bits of hair with tobacco and rolled a spliff. After slowly smoking it, she glanced at Eva's picture staring at her from next to the laptop and ordered a taxi for the airport.

As the wind chimes jangled, the patches on the armpits of Marion's white blouse grew. Alvar had come to the salon to pick her up for a client meeting, and as always, the omens of a bad night were building. The banana bun she had rolled her hair in couldn't hide the dampness and rancid oil of her unwashed scalp.

"Ready?"

"Of course."

Marion went to spray on another layer of hair gloss. She was stalling. She didn't want to leave, and everything in her screamed that one desire. Since her return from the airport, Norma realized she'd misinterpreted Marion because she didn't know what to look for. But the smoking helped. Anita had been right about that. Without it, her roots wouldn't be so calm or her thoughts so clear.

After being left alone, Norma pulled Marion's car keys out of her pocket. She had stolen them from Marion's bag while she was finishing her makeup. If Marion missed them, she would think she'd forgotten them in her agitation, along with the blotting papers and lipstick she always carried but had left on the edge of the sink.

Norma grabbed a brush, dustpan, and handheld vacuum in case anyone wondered what she was doing and went to search Marion's car.

In the trunk she found a carry-on-size roller bag. Norma put it in a garbage bag and carried it to the back room of the salon. The baggage claim tags had all been removed, and all that was inside were a few hotel and travel brochures from Kiev, Tbilisi, and Bangkok, a hairbrush, and a stack of Source Agency brochures with the same titles in several languages. The agency address was located in Kiev, with offices in Bangkok, Mexico, Ukraine, Poland, and St. Petersburg. Norma opened the Finnish brochure and glanced over the biographies of the staff who presented themselves as surrogacy experts. The head of the agency reported getting the idea to start the company after going through the same thing as her clients—a surrogate mother had been the only way for her to experience the joys of motherhood, and now she had two children. The staff at the partner clinics also gave convincing accounts of personal experiences that helped them relate to their clients' difficulties. The final pages listed the client coordinators, the medical advisers, the area directors in charge of surrogates and donors, and the customer service representatives. All the necessary legal counsel, travel documents, and arrangements related to the child's nationality were included in the package. Above the picture of the ideal family on the back cover read the words: MAKING DREAMS COME TRUE. Nothing in the information presented made any direct mention of Lambert or gave any hint of dubious practices.

Norma went out back to smoke another roll-up and then got to work. The bag had never been vacuumed or cleaned. It was a treasure. The first hair she found was Vietnamese. Definitely from a pregnant woman who was young and well nourished.

There was some sort of chemical, too, but Norma didn't recognize it. Pregnancy hair should have a springtime buoyancy, but this one was similar to the Vietnamese women at the nail studios, and the stress level was higher than expectant mothers generally. The next hair protruded from the hotel brochures. It belonged to a Nordic woman on a low-carb diet who was probably infertile. Norma had learned to recognize polycystic ovary syndrome ages ago from excess hair growth. Although the disease could be controlled with medicine, it was obvious from the woman's hair, as were the clomiphene tablets she was taking. The third and fourth women's conditions resembled menopause. The fifth was taking pituitary hormones and enjoyed cheese and organic wines. From the sixth, she picked up at least clomiphene, and from the seventh, pituitary hormones again. All were over thirty, two over fifty. The third and fifth could cut down their alcohol use, and the sixth was a lactose-intolerant anorexic who suffered from magnesium and several other trace element deficiencies. There were seven women in total, all with traces of infertility treatments in their hair. Norma also found a few hairs that belonged to men. One was Alvar's, the other two from unidentified Scandinavians. The men's standard of living and diet was similar to that of the women. And then it hit her—a strong scent memory. Her mother's handbag, which Norma had torn apart searching for her mother's last message. The Scandinavian hair stuck in the zipper. No chance of children, lots of grapefruit juice, too much aspirin, classic home remedies for infertility.

This roller bag was not the luggage of a hair dealer. The hairs were not extensions. They were missing the taint of silicon and chemicals. Earlier Norma had thought Marion's almost daily work meetings had to do with wholesalers from the large network Alla had created. But Marion joked around with the Nigerian braiders, and she seemed lighthearted whenever she went to the warehouse. Norma picked up the hairbrush from the suitcase. It proved the same thing: the meetings Marion had gone to with this bag made her nervous.

Norma slammed the suitcase shut. Although the evidence covered a long period of time, there was no mistaking Marion's complicity in the clan's surrogacy operations. They were all the same.

She had fifteen minutes until her next customer. Norma returned the roller bag to the trunk, then glanced at the jackets hanging in the car—they were still in their dry cleaning bags and wouldn't provide anything interesting. Then she went back inside and put the car keys on the floor under the counter where Marion usually kept her purse.

The customer with the tangled hair was one of those who dreamed of a career in Hollywood, who found Finland stuffy and narrow-minded. For some reason, every one of these types was sure that a career path would open up in America just so long as they had the basics sorted out, meaning white teeth and long, shiny hair full of body. This one was too short for the catwalk, but she was certain she could succeed as a lingerie model. She had already spent her inheritance from her grandmother on silicone. She had gone to Tallinn to get them with her mother.

Enduring the girl's chatter was more difficult than usual today. A one-minute clip from her mother's pink vacation camera played in Norma's ears: "After the baby, I go to America. America after the baby." The Asian girl in another clip was in bad shape and had no English. The room looked like a hospital, and she was in hospital clothing. She was late in her pregnancy, and her wrists were cuffed to the bed. Norma's mother showed the girl pictures and also flashed them at the camera. Norma recognized only two of the men in the pictures, Alvar and Lambert. "Have you seen any of these men here? Have you been talking to any of these men?" The girl nodded toward Lambert's photo and spat at it.

The contents of her mother's vacation camera and the glimpse of Alla on Kristian's widow's video proved that the livelihood of the Lambert clan was not simply a story that could be chalked up to Helena's insane ramblings. But getting mixed up in it was insane. Norma couldn't afford that.

Norma removed all the videos from her mother's computer that referenced hair, the straightening irons of Harlem, and the extra-strength hairnets Eva used. She removed the video in which her mother ordered her to go to Bangkok if anything happened. She removed all mentions of Grigori. The talk about Helena's accent was true, she couldn't erase that, and she left most of the clips that included Helena herself. The cigarette in Helena's hand looked normal, so it could stay, as could the pipe that Helena seemed to carry with her everywhere. The scenes with too much Finnglish in Helena's speech went into the recycling bin, as well as the ones where madness or drug-induced stupor was too obvious in her eyes. That didn't leave much, but there was enough.

Norma went through the material left on the machine one more time and quieted the incessant pounding in her head with painkillers. Occasionally she browsed the departures timetable for the airport, while listening for sounds in the stairwell. The doorbell remained silent, and only the sounds of her neighbors came from the stairs. Still, she expected that at any moment someone might appear on her threshold. She had a bread knife in her jacket pocket and another in her bag. They had a calming effect, as did the cigarettes she rolled from her hair. They didn't make her see visions or hear voices. She didn't know whether she hoped for that. When she opened her mouth, her own voice came from her throat, not Eva's American accent with its higher pitch. Helena's and her mother's madness hadn't taken her.

From the vacation camera, she removed nothing, instead copying the contents onto two memory sticks. One of the sticks she hid in her bra, the other in her suitcase, already packed with bundles of hair, her best scissors, and Eva's pictures hidden in envelopes—Norma didn't want to look at her face just now.

She was almost ready.

Marion hoped to get a moment to herself before dinner. She needed only one moment, plus a little something from the sauna bar. Norma had called in sick, so the final customers before the Midsummer holiday had fallen to Marion alone. She was tired, and she would have liked to stay at home and sleep through the holiday, but everything had to seem normal. The clan couldn't suspect anything. That was why she was cleaning Alla's scalp with firm, professional strokes, then turning off the faucet with a flip of her wrist and grabbing the blow-dryer. She would act when Alla and Lambert returned from Hanoi and would definitely be on Finnish soil. By that time, she would have her own affairs arranged and in the best-case scenario would have succeeded in getting the girl to understand the benefits of her plan.

Just as she was inserting the plug into the wall, Alla turned to her.

"I just have to ask. Have you been having any symptoms like Helena did back then?"

The question came out of nowhere. Alla never spoke about Helena.

"Don't take this the wrong way. We're all under a lot of pressure, and that can trigger mental illness."

Marion's fingers clenched around the blow-dryer so hard, the plastic creaked like the ice crust on a lake, and for a fleeting moment, she saw herself grabbing the file from the table and jabbing Alla with it, even though she wasn't Helena and didn't act like Helena.

"Max can't stand the idea that you might end up in an institution."

That was a threat. Marion recognized the Lamberts' intimidation tactics, and they always worked on her like a stun gun. They wanted her to understand that Lambert could institutionalize her. Not in Finland but somewhere else. That would be her vacation.

"Luckily you don't have any children. Who knows what would have become of them," Alla said with a sigh, picking up her guide to Japan, which opened to a picture of cherry blossoms. "I think of you every time we have a client come in who's afraid of passing on schizophrenia. But let's not speak of that anymore. I've continued conversations with Unno, Mr. Shiguto's representative. Max also thinks she's a little strange. Alvar thinks the two of them are only going to put Interpol on our tail. On the other hand, Shiguto's father is the nineteenth-richest man in Japan."

Marion's hands were stiff, and she couldn't get the plug in the power outlet. She poked at it over and over, then heard Alla stand up and throw the book onto the table. She took the plug out of Marion's hand and inserted it into the wall. Her lips, swollen with hyaluronic acid, melted into a friendly smile.

"Shiguto has an excellent apartment for the surrogates, a home or residence or whatever you want to call it, and has hired nannies so the girl won't even have to worry about changing diapers. He's also promising money, five hundred dollars per month of pregnancy, and all expenses. The girl will get the same treatment as all the others. Plus Lambert has promised to reduce her debt by that amount."

"And after Shiguto?" Marion asked.

"Shiguto will probably want to keep going. He wants a large family. We'll just have to see. At least Unno likes the girl's picture."

This was the news Alla had been building to. The clan had already decided, and Alvar hadn't kept his promise. Norma wasn't sick. She was probably already in the hands of Lambert's mongrels. Maybe in the same place Anita had been. Marion would never find her. Her lungs hurt as if she were caught out in the cold. Her eyes itched, and she started rubbing them, until Alla grabbed her wrist.

"Max thinks we've been neglecting you. What if we go on vacation together when all this is done? Or what if you came with us to Hanoi?"

Marion felt the taste of blood in her mouth. She couldn't wait anymore. She had to act before the Hanoi trip, as soon as the holiday was over. The Big Bang would sweep Alvar up, but she would send Lasse a message on Sunday that it was time to keep a low profile and get rid of his agency phone.

Fifteen minutes remained until her ride. Norma was early. Over the course of the day, the city had emptied family by family, couple by couple. The man running across the street must have been headed for the liquor store before it closed. In Finland even the Kallio neighborhood emptied on Midsummer, and the Chinese restaurants locked their doors. If everything went well, by the beginning of the week Norma would be on her way to someplace where there would be so many immigrants from every corner of the world that it would be impossible for the whole country to sink into a holiday coma. Her mother's habit on holidays like this had been to book them foreign vacations to places where the solitude of single women didn't feel like a stone in the stomach and some store or bar was always open. Norma didn't remember the last Midsummer she had spent at home.

She peered into her handbag. Eva looked satisfied, and her pouting lips were just opening as if she wanted to say something. Norma snapped the purse shut. She now knew everything she needed to, yet something she couldn't figure out rattled around in the back of her head. She knew her mother's reason for her stupid plan, and she understood the selling of the hair. Her mother must have gotten caught, and that was why she jumped in front of the metro train. She had been no match for the clan's professionals. She had known she would never escape their clutches.

"I have no intention of going to Bangkok."

The words just slipped out. Norma glanced around. The neighbors were packing boxes of beer and bags of charcoal into their car. No one had noticed her talking to herself. She tried her voice again. It was still her own, not Eva's. Norma glanced into her bag again. Eva's round eyes looked back at her as if she were a fool. As if Eva were saying that surely no one could be so silly as to let some bush doctor operate on her, no matter what her mother thought.

Time passed slowly. Norma didn't dare roll a third cigarette, despite the urge. She didn't want to investigate what her hair could do anymore. She wanted to be done with the visions. The heat swelled her legs, and her nervous pacing chafed her toes just as a vague idea nagged her mind. She checked the time—ten minutes to eight—then realized what she'd overlooked. She went running for the metro station, hurrying down to the deserted platform and standing next to the bench where her mother had jumped. It was the same bench she stopped in front of every day on her way to work at ten to eight. After the labor negotiations, she'd been later and later, and on her mother's last morning, Norma had been off with her one-night stand and her alarm hadn't woken her. Otherwise she always waited for the metro in the same place because the train car that stopped here also stopped right in front of the escalator at the other end of the line. Her mother could have run into her that morning. Had she come there to tell Norma everything? Why then? Why not some other time? Why hadn't she picked up the phone? Had she tried to find Norma at home? Had she rung the bell? Could Norma have prevented it all if she'd slept in her own bed that night, if she'd arrived on the metro platform at the right time that morning? But why was Norma still trying to find sense in her mother's random reasoning? Hadn't she just decided to leave all this behind?

Norma pulled a lighter out of her handbag. As the metro rushed up to the platform, she threw Eva's photo onto the tracks and saw her smile arc through the air before the flame burned the face from the picture.

Norma sat on the bench to recover from the shock. No smoke alarms had gone off—the flare lasted only a moment. But it had still managed to catch a few wisps of hair at her temples, and the stench was obvious. Two guards who had arrived on the platform regarded her from a distance. She began to rewrap her turban and tried to seem normal. The illusion was still vivid. In the flames, she had seen a smile like one in a photograph taken on a sunny day. Her mother's cheeks had burned with light, her skin had smelled of lemon, and her silhouette had melted into the mandarin color of the platform wall panels. Norma had heard her panting as if after a run. Her mother had tried to steady her breathing and said she made it at the last second. She had guessed she would find Norma here. She was in a hurry. She had to leave, and fast. The sound of the approaching metro was already audible, and people gathered closer to the tracks. Her mother was having an increasingly hard time maintaining her smile, the smile all mothers used to calm their frightened children, and she glanced at the clock on the information display. The air current grabbed her hair, and her mother wasn't alone after all. The curls waving in the air were Eva's. Eva was next to her, with Norma's mother's purse on her shoulder and wearing her mother's shirt, and they looked at Norma as if wanting to confirm that she understood they couldn't delay. Someone was running toward them through the crowd, and her mother's breathing quickened again. Eva kicked the shoes off her feet and said they had to run fast. Everything depended on not being caught. Just as the metro arrived, her mother lost her balance—clattering and brakes and cries and Eva's hand hanging in the air. Eva's sigh: *What a tragedy. But you'll always have me, and we'll always have each other. I will always save you.*

As she climbed into the taxi, Norma wondered whether she was making a mistake. Her brain tried to make the conversation ahead of her easier, to reassure her that she wasn't on her way to negotiate with the person responsible for her mother's murder. But the vision made sense—it fit with her mother's crazy world. Eva had pushed her mother onto the tracks. Eva, who had just spoken to her.

The driver didn't reply when Norma asked where they were going. Norma leaned back and tried to calm down. Maybe smoking wasn't for her either. According to Eva, it had been easier with Helena than with Norma's mother, who was stronger-willed and had stopped listening to Eva when she said Grigori was a con artist and that the woman who had supposedly been cured of hypertrichosis had never been like them. Her mother had forced herself to believe that Grigori was the one. She was sure time was running short and she would be found out soon. She had so desperately wanted to be right.

Marion stopped to lean on the shopping cart. Her purse rested on boxes of beer, and the metal box was inside the purse. She kept it with her all the time. Marion began pushing the cart again and continued collecting the items on Alla's shopping list, heading between the freezer islands toward the dairy section. The pudding cups were the same ones Alvar used to steal from the corner store as a child. Right now Alvar was probably torturing information out of Norma, and he would receive a nice reward if he succeeded. Otherwise he wouldn't be skipping the family party—he'd have left the dirty work to the mongrels.

The supermarket aisles were overflowing with Midsummer holiday favorites: charcoal, sausages, bunches of dill. Other customers' heaped shopping carts bumped Marion's, and kids ran into her legs. Families formed tight, coordinated units with one parent corralling the children while the other waited in line. Solo shoppers inspected lists written by spouses and called home occasionally for more specific instructions. Marion would receive a call soon, too. Not from her husband but from Alla, who wanted to get on with curing the salmon and making her herring caviar. Marion had lingered too long and wanted to linger even longer, but she had to keep up her act for just a few more days. She would soldier on, even though Alla might have spent this time waiting for ingredients to arrange drugs from Russia for Alvar to use. Or maybe Alvar would choose amobarbital, something that wouldn't require a hard approach. They had to keep her face in salable condition. Scopolamine had made Anita babble about Helena's voices as if they were actual people, so they would hardly choose to use that this time. Even Lambert had discounted Anita's nonsense, including when she talked about Marion. That had been a stroke of luck for her.

At the fish counter, another happy family waited ahead of Marion. A boy ran around and shoved Marion's cart, sending the purse falling off the cases of beer. The metal box clanged as it hit the floor. Marion turned her eyes away. She could have screamed when she saw Lambert take Anita at the airport. She could have rushed to get the box and then run straight to the police station with it. She could have exposed the whole clan, and the police would have found Anita alive. But then the authorities would have wanted to know where the information came from. They would have wanted her to testify. The clan would have taken her out before the case ever went to court, and that would happen now, too, if she left her shopping cart and rushed to the police station with the metal box.

Marion took her salmon and roe and went to stand in line at the meat counter. She didn't have it in her to sacrifice herself for Norma. The clan could wait to get caught until the workweek started. Then the mail would be moving, and she would be safe.

As she searched for bitter almond extract, Marion's gaze fell on a bag of almonds. Norma was always hauling nuts and seeds around with her and pecking at them like a bird. Memories of Albino haunted her in the same way: after the Colombia trip, the tree frogs would start their tinnitus whenever Alla made margaritas and dumped ice cubes into the blender. Marion shook her head. This was completely different. She'd tried her best—that had to be good enough. Norma would not trouble her eternally as Albino did.

Anita didn't weigh on her mind either. With Anita, she had done what she could. She had tried to save her.

The lapping of the waves and the unsteadiness of the dock were like something out of a childhood memory of summer, but the mood wasn't. Norma swayed on the splintering boards. Farther off, a Tallinn-bound ferry glided, full of drowsy migrant workers and drinking tourists. Kulosaari Island with its expensive real estate. Sailboats. The high-rise apartment buildings of Merihaka, the Kallio Church tower. Tomorrow anyone left in the capital would flood to Suomenlinna Island, and the rest of Helsinki would turn into a ghost town.

"Midsummer plans?" Alvar asked.

"No. I don't care for holidays."

"I don't either."

Norma focused on her goal, which was seeing the next Midsummer. She opened her mouth to get down to business, but instead raised her glass to her lips, keeping her sips small so the wine would last a long time. After emptying it, she would present her proposal. That was why she had come here, yet she hesitated. She hesitated, even though the sea air and the wind calmed her hair, and the world felt freshly painted, the exposed bedrock newly formed. The incessant knocking in the back of her head that had started after she began winnowing the videos had stopped. And the fear associated with this meeting place had faded—its desolateness was lovely, and Alvar's conviviality was calming. He had been waiting for Norma in front of the sauna on the shore and opened a bottle of wine, which was now half gone.

"If Helena ever gets out, this will be a good home for her," Alvar said. "At Villa Helena, she can pretend to be a retired singing star."

Norma had noticed the security cameras and high fence around the building. A safe home for Helena. But she hadn't expected this expensively restored villa in the middle of a deserted neighborhood filled with ornate mansions from a bygone world. Alvar didn't seem like a man who pored over renovation manuals and researched traditional paint colors.

"Perfect. This is perfect," Norma said.

"Perfect for people who don't like people. For people like you."

After the car stopped at the edge of the forest, Norma had been sure this was the end and decided that perhaps dying at the hands of criminals was better after all. Shady characters like these didn't want paparazzi and police officers swarming over their victims any more than she did. The driver had led her to a forest path with a mat of pine needles that reminded her of her mother's funeral, and they had passed a crystal-clear pond. For a moment, she considered jumping into it, all by herself, without any help.

"Do you want to hear more about Helena's madness, or is there some other reason for this meeting?" Alvar asked.

Norma tossed back the rest of her wine, then focused on a northern wheatear hopping around on the rock near the shore. She had rehearsed this conversation many times. She could do this.

"Or maybe you came to say goodbye, because you think you're going somewhere?"

"I don't understand."

"You stopped in at the airport."

The wheatear disappeared along with Norma's prepared opening. Alvar refilled Norma's glass. He acted as if this were a completely normal occasion for drinking wine on the shore. And perhaps it was, for him. Perhaps he held conversations like this in front of his sauna all the time. Norma wasn't sure whether to be surprised that one of Alvar's hirelings had kept track of her comings and goings.

"Calm down. Let's continue," Alvar said.

"So what if I did visit the airport? I have to plan my future. I want a new life. A passport, an identity, the freedom to leave."

"Disappearing is expensive."

"Is it possible?"

"Of course. What do I get out of it?"

"Anita's camera and videos."

"Videos?"

"You'll want to see these."

"And the Ukrainian supplier?"

Norma shook her head.

"Lambert won't agree to that," said Alvar.

"I'm not making a deal with Lambert."

"I don't decide things like this myself."

"This time you'll want to, though."

"Fine. But only if this footage is valuable enough."

"It is."

"Then we have a deal."

Alvar clinked his glass against Norma's. Norma took a deep breath. She'd made it this far. She was going to succeed: she would be around for next Midsummer. But in order to be sure of that, she had to have insurance. She moved behind Alvar and pressed her nose to his temple. He flinched.

"Repeat what we agreed," Norma said.

Alvar bit his lower lip.

"I have a good intuition," Norma said.

"Most people would consider this strange."

"I'm sure. Does it matter? I want to hear you say it."

Alvar's dog came over to them, but he ordered her to stay. Norma smelled vetiver, she smelled nicotine, tannin, and sulfur, but no lie in any word when Alvar repeated what they had agreed. Norma dropped a key in his hand. Just in case, she had taken her mother's vacation camera and the videos to attic storage locker number twelve.

"I'll send someone. You stay here. Are you hungry?"

The dog jumped up and came closer when Norma tried to raise her head. Sleep instantly disappeared from her eyes. She never nodded off in strange places—her hair always woke her. The dog recognized her distress and cocked its head. She couldn't sit up. Her hair had coiled around the rattan legs of the sofa like a drowsy vine.

"Do you need help?"

Alvar sat on the porch steps smoking.

"What time is it?"

"Almost midnight."

Norma felt her hair. She'd cut it in the bathroom a couple of hours ago, and the growth wasn't noticeable yet. The color of the tips looked strange in the blue light of the mosquito lamp. She hadn't been found out, just snagged her hair on some rattan, so there was no reason to panic. Only then did Norma remember that Alvar now knew everything. He'd disappeared to inspect her mother's vacation camera and videos as soon as he got his hands on them, and that was several hours ago. During that time Norma had cut her hair, walked in the yard, and napped. But nothing about Alvar had changed. He looked the same as before, and his pulse was the same when he came over to Norma and asked if she needed scissors. The vetiver smelled precisely the same as it would normally. There was no change in the heat of his scalp. He didn't smell like a man who had just learned of his sister's betrayal.

"Are there phones or anything else in your suitcase I should know about?" asked Alvar, as he handed the scissors to Norma.

"What?"

"Do you use any phones other than that one on the table."

"Does that question mean that our agreement is still in force?"

"Of course. Why wouldn't it be?"

Norma began extracting her hair from the rattan, cut out a bee stuck in it, and pushed it away. Alvar's imperturbability was incomprehensible. He had just watched his mother's peculiar monologues in the garden at her insane asylum. Surely that had to affect him in some way.

"I'm sorry that Anita taped Helena," Norma said.

"Helena wouldn't care."

"That's exactly why she shouldn't have done it."

Alvar sat in the facing chair and bent down to scratch the dog. "Make a list of the clothes you need. A new suitcase is waiting in the entryway. You're disappearing today."

Alvar took Norma's phone and gave her a burner instead.

"I'll call this when everything is ready. You'll get a ride to Vuosaari. There's a studio apartment there where you can be alone. If you need something, send a message to the number on this phone. Don't go out, don't open the door to anyone, don't contact anyone. The rest depends on you. I'll bring you a passport and credit and debit cards. There will be some money in the account."

"I don't want money."

"Do you understand?" Alvar seized her by the jaw. His hand was warm, his skin dry. "You're never going home again."

The first time Alvar made this move, Norma had been sitting in the backyard of the salon. Her eyes had been wandering, looking anywhere but at him. The asphalt at her feet had seemed to boil, and she'd feared she could sense Helena's madness in him. This time she heard her breathing and the beating of her heart and the tiny birds and the waves of the sea, and her gaze did not so much as stir. Alvar's grip slackened, and at the same moment the thought flickered in Norma's mind that she would always remember how that vetiver smelled on Alvar's skin. She would probably fall for a man someday who reminded her of it.

"Who will miss you?"

"No one."

Alvar released her and opened another bottle of wine. The cork popped, and wine gurgled into the glass. Norma felt like smoking, to banish the echo of her last thought, but she didn't dare take out the cigarettes she'd rolled. She wouldn't rewrap the turban that had fallen to the floor either, even though being in Alvar's presence with her hair down agitated her.

"There's always someone," he said. "Say you're going away on a surprise trip, everything that's happened this year has taken its toll, and you don't know when you're coming back. Or I can write the message for you now."

"Is it so strange there isn't anyone?"

"Yes. What should we write? To whom? To everyone in your contact list?"

"No one will wonder—"

Alvar had come to sit next to Norma. The phone display shone like a moon in the dimness. The chemicals of the mosquito candle caused a slight dizziness, but that was all. Her senses worked normally, and Norma noticed that her hair was attracted to Alvar, coiling toward his hand as if to comfort him. She sensed his sadness. That had to be because of Marion. No rage, no anger, just sadness. Alvar had lost his sister.

Alvar showed Norma the message he had written: "Happy Midsummer! Tomorrow this girl is headed to Asia for a break. See you in a couple of months!"

"Does that sound enough like you?"

Norma nodded, and the message whooshed away to everyone except Marion. She remembered her mother's final message. Maybe her mother hadn't sent it at all. Maybe someone else had written it. Someone who had thought a daughter might wonder if she didn't hear anything from a mother after a trip.

"Questions?"

This was her last chance to ask how her mother had been found out, but Norma didn't ask, not about her mother, not about the girls in the pictures on the camera, and not about what would happen to Marion. She didn't want to know. She already knew too much.

Alvar's phone began to buzz. Marion's name flashed in green in the middle of the table.

"You could have gone to Marion and worked with her," Alvar said. "She would have taken you on as her partner in her new business."

"Marion already failed once."

"Guess how many of our doctors have been arrested at some point? Every one of them is still working as a doctor. Marion's plan was doomed from the start. Men like Lambert never get caught, even when others do. The Lamberts of the world carry on."

Norma's phone began to ring. Margit. Alvar turned off the phone. It was time.

Marion scanned the men walking around Lambert's property and took a more comfortable position in her lawn chair—the mongrels didn't seem to be paying her any notice. When Lambert and Alla took Ljuba to the doctor after she suddenly fainted, Marion had been left to look after the children playing on the lawn. If the clan suspected her, this could have been part of a plot to ensure Marion was kept under watchful eyes, but Ljuba wasn't that good an actor. Marion watched the progress of Midsummer as if it were a long-awaited play. She was no longer disappointed that her brother hadn't answered her calls and that everyone was lying to her. She would witness the last gasp of Alla and Lambert's dream life—the final family dinner and the final hugs they exchanged, the final games in the yard with the rug rats—and if all went well, she would hear the final conversations about how Lambert would soon be the king of an embryo empire.

This time Lambert wouldn't have the chance to empty his safe or erase his computers, or Alla to pack the children's things. Marion wouldn't see Alla's expression when the police came. She would be able to imagine it, though. After Anita was caught, Marion had rushed to the Lamberts to get clarity on what had happened, and Alla, the one she found at home, had been a sight worth seeing.

Waves of mascara collected in the wrinkles around her eyes, rouge striped her cheeks, and her voice sounded like a trapped wild animal. One of the suitcases was already full of children's clothing; Minigrip bags stuffed with dollars and passports lay on top of them. The snap of a fingernail as it hit the side of a suitcase was that of a lion, her hair streamed like a mane, and Marion thought that if Helena had been more like Alla, Marion and Alvar's lives would have taken a different direction. Or if Marion had been like Alla herself, her maternal instincts would have told her that Helena's relationship with small children wasn't healthy. Alla would have remembered the time when Helena tried to take someone's kid straight out of a stroller at the train station. Alla never would have given her baby to Helena, and if Helena took the child anyway, Alla would have been on her before she could get to the balcony. Marion, on the other hand, had stood like a statue. But all that was in the past now. She had learned to fight.

Ljuba was the only one who gave her pause. Ljuba would have to return to St. Petersburg and give birth to a baby that would probably be sent to an orphanage for someone to buy. But Alla wouldn't get any money from it, and no new embryos would be implanted in Ljuba from parents Alla had already chosen for her. That would be only a detour, though, as some other clinic was sure to take her in. Ljuba was young and healthy—she would get her happy ending and go to America.

Marion took out her phone and started to browse flights leaving Frankfurt. Everything needed to go normally until Tuesday. Mail wasn't delivered on the weekend, so she couldn't send the envelopes until Monday. On Tuesday they would arrive, and then she would already be on her way.

She awoke to chirping. A little bird, a delicate sound. Just outside the window, perhaps on the eaves. The chirping was the color of the rising sun, but afternoon light streamed in. Norma's eyes fluttered open. She had fallen asleep again. The ceiling was unfamiliar, as were the sheets, and her skin against the sheets was bare. She felt a crackle all the way down to her lower back when she tried to lift her head, and understood that she was finished. The end of the world had come—it had Alvar's eyes. Alvar's elbow rested on the nightstand. He looked at Norma as if seeing her for the first time.

"You should leave," he said. "I tried to wake you earlier."

His voice sounded distant. Norma's ears were clogged, as was her nose, and the hair rippling across the floor rose in garlands up the feet of the chest of drawers, sprouting from the foot of the bed, and undulating around her like sea oak. It hadn't raised any alarms, not even yesterday, when she'd thought that she would never see Alvar again, that in a couple of weeks she would already be far away, in a new life as a new person, so why not, just this once? Alvar's hands on her neck had felt like a caress, his kiss had slid deep into her heart, and her hair had squeezed and pushed and tangled around his arms, even though it should have known what would happen. And now it knew, now it knew what level these people operated on. It knew that rhinoceros horn cost one hundred thousand euros per kilo, elephant tusk only a thousand, and no dodo birds were left at all. Impotence pills, a cure for HIV. They knew a million ways to use mystical hair, countless ways to use the woman who bore it. She couldn't understand what had happened.

"You could have warned me," Alvar said.

"This is the first time."

"The first?"

"No, I mean, it grows, but not like this. Not this way. Not ever."

Alvar took the scissors from the table.

"They will never stop chasing you, my little Ukrainian."

The drawing room downstairs was in a shambles. Norma leaned on the doorjamb and stared at the destruction. The glass of the desk clock was broken, and the iron umbrella stand was knocked over, as were the flower table, the snake plant, and the billbergia. Soil and pottery fragments were strewn across the floor. Bundles of hair lay coiled on the couch, but they had a strange tint, an amorous red. Next to them were a pair of scissors. Alvar had cut her hair, and it hadn't resisted. It hadn't attacked him or played difficult. It hadn't woken Norma, and she didn't know whether this was because of Alvar, the smoking, or both. Eva could have warned her, or at least hinted.

"You probably don't remember."

"I'm sorry."

Norma tugged Alvar's bathrobe tighter around her as her skin rose in goose bumps. She was dizzy and still waiting for her hair to begin to hiss, to understand that the nightmare had begun. But nothing happened. The hair purred next to Alvar, against his stray dog's ribs, rocking her toward him, pulling her head into his arms, and she heard his heartbeat, felt his slightly higher body temperature, his elevated cortisol level, more adrenaline than normal, but nothing else. Norma was unable to feel fear. Maybe that was a result of Alvar's skill in calming unbalanced women. Alvar's approach to overcoming obstacles and surprises was something dazzling. No one had ever had this effect on Norma. She didn't dare ask what had happened or how.

She stood on her toes and pressed her nose against Alvar's hairline. "It tells me things."

"Your nose?"

"Your hair. My nose is sensitive to hair."

"Do I pass the test?"

"Either that or you're a good actor," Norma said. "You should be afraid or shocked. That would be normal. Psychopaths, narcissists, and professional actors react in a different way from other people. But you aren't any of those."

"At first I thought you'd died. Then I thought I was going crazy. Does that help?"

"A little."

"Marion has the same thing. All children of insane parents do. We look for signs and constantly doubt our own minds. No one can live that way, which is why I decided to stop doing it."

"How?"

"Through will and logic."

Alvar had thought he was hallucinating when Norma's hair continued growing after she fainted on the rug. Then he forced himself to figure out what was going on. He had samples of old raw bundles, and they matched Norma's hair. Now all the oddities of the Ukrainian hair Anita supplied made sense.

"And besides, Anita talked about your hair."

"When?"

"When she got caught. She was so confused, though, that no one believed her. Not even Lambert. They thought it was the rambling of an addled mind."

Norma sat on the stairs to wait for the panic to set in. Her hair should stop pushing and purring. It should react to Alvar's words even if Norma couldn't find the lie in them.

"Lambert snatched Anita at the airport," Alvar continued. "She'd just returned to Finland, and they gave her a truth serum. Which isn't dangerous."

"Is that some sort of defense? My mother always protected you. She thought about you every day—she thought she was responsible for what happened to you. And you let her die!"

"She jumped onto the tracks herself. She ran away and jumped."

"And you couldn't do anything to stop her?"

"No. That wasn't within my power."

"You could have let her go."

"Anita wanted to put me behind bars."

Now should finally be the time for rage. Norma grabbed the railing and waited.

Nothing happened.

The car would come in an hour, and Norma's new suitcase waited on the threshold, a new dress and new shoes in the bathroom. She restrained her desire to grab the raw beef she had glimpsed in the refrigerator, but she took a risk and pulled a cigarette out of her tobacco case to clear her head. She would never see Alvar again. She'd known that yesterday. She'd known it as she undressed, she knew it now, and that knowledge became unbearable even though it was unavoidable. If Alvar wasn't already thinking of ways to profit from her hair, it was an inexplicable moment of weakness, and he was sure to recover. Norma had to leave primarily because of Lambert, but now also because of Alvar.

"If you need something to help you sleep, text me," Alvar said.

"Don't go looking for anything yourself. Do you promise to stay in the apartment?"

"Will you tell Lambert?"

"I'll keep to my part of the agreement. Always. But Anita took a big risk when she started selling your hair. Lambert has customers who would pay anything for a child with your genes. Has your DNA been studied? Did all that hair come from you, or are there others?"

"There aren't any others. But I don't want to talk about it."

"I have to know, my little Ukrainian. You have to help me make you disappear. Listen, Anita chose suicide because she knew Lambert would catch her again and she would talk. She would talk about you, and before long Lambert would have believed."

Alvar held Norma's head. Norma's nose had cleared, it worked, and now it trusted.

In front of the mirror, Alla considered how the top and bottom parts fit. Alla's lucky bag was also going to Hanoi, a snakeskin Birkin acquired at a luxury purse auction.

"I like that Vietnamese deputy health minister. We need more men like him in politics," Lambert said. "That nursing analogy was really good."

Lambert showed Marion the news on his phone. According to this minister, surrogacy should be compared to breastfeeding: there had always been wet nurses, so why couldn't a woman bear children for those who weren't able? Fertility had dropped radically in Vietnam, and demand at infertility clinics had multiplied several times in the past decade. The media was reporting on cases of illegal surrogacy in Hanoi.

Marion dropped the phone onto the table. She couldn't concentrate. "I haven't seen Alvar all weekend," she said.

"He has some new fling," Lambert said, giving a wink. "Let the boy have a little time off. He's earned it."

"Let's focus on Vietnam," Alla said. "Think about your wardrobe. You're going to come along to meet the minister of health."

"You should get a feel for this side of the business," Lambert said. "We'll meet with all our old partners and ponder strategy.

There's potential. If husbands are prepared to sell their wives' hair for twenty dollars, what will they take for a uterus? That's no small shit."

Lambert tossed his Panama hat in an arc onto the couch. The black hatband woke the tree frogs in Marion's mind. "Get a feel for the business," Marion had told Albino before the Colombia trip. Norma probably gave up her secret, which would explain Lambert's good mood. But he could walk on sunshine for all she cared—the clan wouldn't have time to do anything with the girl's information.

"What do you think, Marion? About Vietnam?"

Marion was startled.

"You didn't read the whole article," Lambert said.

Marion picked up the phone and focused her eyes on the screen.

"Clever that the minister focuses on the worries of local couples," Alla said. "It avoids the image of rich foreigners taking advantage of Vietnamese women."

Lambert was already looking far into the future. He had an advantage because of the hair trade. Years of experience and relationships would make him king of the Vietnam embryo market. And after that, Japan. Marion would remember that smile forever, the dilated pores around his nose, the eyebrows grown bushy with age, the hand that rattled ice cubes in his glass like the bell of a colonial master calling a servant. Marion would never know whether the decision about her vacation had been made because Lambert knew the truth or simply because she was considered a risk. She would never know if Alvar was gone because he didn't want to participate in this or because the girl and the information she had given were keeping her brother busy. At this point, Alvar would have called Lambert "Dad" to awaken childhood memories, but Marion didn't need to grovel anymore. Today was the last time she'd ever see this pair. During this last father-daughter meeting, each had a plan for how to get rid of the other. This time, though, Marion would prevail.

"And we're leaving Nigeria," Lambert said. "I fully admit the water bottle factory was a mistake. We'll liquidate it and forget the whole thing. We can't sell black kids here anyway, and what the hell are we supposed to do with Nigerian ritual murders or virgins as a treatment for erectile dysfunction? Nothing. At least the Vietnamese are civilized. So get packed, Marion!"

Ljuba was still in the hospital, and Marion was in the kitchen making sandwiches for the kids when she heard Alvar's car drive up. Alvar made straight for the backyard, where Lambert was sleeping off his Midsummer hangover with his hat over his eyes. Marion set the bread down on the counter and looked out. The yard swing swayed empty. Lambert had jumped up, and Alla had removed her sunglasses. The conversation was audible through the open window.

"It's confirmed. The Ukrainian hair is coming from Dnipropetrovsk," Alvar said. "The family Anita talked about lives there. They've been fighting with the tax authorities. Apparently the problems have something to do with Oleksandr Yanukovych's businesses."

Lambert paced the lawn. The languor and boozy haze had disappeared in an instant.

"Dnipropetrovsk," he said, savoring the name as he turned his hat in his hands.

Marion shook the tree frogs away. In two days she would never have to hear them again. Alvar was Lambert's golden boy again. And this time maybe hers, too. She wouldn't go to Frankfurt. She would go to Dnipropetrovsk. She would find the Ukrainian supplier. She was sure of that. Once Alla and Lambert were out of the way, she would have time to turn over every stone in the city.

"Guns, nuclear weapons, the arms industry," Alla said. "The mafia is mostly interested in dividing up state property. That region practically breeds politicians. Even Tymoshenko, the one with the braids, started her career there." Alla made her hand into a pistol and cocked her thumb. "That's how they handle things. But we have good contacts. I should have heard about this."

Lambert placed his fingers against each other and nodded. "It is strange. So do we have a secret competitor in Dnipropetrovsk? Why do I have the feeling we're still missing a piece of this puzzle?"

"All Norma knows is that the hair comes from there," Alvar said. "She goes to the bus terminal and picks up the deliveries, and the money moves through a dummy account. I sent the boys to look for the woman whose name is on the account. The middleman is probably on the take. Norma believes that's who's behind Anita's accident—I think the same person must be trying to muscle in on our territory. But we can contact the supplier in Dnipropetrovsk directly and try to cut a deal. We make it clear that without us they won't be able to operate here, and that we play by our own rules. No one elbows out the Lamberts."

Her brother's voice was normal, but something was off. Marion just couldn't put her finger on what. She couldn't see his pupils. But his voice was clear, and he wasn't twitching.

"I'm sending you right now the address in Dnipropetrovsk I got from Norma," Alvar said, then started typing on his phone.

"We'll go there directly after Hanoi," Lambert said.

"And let's get the girl's auction out of the way before then. Alla can make her look presentable. Shiguto can't resist blondes. Or do we need more time? Her face is still okay, isn't it?"

"Should we get her out of the country now?" Alla asked.

"Maybe not right this instant," Alvar said.

"So she does need to heal up. We can wait awhile, then."

Her brother was effective and competent, a perfect member of the clan. She didn't have anything in common with him anymore, and he would never reveal where he was keeping Norma. At that exact moment, Marion knew what the name of her hair salon would be:

Thelma and Louise.

Marion pushed across the table a nondescript folder containing ultrasound images and information about the progress of the pregnancy. Alvar had left her in charge of the meeting with the Down syndrome client. Marion guessed that he was avoiding her because he was afraid she would quiz him about Norma.

"My luck can't be so bad that the same thing is happening again," the woman said.

"No, of course not."

Marion patted the woman's arm consolingly, then continued delivering her standard litany, all the while wondering what this woman would do when she read about the Lambert clan's businesses at her breakfast table. The media would start calling and whispers would follow her at work as her bosses wondered how to get rid of her legally. The neighbors would stop saying hello. Soon the whole country would want to know what happened to her first child. The headlines would suggest an orphanage, and if things went according to plan, questions about organ smuggling would surface. Marion had no clue about the child's current location, but the key piece of evidence was in the memory sticks stored in the metal box: a recorded conversation demonstrating the woman's disgust with her Down syndrome baby.

Marion smiled. She was smiling more all the time, and her smile was already borne aloft on airplane wings. She would leave. She would go to Dnipropetrovsk and find the Ukrainian supplier. *Vogue. Harper's Bazaar. Cosmopolitan.* The covers of the hair magazines, styling for Paris Fashion Week! The next generation of supermodels! Nicki Minaj's wig master, Terrence Davidson, would become a regular customer, and Ursula Stephen would order hair from them to do Rihanna. Madonna was a foregone conclusion. How many nights had Marion and Anita spent browsing glossy magazines and planning their future conquests? And now the future was here. She'd been able to finish everything herself after all. Without Anita, without a partner. She'd already emptied the accounts, and she no longer regretted withholding the remaining money from Norma. Norma didn't have a use for it anyway; she wouldn't need anything anymore.

They were supposed to open the metal box together. They'd planned to pack the flash drives into envelopes and mail them on Marion's birthday, the fourth of August. They settled on the date before leaving for Thailand. That should have been the start of her new life. Marion opened a bottle of sparkling wine and poured two glasses.

The eggshell-white envelopes waited on the table. She had already put stamps on them and was starting to write the addresses. One was meant for the National Bureau of Investigation, another for an activist who specialized in leaks, a third for a news organization she hadn't chosen yet. Anita had jumped in front of a train before they could decide. A tabloid or a newspaper? A magazine or a local rag? Maybe somewhere in Denmark? Or Sweden? They'd tried to look for Finnish-language search results, but even *baby factory* was such an obscure term that articles put it in quotation marks. A few of the raids on Nigerian and Thai baby farms had been mentioned as column filler with no mention of how many Finns had acquired children from these countries. The Danes and Swedes would take up the story more eagerly.

Marion decided to play it safe. She would send one envelope to the *Expressen* in Sweden and another to one of the Danish papers.

She would get more memory sticks in Kiev, make more copies, and send them to every country where the agency had operations. Lambert would soon become the public face of rent-a-womb tourism.

When everything was ready and her bag was packed, the doorbell rang. Through the peephole, Marion saw Alvar, who didn't take his finger off the bell until she opened the door. Marion remained unconcerned. She had pushed the envelopes and suitcase into the closet, and otherwise nothing else in the apartment revealed her intentions, so she simply let him in and began giving a detailed report on the meeting with the Down syndrome client. Her brother said nothing. Marion continued her speech until his silence made a familiar stiffness spread through her limbs, and she trailed off.

"Are you finished now? You didn't really think your plan would succeed, did you?"

Two of Alvar's men came in and began tossing Marion's apartment shelf by shelf. Her life was turned upside down one drawer at a time. They even cut open the mattress. Feathers cascaded from pillows like snow, coins rained from pockets, glasses smashed on the tiles, flour and sugar frosted the kitchen, and powder dusted the bathroom mirror as the men opened jars and tins and poured their contents on the floor. Marion stood against the wall, like a tongue frozen to a metal railing, and watched. Alvar sat in front of her and went through the envelopes they found in her suitcase. Then he inserted the memory sticks into a laptop, and the recordings began to play.

"You can go."

Marion didn't understand.

"You can have ten hours' head start. I'll take these to Lambert in the morning."

One of Alvar's men brought him some papers: Marion's tickets to Kiev. Alvar glanced at them and dropped them onto the floor.

"Go wherever you want."

Marion peeled herself off the wall and picked up the tickets.

"Make sure she doesn't take anything with her," Alvar told one man. "Passport, phone, and credit card, but that's it. Take her to the airport, then check her pockets and hair again."

On the screen in front of Alvar, a Mexican girl cried about the abortion she'd been forced to have at seven months. Alvar jumped to the next video, the next cascade of tears, and then to the next girl, who said she'd received a passport and a trip across the border as payment.

Marion shook the pillow feathers from her skirt and took another step toward the entryway, then a third.

"I sent you that address in Dnipropetrovsk," Alvar said as Marion reached the door. "There's no point going there, but you will anyway."

Epilogue

The weather had decimated the service station's selection of ice cream. Norma stood in front of the freezer, leaving the door open until the tongue of sweat on her back cooled a bit. At the checkout she cast a passing glance at the headlines. Heatstroke deaths, thunderstorms and silicone implants, divorces and weddings.

"Anything else, ma'am?"

A moment passed before Norma realized the clerk, face turned toward the ineffectual fan, was talking to her, and she smiled. Nothing else. *This is all. Coffee for two. Water for two, one sparkling, one still. Cigarettes for two, with menthol and without. Everything for two.* Plus pig ears from the pet aisle for the dog—who was standing outside on the asphalt lifting each paw in turn.

Alvar's smile knotted her stomach in a good way, and as she crossed the parking lot to where he was smoking next to the car, Norma imagined herself as any woman leaving on a summer vacation with her lover. The station wagon that pulled in behind them interrupted the daydream. A sudden nausea forced her to crawl into the front seat and fumble for a motion sickness pill. It was caused by the woman who got out of the wagon to walk while the children bounced inside with her husband.

"That woman is sick."

Then Norma snapped her mouth shut and turned the air conditioner on high. Alvar had climbed into the car and put his arm around her waist. The heat of July was melting her head. Or maybe Alvar was to blame. Water for two, beer for two, coffee for two, rooms for two—her hungry heart was prepared to reveal everything.

"She won't see next summer," Norma said.

The children ran to show their mother their juice boxes, but she was busy arguing with her husband in Russian. The woman wanted to fill the tank now, the man didn't, and the woman asked whether he really intended to drive around looking for the cheapest gas in Finland or if he'd try to make it all the way home without filling up in order to get a better price on the other side of the border. Years later the children would remember their parents' constant arguing through their mother's final summer, and they would come to hate the stepmother who would enter the picture before long.

"Do you remember the heat wave in 2010? I was drunk practically the whole summer. Heat makes everything stronger. Death, alcohol, sex. Winter is better for me." Norma instinctively clapped a hand to her mouth and glanced at Alvar. He wasn't looking at the family—he was looking at Norma.

"So you can smell diseases from people's hair?"

"I'm not making it up."

"You shouldn't tell that to anyone, kitten."

Alvar made everything sound normal. Norma told the story of how, when she was a little girl, she'd seen the fatal illness in the store clerk and kept it to herself. Just as she was staying silent now, looking at this family about to lose a wife and mother. She could intervene. The woman might recover if she went to the doctor in time. Norma could get out of the car and tell her now.

"You aren't going anywhere," Alvar said.

"You don't care at all."

Alvar shrugged. "I care selectively."

Coffee cups in hand, they watched the family squabble as if it were a spectator sport. Alvar would never judge Norma for not rushing to the woman and ordering her to the doctor. He wouldn't harp on how much good she could do. She could walk right past people she knew were doomed; she could also ignore the ones whose problems would be solved by a change in diet. With Alvar, she could be indifferent without the guilt, and that made her feel weightless. Before, she'd always feared seeing a disease in someone she was close to. It happened sometimes: she'd remained silent, and it had always been pure torture.

The pond at the farm was exactly how Norma remembered. More than ten years had passed since her last visit. Now there were more waterlilies and reeds—the shore hadn't been dredged in decades. The pond was still swimmable, though. After Alvar and the dog splashed into the water, Norma tried the car radio again, but it just continued its frivolity; nothing about a Finnish businessman found dead in Ukraine, his wife, or his daughter, or a violent gunfight involving Finnish citizens. The radio went silent, perhaps because of the approaching thunderclouds, and Norma walked to the beach. She dug a cigarette out of her pocket. It controlled the fear that occasionally burst its restraints. If Lambert had survived after all, or Alla, they would come after her. After them. Eva encouraged her to trust Alvar. He was one of those men who knew how to handle things.

Norma stubbed out her cigarette when the dog climbed onto the shore to shake off her coat, and Alvar followed.

"You have that look again," he said. "But Lambert isn't coming back."

"You haven't seen the body."

"I trust my men."

"What if Lambert paid more than you did?"

"It doesn't work that way."

"How does it then?"

Alvar dropped his towel to the ground and began to dress. Norma realized this wasn't a conversation worth continuing. Alvar wouldn't tell her everything. But Norma wanted to be able to sleep alone. She didn't want to worry every time he went out of the room. She didn't want to listen for sirens constantly, to flinch at the sight of every police cruiser their car happened to pass. The certainty that Alvar would be arrested sometimes made her heart burn with rage, and it wouldn't relent until she felt the familiar ribs of that stray dog under her fingers.

"I have to know how it happened."

"It's better if you don't."

"I have to!"

"How do you think Lambert would react to Anita's videos?"

"Lambert would want to kill Marion."

"Exactly. So you already know everything you need to, kitten."

The success of Alvar's plan still felt just as improbable as when he'd explained he'd given Anita's videos to Lambert. Norma had been startled, and Alvar tried to calm her down. Lambert and Alla were already on their way to Dnipropetrovsk, where Marion had gone a little earlier. Alvar sent all three to the same place at the same time. That could only result in the trio slaughtering one another.

"But what if Marion managed to send those files to someone before she left?"

"Then we'd hardly be sitting here right now."

"I couldn't stand it if you went to prison."

"No one is going to prison."

"How can you be sure?"

Alvar pulled her into his arms and, despite Norma's resistance, tickled her so that her worry faded momentarily behind laughter. He had sent his men to Dnipropetrovsk to clean up the evidence, and Norma expected he'd receive news that would concern, upset, or relax him. Instead, nothing happened. Alvar had taken over the entire empire as if Lambert and Alla had never existed, as if it had always belonged to him, and Norma felt certain that Alvar had been planning his takeover for some time. He'd just been waiting for the appropriate opportunity.

The Naakka home was the same as always, except that the only cups in the kitchen had their handles broken off, and the floorboards squeaked in new places in addition to the old familiar ones. Alvar began to light a fire in the stove, and Norma looked at the vertebrae visible through his shirt. She wasn't sure why she was here and not abroad. Her new passport was still in her purse, as were the bank cards Alvar had given her the week after Midsummer, when he'd come to the door of her hideout and said that Lambert and Alla had been in an accident in Dnipropetrovsk.

After handing her the passport, Alvar had asked whether she wanted a ride to the airport or if she'd be interested in going to dinner first. She chose dinner and never made it to the airport. She slept that night by Alvar's side, listening to his dozing. This time she was careful not to lose control of her emotions, and her hair didn't repeat its wild display, even though she knew it could become besotted again. But not now, not yet. Perhaps before this game ended, though. Once or twice. For a moment longer, she'd allow herself to imagine she was a normal woman on a summer vacation with her lover. Even Eva thought she deserved a short rest and a little merrymaking after all the difficulties Anita had caused.

Once the stove was smoking, Alvar straightened his back, and Norma opened the window for a bee that had come inside and now buzzed on the ceiling. They knew too much about each other, and before long she would remember that. She would realize that knowledge of her DNA must have reached others, and someone outside the clan could come after her, someone she wouldn't have to worry about if she were far away with her new passport. Before long she would forgive her mother and grow bored of blaming the madness she herself had caused. She would want to blame Eva or Alvar. She would wonder whether Alvar could have prevented her mother's fateful end, if he would have stepped in if he could have. But just for this moment, she wanted to live out her fantasy. As long as she couldn't be completely sure that Lambert and Alla were dead, she wouldn't be safe—unless she stayed with this man who knew how to deal with such people. So she told herself, not knowing whether it was true.

Tomorrow Norma would see Helena, who had deteriorated and now constantly asked after Anita. At first, Alvar opposed the visit. Nevertheless Norma had insisted, and she'd wager that Alvar was actually pleased she wanted to see Helena.

Eva looked forward to the meeting with enthusiasm. There was so much to say, and Helena would tell Norma everything, including where she should start looking for Eva's daughter's descendants. Eva missed them, and Helena needed her pipe filled.

A NOTE ABOUT THE AUTHOR

SOFI OKSANEN is a Finnish-Estonian novelist and playwright. She has received numerous prizes for her work, including the Finlandia Prize, the Swedish Academy Nordic Prize, the Prix Femina, the Budapest Grand Prize, the European Book Prize, and the Nordic Council Literature Prize. She lives in Helsinki.

A NOTE ON THE TYPE

Pierre Simon Fournier *le jeune* (1712–1768), who designed the type used in this book, was both an originator and a collector of types. His services to the art of printing were his design of letters, his creation of ornaments and initials, and his standardization of type sizes. His types are old style in character and sharply cut. In 1764 and 1766 he published his *Manuel typographique,* a treatise on the history of French types and printing, on typefounding in all its details, and on what many consider his most important contribution to typography—the measurement of type by the point system.

Typeset by Scribe,
Philadelphia, Pennsylvania

Printed and bound by LSC Communications,
Harrisonburg, Virginia

Designed by Cassandra J. Pappas